RIDE TO GLORY

RIDE TO GLORY

MICHAEL J. GILHULY
&
MARILYN CLARK GILHULY

LONGSTREET PRESS
Athens, Georgia

Published by
LONGSTREET PRESS, INC.
325 Milledge Avenue
Athens, GA 30601

Printed in the United States of America

1st printing 2004

Book design by Burtch Hunter Design LLC

To Tiffany and Jennifer Gilhuly

RIDE TO GLORY

CHAPTER ∞ 1

Clayton Wiley's memorial service was held on a dismal gray day. The wind fluttered the black garments of the friends and family who had gathered by the stone which marked the empty grave. Leroy's eyes never met those of his parents. In spite of repeated assurances from his brother, Carter, and his wife, Mindy, that he wasn't to blame, he still felt guilty While listening to the minister recite the burial service, Leroy made a silent promise to his brother, Clayton, that he would track down and kill every last one of the murdering savages who had butchered him.

"It is not for us to take upon ourselves the act of revenge," the minister intoned in a high-pitched voice, as if reading Leroy's mind. "The wrath of God will deal with all who commit violence upon others."

Carter raised his head and looked across the grave at Leroy. He watched Leroy stiffen when their eyes met.

That's not what he's thinking, Carter thought. *Leroy, it's not your fault. Can't you get that through that thick head of yours?* Then he wondered how Leroy could possibly accept that it wasn't his fault when he still had questions about it himself. He shook his head and tried to push those nagging questions to the back of his mind.

Leroy turned and looked away. He found himself staring at a large oak tree with raised branches reaching toward a sky filled with dark gray clouds. He felt Mindy shiver, as she clung to his arm. For a minute there was silence. Then his mother reached down and picked up a handful of earth to throw on the coffin containing letters from the family to Clayton.

The wind began to howl through the withering leaves and branches, causing a mournful sound. Out of the corner of his eye, Leroy saw the men come forward with shovels to close the grave.

"That's about all I can take," Leroy whispered to Mindy.

Before she could resist, he gripped her arm and hurriedly walked her back to the wagon.

"You can't leave now," she whispered. "You have to stay at least until the grave is closed."

"What do you want me to do?" he demanded angrily. "Stand there and watch them throw dirt over what should be my brother's coffin?" He glanced back toward the grave site and the people standing around it. Several mourners had turned and were staring at him.

"Everybody knows that he's not really there. Hell, there wasn't enough left of Clayton to bring home to bury. And I damn sure didn't want my Mother and Father seeing what the Comanch had done to their favorite son." He turned back to Mindy, pain choking his words. "How do you think I feel right now?"

"Leroy, are you all right?" Carter walked up behind them and reached out to touch Leroy's shoulder. Nancy, Carter's wife, stood beside her husband. Her golden hair was tucked under her black bonnet. Her face was pale, and her brown eyes were filled with sadness.

"Yeah," Leroy answered, never taking his eyes off of Mindy. "Carter, will you take Mindy and the folks home? I've got some unfinished business to attend to."

"Leroy," Carter started to argue, but Mindy spoke first.

"Your place is here with your mother and father. Do you think going off and killing a bunch of Indians will bring Clayton back?"

Leroy's hands circled her waist and lifted her up onto the wagon. Then he turned to Carter and said in a flat, emotionless voice, "Tend to the folks for me, Carter. This is something I gotta do."

"I don't agree," Carter said firmly. "But you know I'll take care of things here until you get back."

Leroy brushed past Nancy and walked to a waiting horse. "This paint belongs to Gaston Cave," he said while climbing into the saddle. "Tell him I'll bring it back when I'm finished with the Comanche." Without saying another word, he rode off.

The Leroy Wiley that left his family behind that cold, gray day at the family cemetery was a man in pain. He was hurting for so many reasons, most of them he couldn't explain to anyone, not even to his wife.

He was a handsome man, not quite six feet tall, with rugged features. He had squarely set shoulders and piercing blue eyes that turned to steel gray when he was angry. His sandy brown hair had been bleached lighter by the sun and had a windblown, tousled look. But it was his smile, more of a devilish grin, that people seemed to remember.

For the next two days Leroy rode west, stopping only to rest his horse. His eyes took in the pleasant sight of copper beech trees, spider-limbed this time of year, clustered along with big elms that reached upward into the cloudless Texas sky. He allowed his mind to drift back to the days before the war.

"The good times," he said softly as he led the small paint through the Texas prairie grass. In his mind's eye he pictured his brothers, Clayton and Carter, working the stock and doing the chores. A big lump swelled in Leroy's throat. Wiping away an unwanted tear, he took in a deep breath and made an effort to bring his mind back to the present.

There were so many pleasant memories of Clayton that he wanted to enjoy, but there would be time enough for that later, after the killing was done. Right now he didn't want to let anything or anyone distract him from the mission he had set for himself.

"Try to stop dwelling on all the hurts," Mindy had told him before the funeral.

"Mindy doesn't understand." He sighed. "No need trying to tell her. She just doesn't understand."

"Gotta tend to business," he said in a resigned tone. "If there ever is a judgment day, I've got some hard questions for the Almighty—savages going around butchering innocent folks. Yankees running roughshod over Texas and the rest of the South. Why does He lets things like that happen?" The thought of Clayton being tortured and dying alone, hit him like a thunderbolt. "What those Comanche did to my brother is beyond the pale of human behavior." A thin smile crossed his face as he spoke these fancy words. The words reminded Leroy of something his lawyer brother Carter would say. The smile quickly vanished as Leroy braced himself for what lay ahead.

I intend to keep my promise to my dead brother or die trying. Anyone who knew Leroy Williams Wiley would tell you that he meant every word.

It was late afternoon on the third day when he finally stopped to camp. He built a good fire and for a few moments, he sat on the ground and gazed at the flames licking up around the coffee kettle. Just as he opened a tin of biscuits, he heard a rider approaching from the east. Leroy reached for a piece of firewood and covered his Union Army issued Colt pistol which he had placed in front of him, keeping it hidden until the time came to use it.

"Don't draw down on me, Leroy," a familiar voice called out. "Knowing you the way I do, I figure you got that Yankee Colt pistol ready to blow me in half."

Leroy smiled as he stood and stretched his lean, muscled body up to almost six feet. "Sorry, old man, but I don't have any grub to spare so you just better turn around and go on home."

"I figured you'd be traveling light," Willis laughed as he tipped his hat in a mock salute to Leroy. "I brought enough grub to keep both of us alive for awhile. Put it this way, I figure it's a lot more likely that the Comanch will get us before we run out of food."

"This ain't gonna be no picnic, Willis," Leroy walked over and began to untie the heavy saddlebags attached to the big Roan that Willis was riding. Willis was a man of medium height with a stocky build. His thin wisp of silver hair framed a weathered face highlighted by steel blue eyes.

"Hell I know that. But you can't do this by yourself." Willis put his hand on Leroy's shoulder. "I followed you from the funeral, Leroy. I took just enough time to explain things to Patsy then I made my way out here."

"How'd you find me?"

Willis shook his head, "Leroy, you ain't exactly trying to cover your tracks."

Leroy thought about the three long days that he had spent on the trail. "Guess not. I've had a lot on my mind. I've been trying to sort things out."

"Well," Willis walked over to the campfire, "You're gonna have some help come tomorrow."

"What kind of help?" Leroy asked.

"The kind of help you'll need if you're gonna sort things out," Willis laughed. "What's left of our Ranger Company together with a few more good men that Captain Johnson and Dave English managed to round up are headed this way." Willis gestured back toward Tyler. "I figure they ought to catch up with us by the time we set camp tomorrow—that is, if you let 'em."

Leroy shook his head, then smiled, "I'll let 'em."

Willis remained silent.

"I'm mighty grateful." Leroy's voice grew suddenly husky.

"They know that," Willis said as he handed his friend a hot cup of coffee. "And so do I. Ain't no more to be said 'bout it."

For the next three days the weather remained decent. At the end of the third day, Leroy and the other Texas Rangers crossed the River Brazos putting themselves directly in harms way—they were now in Comanche territory.

"Tell me about the Comanche, Leroy," one of the young Rangers asked as he rode up along side a silent Leroy Wiley.

"Don't know if I can tell you all that much about 'em, Derrick," Leroy said in a dry, expressionless voice. "I guess they got their ways and we got ours." He paused, then looked over the sweeping North

Texas plain before finishing his thoughts. "I do know it's near the end of their way of life."

"What makes you think that?" Derrick asked.

"The Yankee Army, that's what." Leroy shook his head. "Pretty soon Texas is gonna be filled with farmers all wantin' law and order and such."

"But ain't that a good thing?" The young Ranger sounded confused.

"Depends on how you look at it. Some folks might not be happy with that." Leroy continued to search the horizon.

"Does that include you, Leroy?"

Leroy thought for a moment then tilted his head back and laughed. "Well, now, Derrick," Leroy's tone had a hint of sarcasm. "We ain't exactly outlaws, are we? We are, whether the damn Yankee Army likes it or not, the law in these here parts."

"Leroy, quit filling the boy's head with disrespectful talk about those unwanted visitors to our fair state of Texas," Captain Johnson pulled up on the other side of Derrick and gave him a pat on the back. "Leroy ain't never gotten over the whippin' we took during the war, Derrick. But don't pay him no mind, he'll get over it, someday."

"Yeah," Leroy grinned, "I'll get over it someday. You can count on that, Captain. But for right now if you put a Yankee hat on each and every one of the Comanch, I have no doubt that my aim would improve."

Leroy turned to see a huge grin on Derrick's face. Derrick was like most of the other young men who had recently joined the Rangers, too brave for his own good. *Young and stupid,* thought Leroy. *Most of them were too young to have fought in the war so they're too stupid to be afraid. I figure one run in with the Comanch ought to cure 'em or kill 'em.*

"You never did answer my question, Leroy." Derrick brushed back a wisp of sandy colored hair, then replaced a weatherbeaten, sweat-stained hat low on his brow.

"I got distracted thinking about the Yanks, Derrick, my boy," Leroy laughed. "I'll tell you what I know about the Comanch, which ain't much, you understand."

Derrick noticed how easy Leroy sat in the saddle. Leroy had a manner about him that Texans admire. It was difficult to put into words exactly what this entailed—it was enough to say that nothing about Leroy Wiley was put on. Leroy was the real thing. He was a true Texan down to his worn boots and silver Mexican spurs.

Wonder where he got those spurs? Derrick asked himself. He pictured Leroy taking them off of some dead Mexican outlaw after a gun fight.

"The Comanch," Leroy began his description of the character of the Comanche Indians, "ain't got much to look forward to, so he's gonna make the best of what he's got at the present. By that I mean—"

Captain Johnson's mind drifted away from Leroy's words. He was thinking of what lay ahead. *Knowing the Comanch, they'll probably make their play near the next watering hole.* He tried to clear his mind of the dangers that he and his fellow Rangers would soon face and allow himself a few moments to enjoy the view of the Great Plain that surrounded them. This broad stretch of northwest Texas had few abrupt changes in elevation. However, the trail followed by the Rangers was lower than the land on either side of them. Gradually, the terrain developed a gentle slope upward toward a distant plateau the color of desert sand. Patches of trees dotted the landscape, mostly pines and other cone-bearing evergreens. Just as he was gazing at the thick prairie grass beneath the horses hooves and thinking of home, Leroy's tone of voice grabbed the Ranger Captain's attention. It wasn't that Leroy had raised his voice, quite the contrary, his voice was almost a whisper. But there was an edge to his words that made Captain Johnson snap back to reality.

"Captain, we got a war party coming towards us from that plateau up ahead. From what I can see they're all decked out in war paint and feathers. Hell, even their ponies are painted for war."

"I see 'em," Johnson sighed. "So much for them waiting until the next watering hole. Nobody make any sudden moves. Just keep riding 'till I give the word."

Leroy looked at the young Ranger beside him. Derrick's eyes were wide with fear. Slowly, he reached over and touched Derrick's arm.

"Derrick, speaking of the typical Comanche, he's more afraid of us than we are of him," Leroy lied. "Just stay alongside me and you'll be riding back to Tyler with all your hair, or at least most of it."

"Jesus, Leroy," Derrick whispered. "They ain't getting near enough to me to get any of my hair."

"I'll see to it," Leroy laughed.

"How long, Leroy?" Captain Johnson asked.

"Can't be sure, but probably at the next bend. That's all the cover they'll need and from the looks of it that would leave us without any."

"Without any what?" an obviously frightened Derrick asked.

"Hair," Leroy laughed.

"Shut that kind of talk up, Leroy," Willis had ridden up and was directly behind them. "Derrick, don't you pay no mind to Leroy. He was talking about cover."

"What cover? That's the problem, Willis. Or hadn't you noticed? We ain't got none," Leroy replied. "I seriously doubt that the Comanch is going to oblige us by waiting until we find some before they make their move. They might be savages but they sure ain't stupid."

"Leroy," Captain Johnson stretched up in his saddle to get a better view of the trail ahead. "What do you think about us making a run for it. The horses are fresh."

"Captain, I'd hold off 'till we have to," Leroy gestured toward the Comanche war party that was now keeping pace with them on their right flank. "Right now, we ain't got anywhere to run to. I'd rather wait 'till I see something."

"Thought I'd never say it, but damn Texas," Willis spat a wad of tobacco juice in anger mixed with frustration. "Right now I wish I'd stayed in Tennessee. At least a man can always find something to hide behind in Tennessee."

"If we get out of this, Willis," Leroy laughed, "I'll personally take your sorry butt back to Franklin. Now there was one hell of a place." Leroy looked over toward Derrick. "Lots' of Texans still talk about the time they spent in Franklin, Tennessee, Derrick. That is, what few Texans ever made it out alive from that hell hole."

"I hated Franklin," Willis appeared in deep thought, "I meant

Arkansas, Leroy. Ain't no place like Franklin in Arkansas. And there's still plenty of places to hide in Arkansas."

"Get ready men!" Captain Johnson shouted. "I can see a river up ahead. We'll make our stand there."

That's at least five miles away, thought Leroy. *There's no way in hell we're gonna make it to that damn river.*

Leroy had already spotted a second Comanche war party lining up on the left side of the Rangers. Suddenly, the Comanche chief gave the signal to attack.

In spite of Captain Johnson's attempt to maintain control, Derrick quickly rode to the front of the column. He could think of nothing but getting away from the charging Comanche. He suddenly changed direction when he spotted a cluster of rocks and trees a half mile ahead and to the right of the direction they had been headed. Derrick raced toward the rock and trees while the other Rangers followed his lead. The abrupt change in direction of the Rangers seemed to momentarily take the Comanche by surprise.

Derrick's pony surged ahead of the rest of the Rangers and easily outran the Comanche to the cluster of rocks. The young Ranger had barely dismounted before he was firing shot after shot in the direction of the Comanche chief who was charging towards him on his painted war pony. Derrick was so frightened that he hardly bothered to take aim before he fired his Winchester. Against all odds, one of the rounds found it's mark and the Indian Chief's chest exploded in bright red as he fell over backwards onto the ground. Derrick kept firing until he ran out of ammunition. By that time, the Rangers had formed a firing line behind the boulders and trees on either side of him. Willis and two other Rangers tried their best to keep the horses under control, but in the end, all but four of the terrified animals managed to break away and run off.

The Texans were trying to stay alive when the Comanche halted their attack in order to recover the body of their fallen chief. When the smoke cleared and the dust finally settled, Leroy figured that unless they ran out of cartridges they just might be able to hold off the

Comanche. *Three to one ain't bad odds,* Leroy thought. *We can handle this bunch, that is unless more of 'em show up.*

Captain Johnson was busy making preparations for the next attack. *Thank God nobody's been hurt,* he thought. At the moment, the only thing he had on his mind was making sure that as many of his men as possible made it through this alive.

"How much ammunition do you and the other men have left?" Captain Johnson called out to Leroy.

"'Bout enough for another charge," Leroy answered.

Turning to Willis, Johnson asked, "Got any cartridges on those horses?"

"There ain't any on these horses," Willis shouted. "The extra cartridges were all on the two pack horses and they were the first to run off."

"I guarantee you them horses ain't going far," Leroy looked around. "Spread some grain out and give a whistle. They'll come back if they can. If the Comanche's got 'em, well, that's another story."

"What story are you talking about, Leroy?" Derrick asked excitedly.

"The story of the Comanche attackin' with plenty of cartridges and us trying to hold them off without any, Derrick," Leroy replied with a grin on his face.

Willis was about to tell Leroy to shut up again when he spotted five of the horses including the two big pack animals trotting toward them.

"Well boys, looks like we get to keep our scalps and fight another day," Leroy laughed. "The Comanch ain't got us yet."

Leroy motioned to Captain Johnson. "The Comanch are long gone. There's no way they'd let them horses come back to us if they were still anywhere out there."

Leroy was right. The Rangers were going to have to ride deeper into Comanche country if they intended overtake and kill the remaining warriors of the raiding party.

CHAPTER ∞ 2

Any word from Leroy?" Carter asked Mindy as she opened the door.

Mindy frowned. "No, I don't expect him back for a month or two. You know the humor he was in when he left." She turned on her heel and put her hands on her hips. "I could shoot him sometimes."

"No one would blame you," Carter laughed. Reaching into a small bag he pulled out a sack of sweet rock candy. "I brought this for Ma and Papa. But there's plenty for you too. Although as sweet as you are, dear sister-in-law, you probably don't need any candy."

"Oh, you!" Mindy smiled. She walked over to hug Leroy's tall brother. "If you think that's going to make me any less mad at Leroy you're wrong."

"I wouldn't think of helping Leroy," Carter grinned as he walked past Mindy and headed toward the kitchen. "Where are the folks?"

Mindy dropped her head and answered softly, "Your parents are visiting Clayton's grave. They just can't seem to let him go." Tears begin to fill Mindy's brown eyes. She looked up at Carter, seeing him through the tears which were now running down her face. She looked around the room in vain for a handkerchief to wipe them away. Carter reached into his waistcoat and handed her a soft cotton handkerchief that Nancy had sewed with his initials. He gently put his arm around her shoulders.

"Thank you," Mindy whispered. "I thought I had cried all that I could, but every time I think of dear, sweet Clayton I start all over again. I can't keep acting this way. I have to think of Mama and Papa Wiley."

Carter sighed. He shifted his new gray Stetson into one hand and reached for Mindy's arm with the other. His voice filled with sadness, he nodded toward the family cemetery and said, "Let's go see about them."

Mindy put on a warm shawl and took his arm. "Leroy ought to be here," she muttered softly. "They need him more than they need us."

Carter looked down at her with a quizzical expression on his face. He didn't understand why his parents would need his brother now more than him. After all, wasn't Leroy in some way responsible for Clayton's death?

Carter Wiley was the eldest of three brothers. He was a lawyer by trade, but during the war he had served in the 28th Texas Cavalry with his brother, Leroy. Carter was tall with dark hair and considered quite handsome. He had married Nancy, an attractive woman from Tennessee, whom he had met during the war. He had a close, but at times difficult relationship with his brother, Leroy.

Carter had always resented what he perceived as his parent's favoritism toward their youngest son, Leroy. He was wrong. Clayton was the "good son" and clearly the favorite of both his parents. Leroy always knew this to be true. The difference in their personalities was that any sign of favoritism bothered Carter, while Leroy never gave it a second thought.

Leroy had been the first to leave home, serving with the Texas Rangers while only a teenager. His parents never seemed to stop bragging about that fact. Leroy was the "ornery" one, constantly getting into mischief when he was a young boy. He was also the first son to marry. Leroy had brought Mindy to live in East Texas after meeting and marrying her while visiting relatives in Columbia County, Georgia.

Leroy cared about few things - his wife Mindy, their young child,

JR, and being part of the Texas Rangers. Mindy would probably argue that Leroy's priorities were not necessarily in that order. But deep down, Leroy Wiley was a family man. Although he enjoyed playing cards with the boys and could always be counted on to consume his fair share of whiskey, the saloon girls never interested him. Once he had met and married Mindy, he was a happy man. This being said, Leroy Wiley was basically a loner. The most content hours of his life were spent alone in the Texas wilderness, as far away from civilization as possible. He was seldom afraid. He had spent too many hours of his life facing death. He had an attitude shared by most men who had fought on both sides of America's Civil War - "you either live or you don't." The best you could do, Leroy believed, was to strengthen the odds in favor of survival. Although he didn't look for trouble, if it found him, he was more than willing to oblige. When angry, he usually displayed a grin instead of a frown. This tended to unsettle whoever had the misfortune of being the target of his anger.

Mindy thought the family order was mixed up. Leroy was treated as if he was the eldest son and yet he was the youngest. Carter clearly had some issues with his parents turning to Leroy when he felt they should be consulting him about financial and family matters. Mindy resented Carter's superior attitude at times. She, like the rest of the family, had adored Clayton during his brief time on God's earth. Clayton was the son who was able to bridge the gap and find the common ground whenever there was a family squabble. Now he was gone.

Taylor Wiley and Verlinda, his wife of forty years, were like many pioneers who migrated to Texas in search of a better life. They were from Scotch-Irish stock who, with each generation had moved further west—from the Carolinas, across Georgia, Alabama, Mississippi and Louisiana until they finally settled down in the fertile farmland of east Texas.

CHAPTER ∞ 3

"This bothers me, Leroy," Captain Johnson paused momentarily as he pointed to the trail ahead. "They're dragging brush behind 'em." Surveying the horizon, he shook his head, then asked, "Why?"

"Captain, the Comanch is full of tricks," Leroy replied. "Sometimes I think I got 'em figured out, other times I know better."

"Ever ride out this way?" asked Johnson."

"Yeah, a few times before the war. There's a box canyon west of here. That way, he pointed towards the north, leads to the Indian Territory. That other direction," Leroy pointed to the south, "leads you right to that new Yankee fort. It's a ways from here, but I can tell you this much, the Comanch knows exactly how far it is."

"Think they went up into the Territory?"

"Nope," Leroy said in a matter of fact tone. "They ain't gonna go mix it up with the Chickasaws if they can help it. The way I see it, they're probably holed up in that canyon west of here getting ready for another raid."

"But the brush leads north toward the Territory."

"Yep, it sure does, which leads me to believe they ain't going in that direction. The Comanche like to follow a round about way," Leroy made a broad circle with his right arm. "But they've got to hide their women folk and babies. And that there canyon ain't nothing but a maze of deep valleys and caves. Plenty of places to hide a whole village and nobody be the wiser."

Captain Johnson stared intently in the direction of the red rock canyon that was surrounded by sandstone spires. The walls of the canyon appeared to be of red sandstone rising almost three hundred feet above the valley floor. "Leroy, we ain't got the time nor the men to allow for any mistakes."

"I'm as uneasy as you are, Captain, but if we go riding up into the Territory it will be nothing but a waste of time. If we're serious about finding and killing 'em, we gotta go right into that canyon and finish 'em off."

"Leroy," Willis spoke for the first time. "I don't wanna have to say this, but since it's my scalp that's on the line I figure I got a right to speak my piece." Willis had more time in the Rangers than anyone else in the company, including both Leroy and Captain Johnson.

"Go ahead, Willis," Captain Johnson was more than a little annoyed that Willis was addressing Leroy instead of him. The captain was Leroy's age. He had been an officer in Terry's Texas Rangers during the war and had risen to the rank of Major before the war ended in Virginia. He was a small man physically, but he was strong as an ox. The other Rangers had a lot of respect for their captain, but right now Willis was not in the mood to observe rank. He knew that Leroy was acting as the scout and second in command for this patrol. Because of that he wanted Leroy to know exactly how he felt about what they were about to do.

Leroy turned and spoke impatiently. "Go on back to Patsy if that's what you want, Willis."

With that, Willis completely lost his temper. "Damnit, Leroy," Willis threw his hat on the ground as he climbed down from his horse. "You got yourself so riled up over Clayton that you ain't thinking straight nor smart either." He pointed toward the trail ahead, "We ride into that canyon and you can bet not many of us will ride out. Them Comanche will be waiting for us behind every rock. Look around you,

Leroy, there's only twenty of us and we don't know how many of them are in that there canyon."

"Go back home, Willis," Leroy said in a flat tone. "Nobody's gonna think any less of you."

"You're acting as if I've lost my nerve," Willis stiffened and looked up at Captain Johnson, "I ain't lost my nerve. Captain, I'll go into that canyon if that's what you tell me to do. I just think it's stupid to ride in there blind, not knowing what we're up against."

"It's gotta be done," Captain Johnson said quietly, then turned to Leroy. "We'll ride in late tonight."

"What?" Willis asked. He couldn't believe what he had just heard. "Them Comanch are gonna hear us coming a mile off. They sleep with their best pony right by their side. If we go riding in there like that, I promise you that every last one of our scalps will be hanging next to their teepees by sunrise."

"Set up camp over by those trees, Willis." Captain Johnson turned to the rest of his men. "Leroy and I will go on ahead after dark and scout the canyon."

"Did I miss something?" Leroy laughed. "I don't remember volunteerin'."

Captain Johnson smiled, "Sure you did. I heard you, bet Willis did too."

"If you two fools are going, so am I," Willis said in a resigned tone.

"Captain," Leroy dismounted and walked over toward Johnson before continuing. "If it's all the same to you, I'll go in there with just Willis. Sometimes back during the war, I'd know what Willis was going to do before he knew himself. Besides," he added, "your place is here with the men. If we don't come back then I suggest that you ride to that damn Yankee fort and bring back enough yellow legs to wipe 'em out."

Willis shivered. He'd never heard Leroy's voice so cold and forbidding. *Not even during the war was he like this,* Willis thought. *He's about to boil over and when that happens, he's gonna lose control and get us all killed.*

"Suit yourself." Captain Johnson nodded sharply and motioned to the rest of the men to follow him into the cluster of trees.

As soon as the other Rangers were gone, Willis whispered to Leroy. "If anything happens to me you better hope those savages get ahold of you before Patsy does."

Leroy threw his head back and laughed. "That's for sure. Knowing that your Patsy would put all of the blame on me if you lose what little hair you have left, you can rest assured that I ain't gonna let nothing happen to you."

Willis lowered his head, thinking hard. He knew that Leroy was, by nature, a cautious man. But Willis wondered if his friend was cutting a few corners in order to take on the Comanche and settle his score with 'em because of Clayton.

Leroy and Willis started walking their horses toward the campsite. They heard Captain Johnson say, "No fire tonight, boys. We don't want the Comanch to know that we're this close."

"Damn," Willis said in disgust. "Not much food and no hot coffee."

"Willis," Leroy grinned as he spoke. "While we're in that canyon I'll snatch some Comanche grub for you. I hear they eat quite nice now and then."

"From what I hear they ain't eaten much of anything since the Buffalo hunters started coming out here and killing off the herds."

Willis' statement made Leroy pause for a moment. In spite of his hatred for the Comanche, he felt a slight twinge of sadness. But then he remembered what they had done to his brother, Clayton, and he put any feelings of sympathy for the Comanche out of his head. *To hell with 'em,* he thought. *Who cares if all of 'em go hungry? I sure don't.*

CHAPTER ∞ 4

Leroy sat quietly by himself waiting for the cover of darkness. While he waited he began to put together a plan. There would be a full moon tonight. This would help them see where they were going, but it would also mean that they were more likely to be seen by the Comanche. He decided that they would have to walk most of the way to the canyon. Because of this, he realized they would never make it back to the camp before sunrise. That meant they would be on their own until sometime tomorrow morning. He watched Willis packing some gear. Their eyes met briefly. Willis nodded his understanding and continued his preparations. Leroy knew that Willis was thinking the same thoughts. Leroy shifted uncomfortably. *One thing is for certain,* he thought. *Tomorrow is going to be a long day.* He looked up into a crystalline blue sky and then studied the low, barren hills and walled gullies near the entrance to the canyon. *Too many hiding places for the Comanch,* he thought. *But between here and that there canyon all you have is a few bare limbed trees and some scattered brush. Not much cover, that's for sure.* He stood up, stretched, and walked over to Willis.

"Not long now, Willis." Leroy's voice was flat without any trace of emotion. The anger he felt towards the Comanche was gone for the moment, replaced by a cold, calculating determination and an iron will that had been hardened by four years of fighting during the war.

Willis, on the other hand, felt sick to his stomach. "I'm getting too old for this, Leroy."

Leroy didn't immediately respond. When he finally did, there was steel in his voice. "Quit worrying about this little trip into the canyon, Willis. I know what I'm doing. I ain't thinking of Clayton or anyone else - just what we gotta do."

"And what is that, Leroy?"

Leroy looked directly at Willis and flashed the grin that had made him a legend during the war. "I guess the simplest way I can put it is that we gotta see that we both stay alive while getting a little payback. Every Comanch we kill is one less savage trying to kill us, and that's all we have to think about."

"I'll fill the canteens," Willis said in a resigned tone of voice. "I got faith in you Leroy. I got faith that you'll keep us both alive. That's all I'm thinking about."

Leroy and Willis rode into the darkness until Leroy decided they had better find cover for the horses and go the rest of the way on foot. Willis set a picket line in a small ravine where the horses could graze. The two men ducked down into a shallow ravine and started toward the mouth of the canyon. Leroy set a fast pace. After an hour of this, Willis' back was aching and his legs felt as if they would give way at any moment but he kept up with the pace and stayed close to Leroy.

As they approached the canyon entrance, Leroy turned and motioned for Willis to get down behind a granite wall. He pointed toward the right side of the canyon. Leroy had spotted the Comanche.

Willis had been there with Leroy when he found the bodies of Clayton and the other dead Rangers after the Comanche had butchered them. He had no illusions as to what would happen if the Comanche ever got their hands on him.

Willis held his breath as Leroy slipped over the granite wall and made his way as silent as any Indian into the darkness. An hour later, Leroy was back holding a wicked looking Bowie knife. He slipped the bloody knife into his belt and motioned for Willis to follow him as he moved deeper into the dark recesses of the canyon.

After eliminating the two Comanche guarding the entrance to the canyon, Leroy was unable to locate the raiding party's camp. He and Willis climbed to the top of a gentle rise near the canyon wall. Using the moonlight, Leroy began to systematically survey the area. Suddenly, he saw some movement up ahead where the canyon forked. The two Rangers carefully made their way in that direction. When they reached the spot where Leroy thought he had seen movement earlier, they found nothing. Leroy left Willis and again began to climb the wall of the canyon in order to get a better view. He climbed almost a hundred feet up the canyon wall before he found a vantage point that allowed him to see into the right fork of the canyon. His chest tightened at the sight of row after row of scalps hanging from short poles next to a cluster of tepees not a hundred yards from where he stood. Buffalo horns marked the entrance to the chief's teepee. Knowing that several families shared each large teepee, he counted the number of teepees and decided that there were sixty to eighty warriors in the raiding party. Not many more than that number had attacked the day before. It was now time to get back to the Ranger camp.

Leroy quickly climbed back down the canyon wall and ran to where Willis was hiding. Without stopping, he motioned for his friend to follow him. As he trotted along a gully, Leroy whispered, "The Comanche are camped down the right fork of the canyon. We need to put some distance between us and them before they find those dead sentries."

Willis remained silent.

"Willis?" Leroy whispered. "You hear me?"

"Hell, yes. But that don't mean I can answer you. Right now I can't talk and run at the same time. My whole body is about to give out."

"Then think of something else," Leroy said in a husky voice. He was also about to drop from exhaustion. "Hey, Willis, look up at the sky. I can't believe how clear it is."

"Leroy, my guts are in too much of an uproar for me to be looking up at the sky," Willis struggled to speak.

"Get your mind off running," Leroy choked out the words. "As my fancy lawyer brother would say, think of the alternative."

Willis closed his eyes and leaned his body forward. *One foot in front of the other,* he told himself. *Don't stop, just keep putting one foot in front of the other.*

Suddenly, Willis staggered to his right and fell to his knees. Leroy stopped running when he heard his friend fall. For a moment he stayed where he was, bent forward with his hands on his knees as he tried to get his breath. Then he straighten up and walked back to Willis. He grabbed Willis by one of his arms and roughly pulled him to his feet. He whispered into Willis' ear, "Remember what those savages did to my brother and the Rangers that were with him. They'll do the same, or worse, if they get their hands on us."

Willis forced his legs to move on. Thirty minutes later, they saw the first hint to dawn on the horizon. Leroy knew they were near the entrance of the canyon. He turned to Willis, "We're almost there. Just hang on a little bit longer."

Before Willis could answer, they heard the sound of a half a dozen or more Comanche ponies coming towards them at a full gallop.

"Goddamn 'em," Willis cried out. "How can they ride like that at night without their horses stepping' in a hole and going lame?"

Leroy didn't answer. For some strange reason he was reminded of a lesson he had learned at Shiloh. *When it appears that things are going all right, just wait a minute and you'll find out that they ain't.*

Leroy kept running. He knew there was no hiding from the Comanche even in the dark. They could smell a white man a hundred yards away.

Up ahead were the steep three hundred foot walls of the canyon entrance. Leroy took a hard right and fell into a shallow ditch. Willis stumbled behind him. *We're done for,* Leroy thought. He took a last look up at the canyon walls. That's when he remembered the slow running river that ran along the far side of the canyon.

"Willis," he said breathlessly, "Head for the river. When you get across, there's a cave in the canyon wall over in that direction." He pointed with his finger. "Find the cave and wait for me there."

"What the hell are you going to do?" Willis asked, his voice breaking.

"Don't worry about me," Leroy replied. "I'll see you on the far bank of the river in a little bit. Just try not to shoot me. Now get going!"

Willis jumped up and began running towards the river.

Leroy lifted his rifle and carefully took aim at the approaching riders. "Die you sonsofbitches," he snarled.

He knew that this was going to be his only chance to catch the Comanche warriors off guard. Leroy fired twice and two braves fell to the ground. The rest, yelling at the top of their lungs, pulled back to regroup. Taking advantage of the Comanche's momentary confusion, Leroy climbed out of the ditch and began running towards the river. Willis had already made it across and was firing his rifle from the far side. *Damn Willis,* Leroy thought. *He's just wastin' cartridges. He won't hit any of them. But just my luck, he'll hit me.* Leroy threw himself into the river, knowing it would be shallow. *It's been a dry spell around here for about two years,* he thought as he plowed through the waist deep water. *The damn river is just deep enough to slow me down.* His legs felt heavy and his whole body was sluggish. *Gotta move faster,* he thought. *Ain't got much time before they'll be on top of me.*

Leroy was halfway across the river when he heard the war pony splashing through the water behind him. He turned just in time to avoid being trampled by the horse. With only seconds to react, he grabbed the reins of the horse and pulled with all his might. The horse's front legs buckled. The startled Comanche brave, who was trying his best to hit Leroy with a tomahawk, fell off of his horse and onto Leroy. The two men tumbled into the water. Leroy felt the warrior's hot breath on his face as the two men fought. The Indian's shoulder slammed onto a sharp rock protruding from the riverbed. He cried out in pain, but never loosened his grip on the tomahawk. While Leroy struggled to pull the Bowie knife from his belt, another Comanche rode his pony towards Leroy. Willis saw what was happening and carefully took aim and fired his rifle. He missed the

Comanche but hit the horse square in the neck. The horse reared back, throwing the warrior into the water, then crumpled into the river, landing on top of Leroy and the Indian he was fighting. The weight of the horse knocked the breath out of Leroy. He gasped for air, then staggered back to his feet and tried to get his bearings. The warrior he had been fighting was pinned beneath the dead horse with his head under the water, and he appeared to be dead. He had barely regained his footing and was just getting his breath back when the second Comanche charged. Leroy pulled the Bowie knife from its sheath just as the warrior swung his tomahawk, trying to deliver a killing blow to Leroy's head. Leroy dodged the tomahawk, then lunged forward, grabbed the man by the throat and plunged his knife into the Comanche's chest. He caught a glimpse in the moonlight of a man with fierce eyes and flaring nostrils. Blood began to flow from the Indian's mouth and his eyes began to bulge. The Indian continued to struggle for a moment, then fell to his knees. Leroy eased his grip and the lifeless warrior slid under the water.

Leroy felt, rather than heard the remaining Comanche closing in on him. He looked around for the rifle he had dropped, then gave up and ran for the safety of the far shore of the river. His legs quivered. Each one seemed to weigh a ton. Suddenly, gunfire erupted all around him. Captain Johnson was attempting to lead the charge, but Derrick was four horses lengths ahead of the rest of the men.

Halfway across the river, Leroy felt something slam into his left shoulder. He lost his balance and crashed into the river hitting his head on a rock.

Willis had been watching the struggle from the far bank of the river. When he saw Leroy fall, he charged into the water to help his friend.

"Goddamn fool," Willis muttered as he lifted Leroy out of the water. "One of these days you're gonna get us both kilt." Willis continued to curse as he lifted Leroy out of the water and onto his back.

Willis' cussing and being lifted out of the cold water were the last things Leroy remembered before he passed out. When Willis reached the far bank of the river, he laid Leroy down and examined his wound. *It had been a hell of a fight, Willis thought. But them two Comanch are floating belly up somewhere out there in the river. Leroy is a little worse for wear, but he'll survive. Leroy always does.*

CHAPTER ∞ 5

Captain Johnson could hear the rolling thunder of the Texas rain storm that was heading toward them. He went to the cave entrance and looked out across the floor of the canyon. *No sign of the Comanche. Wonder why?* he asked himself. *They know they got us trapped here. What they don't know is that we're nearly out of cartridges,* he thought as he took stock of their situation. *We lost two good men and had three other men wounded in that first attack. Staying here in the cave isn't a matter of choice, we got no other option. They got us beat, wonder where they are?*

The Ranger Captain waited a moment, then walked over to where a group of his men were huddled, all the time keeping an eye on the gathering storm in the west. *Thank God we've got some shelter,* he thought. *The cave ain't much but it's better than being out there in the open especially with that thunderstorm coming.*

"There were at least a hundred of 'em," roared Derrick.

"I ain't so sure," Leroy took a deep breath. His head ached and his shoulder hurt. He made eye contact with Willis while he tried to settle Derrick down. I don't think there were quite that many."

Derrick stopped pacing back and forth in the cave. He felt foolish. He cleared his throat and tried to sound confident. "I ain't gonna say nothing else, Leroy. I know Rangers don't like to hear other Rangers brag."

Captain Johnson shook his head after taking in the dark cave, he turned back to his men. "Let's get a fire going, men It's damp and cold in here. No sense in us being wet and miserable."

"What about the Comanche?" Derrick asked.

"Derrick," Leroy managed a laugh. "Don't you think they know where we are?"

Willis and several of the other Rangers laughed aloud. Derrick shrugged his shoulders trying to shake off the embarrassment he felt before he left the cave to look for firewood.

A few hours later, Leroy was the first to spot a patrol of cavalry riding through the canyon entrance.

"Captain, I guess we know now why the Comanche high tailed it on out of here just when they had us dead to rights."

"Send 'em a signal," Captain Johnson smiled. "They're a sight for sore eyes."

"I wouldn't go that far," Leroy muttered. "But I'll signal 'em just the same."

"Follow me. A column of twos!" A young round faced Federal officer called out.

Thirty-seven cavalrymen wearing Union Army blue uniforms with yellow scarves turned their horses and rode toward the Rangers. The long shadows of the cavalrymen stretched across the canyon floor.

"Ain't they pretty?" Willis walked past Leroy in order to get a good look at the approaching Yankees.

"Yep," Leroy laughed. "The sight of Yankee cavalry still brings back bad memories."

"Leroy, you got a funny look on your face. What's going through that head of yours?" Willis asked.

"I am fighting this overwhelming urge to pick up my rifle and take out a few of them damn Yanks." Leroy stared at the approaching Yankees. "Old habits die hard."

While watching the Federal Cavalry ride toward him, Leroy had time to reflect on some of the things that occurred during the war. He thought back to the rescue of his brother, Clayton, from a Union prison camp and the many battles he had fought in alongside his other brother, Carter, a few won, most lost. "I can tell you this, Willis. Even now with them pulling our butts out of the fire, I still wish to hell I'd seen the last of 'em."

The young cavalry officer, his forehead creased from spending days in the hot sun, dismounted and walked over to the Rangers. Leroy quickly decided that the lieutenant was nothing special. You *can bet that some Comanch is gonna take his hair before too long,* he thought.

"Lieutenant Penny, at your service, Captain." The young man gave a snappy salute. "We encountered your man riding toward Fort Belknap." Lieutenant Penny gestured toward Dave English. "He said you were tracking a Comanche raiding party into this canyon." He shook his head. "Probably not such a good idea. Not with so few men."

"This is about our usual number, Lieutenant - I'm sorry, I didn't catch your last name?" Captain Johnson replied.

Leroy interrupted in a sarcastic tone of voice, "The man's name is Penny."

The Lieutenant frowned. "Lieutenant Penny is my name, Captain." He gave Leroy a disapproving look, then turned his attention back to Captain Johnson. Lieutenant Penny wasn't fond of Texans or Texas for that matter. From what he had seen, Texas was an ugly and Godforsaken place. Nothing at all like his home state of Connecticut. He and his men had been riding since sunup. He had slept badly the night before and was in no mood to be sassed by the Rangers. "If you'll gather your men, we'll rest the horses for an hour and then head back to Fort Belknap."

"We hoped you would join us in tracking down the Comanche," Captain Johnson gave the officer a wary look. "That's what we rode out here to do."

"We'll have to leave that for another day. My men are on short rations. We were at the end of a long patrol when your man asked for help. Besides, it looks like you have some wounded men that could stand some medical attention." As he spoke, Lieutenant Penny was joined by a big red faced Irishman.

Leroy glared at the big Irishman and stepped forward. He rubbed his chin as if in deep thought. "Well, well, Sergeant O'Connor," Leroy grinned. "I can't believe you're still in Texas."

O'Connor opened his mouth as if to speak but not a sound came out. He glared at Leroy. There was plenty that he wanted to say but now was not the time or place.

"You know this man, Sergeant?" Lieutenant Penny asked.

Sergeant O'Connor spit tobacco juice onto the ground just in front of Leroy's boots before he answered, "Yes, sir. I'm right well acquainted with him."

"Whatever the problem is between you two I strongly suggest that you both put it behind you for now. We've got enough problems out here without the two of you going at it." Lieutenant Penny spoke with a voice of authority. Penny was what the enlisted men described as "West Point from his boots to his cap." He wasn't well liked by his men but he was respected. Since Penny had no intention of socializing with any of them, he really didn't care. He was twenty-four years old and a product of his upbringing. He had been raised by well-to-do parents who had instilled in him a dedication to duty. As far as Harold Penny was concerned, there was only black and white with regards to any issue, no shades of gray allowed. He had entered West Point with the intention of making a career out of the Army. He had graduated from the military academy in time to serve during the final campaigns of the war in Virginia. By the time the documents of surrender were signed at Appomattox, Harold Penny had began to have other ideas about his life's vocation. The past few months on the Texas frontier had erased any doubts he might have had about leaving the army. Penny intended to return to his home in Connecticut and start a new life. With this in mind, the young lieutenant was in no mood to take any guff from these Texans, even if they were Texas Rangers.

Captain William Timothy Johnson, in command of this company of the Texas Rangers was as different as night and day from Lieutenant Harold Penny. Johnson, like Leroy Wiley, was Texas through and through. Not only did he not know what was happening in the rest of the United States of America, he didn't care. His whole world was right here in Texas, in the company of men who shared his values. He liked every man in his command and they, in turn, liked and respected him. There was no doubt that they would follow him anywhere.

"Captain, I'll expect you and your men to be saddled and ready to move out in an hour." Lieutenant Penny's tone of voice left no doubt in anyone's mind who was in charge. With that, he turned and walked back to his waiting mount.

CHAPTER ∞ 6

Willis kept his horse beside Leroy's mount as they cleared the canyon entrance and headed south towards Fort Belknap. He leaned to the side and whispered so that only Leroy could hear, "Ain't he the one?"

"You're damned right he's the one." Leroy spit the words through tightly clinched teeth. "That's the sonofabitch that ground us down at Palmito Ranch."

"I thought so," Willis, paused for a second, then looked at Leroy and asked, "What are you going to do?"

Leroy turned and stared back at O'Connor. He wanted O'Connor to know that he hadn't forgotten what had happened at Palmito Ranch.

Sergeant Dan O'Connor glared back at Leroy, then slowly smiled. *When the time comes,* O'Connor thought. *I'll show 'em who's in charge now. Texas Rangers my ass, they ain't nothin' but a bunch of sorry Rebs without their uniforms.*

"Now that I know he's here, I'll just play my cards and wait for the right time." Leroy struggled to get his emotions under control.

"Give any thought as to how you might take him out?" asked Willis.

"When the time comes, I'll probably bushwhack 'em. That's what he deserves." Leroy's expression turned deadly serious. "But until then, Willis, we've got to watch our backs."

"The Captain will take care of any trouble," Willis said in a reassuring tone of voice.

"Not likely," Leroy shook his head. "That damn Yank Lieutenant outranks him. So does O'Connor. You forget that we're all under martial law right now." He turned to Willis and grinned, "This is what my brother Carter refers to as the Yankee Reconstruction of the Southland."

"No matter what you call it, there's gonna to be some hard times for awhile," Willis sighed as he looked down at the sandy clay soil. "Leroy," Willis had turned his attention to thoughts of home, "I sure do miss the sugar maples back home in Tyler. Ain't no sugar maples or willow oaks anywhere around this part of Texas."

Leroy tried to ignore Willis' talk about the trees in east Texas. His mind was on other things. "Forget about the damn trees. We've got enough trouble, what with the Comanch and the Union Army without you worrying about sugar maples and willow oaks. But you're right, these next few years are gonna be hard times for all of us. And it won't end until we kick every last Yankee butt out of Texas," Leroy's face melted into a huge smile. "Maybe the Comanch will do the job for us. You never know."

"I don't think that's likely to happen, Leroy. The Yanks got too many men and too much firepower for even the Comanch."

"If it means killing the likes of O'Connor and smart mouthed Yankee lieutenants like Penny, I might even consider giving the Comanch some help."

"You better watch your mouth, Leroy," Willis warned as he looked around to see if anyone had heard what Leroy had said.

"Oh I can do that just fine," Leroy replied. He took another look behind him at a still glaring Sergeant O'Connor. "I can wait. I'm going to be as patient as a Comanch torturing a prisoner after a raid." Leroy turned back to Willis, "Did you know they can keep a man alive for days while they're working on him. Yep, the one thing you can be sure of is that the Comanch are a patient bunch."

Captain Johnson rode in silence most of the day. He understood the command situation and was carefully weighing his options.

Unfortunately, he didn't have many options to weigh. He smiled when he heard his men, mostly farmers, talking about the lay of the land. *Not many trees,* he thought. *Just a few scattered Mesquite trees surrounded by short grass.* His mind drifted when he heard Willis describing the scarlet and gold leaves on the maples and oaks in east Texas.

Penny did his best to ignore the Rangers. As the afternoon sun crossed toward the west, He began to look for a place to set up camp. He realized that the Rangers knew the terrain far better than he did, but he was bound and determined not to ask for their assistance.

Leroy touched the sides of ol' Captain Jack, his new mount. He liked the horse, and he liked its name. Ol' Jack was the name that the men in the Army of Northern Virginia used to call General Stonewall Jackson. Leroy had never served under Jackson but admired him just the same. Ol' Jack easily caught up with Captain Johnson's mare.

"Think he knows where to find water?" Leroy nodded his head slightly toward Lieutenant Penny.

"I doubt it." The Ranger Captain continued looking toward the countryside that stretched out ahead of the tired riders. "But he ain't going to ask us, and I'm not about to offer any advice."

Leroy thought about the situation for a moment before replying. "Well, if we pass that bluff over yonder without turning east, we'll miss the river and any chance to have water for supper and coffee."

"So be it," Johnson replied. "We've done without before, the question is, have they?"

"Probably not," Leroy laughed. "Maybe it's time for them to find out they ain't right about everything."

"Agreed," Johnson smiled and turned his attention back to the Texas prairie and the trail ahead.

Sergeant Dan O'Connor, formally of the 34th Indiana Infantry, now assigned to the 2nd US Cavalry, planned to stay in the army as long as possible. In a time when most soldiers out west went hungry, he managed to stay big and strong enough to intimidate just about anyone he met whether they were in or out of the army. The tough Sergeant had been part of the wave of starving Irish immigrants arriving in America during the 1850's, fleeing English rule and the famine in his Irish homeland. O'Connor had come from nothing and had nothing to go back to. He was satisfied with the simple pleasures that made a soldier's life bearable. He did, however, expect a little justice and a bit of revenge now and then. Leroy Wiley, in O'Connor's opinion, deserved some good ol' fashion Yankee justice and he, Sergeant Dan O'Connor, was entitled to some personal revenge.

The last major land battle of the war was fought at a place in south Texas called Palmito Ranch. The Confederate Army, composed almost entirely of units from Texas, won a decisive victory against the Union forces that were attempting to invade Texas. Two days later, the Texans were forced to lay down their weapons and surrender to their own prisoners after learning that the documents of surrender had been signed in faraway Virginia. The Texans, under the command of Colonel Rip Ford, were forced to endure the humiliation heaped upon them by the Union prisoners turned victors. Leroy and Sergeant O'Connor had a nasty confrontation after the Texans surrendered. O'Connor had intended to teach the smart mouthed Reb a lesson he wouldn't soon forget. Unfortunately for O'Connor, Leroy escaped, leaving behind a rattlesnake as a keepsake for the Union Sergeant. O'Connor had been seething with anger ever since. He was now ready to explode. Everyone, including Lieutenant Penny was aware of O'Connor's famous temper. The lieutenant was anxious to get to the fort before words led to violence. Penny knew that once they reached Fort Belknap any problems between the Rangers and the soldiers would be handled by someone far above his pay grade.

Captain Johnson was just as concerned about his Rangers as Lieutenant Penny was about his troopers. But while Penny was determined to dump this problem in the lap of the commanding officer at Fort Belknap, Johnson was bound and determined to get his Rangers away from the Federal troops as soon as the opportunity presented itself. While they rode south toward the fort, Johnson was trying to come up with a plan that would allow him and his men to ride east toward his home in Mount Pleasant. Johnson decided that Leroy Wiley's feud with

Sergeant O'Connor might be the answer he was searching for. He signaled Leroy to move his horse close to Johnson's mare.

"Leroy," Johnson whispered. "How's that shoulder of yours?"

"Not bad, Captain," Leroy replied. "You have something in mind?"

"Think you can mix it up with that big, ugly Yankee sergeant without him taking your head off?" Johnson's voice was calm but his body was tense.

Leroy's face broke into a wide grin before he spoke. "Anytime you want, Captain," Leroy answered.

Looking ahead at the big sergeant, then glancing at Leroy's slight build, Johnson shook his head and felt a mix of admiration and pride. Johnson didn't say another word, he just nodded in the direction of O'Connor. Leroy immediately tapped his boot heels into the sides of 'Ol Jack and was on his way to challenge O'Connor.

Leroy gave a slight nod as he passed Willis and Dave English. "Be ready," he said.

"Oh, hell," Willis muttered. "Here we go again. I knew it was coming."

"It was bound to happen," Dave replied as he pulled the reins to his horse in order to follow Leroy's lead. "Might as well get it over with now as later."

Willis felt otherwise but he too pulled his horse out of line. *Damnit,* he thought. *I hope Leroy knows what he's doing.*

Penny, O'Connor, and most of the Union cavalry troops noticed the three Rangers as they rode towards the head of the column. Penny turned to O'Connor, "I suppose they want us to stop for a break, we've been pushing it a bit hard."*It's about time to rest the horses anyway,* Penny reasoned.

"Lieutenant, I smell trouble, it don't take three Rangers to ask for a stop to piss." O'Connor reached down and unsnapped the holster of his Colt pistol in case the opportunity arose to blow Leroy Wiley's head off.

I'll get that sonofabitch first, he thought. *And then I'll get one more before —.* He let his mind skip the rest of the picture.

Leroy rode up beside O'Connor without speaking. The sergeant waited for Leroy to make his move.

Before either man could act, Lieutenant Penny spoke in a loud authoritative voice, "Sergeant O'Connor, instruct the men to walk their horses for one hour."

Immediately, O'Connor roared, "Dismount!"

Leroy grinned. *Better still,* he thought. *It'll be easier if he's on foot.*

The men climbed down and began to lead their tired horses. They were walking on hard packed dirt covered with a thick layer of dust. The Rangers and soldiers who had been raised on farms took note of the dry land.

"Awhile back, we went through some rain," Dave English remarked to Willis. "Ain't much fallen here though."

"Every time I'm west of the Brazos, I'm thankful that I live in East Texas." Willis pointed to the dry land. "Hard enough to make it on good dirt. It'd be darn near impossible to grow anything here."

"Not much good for grazing either," Dave added.

"I'm not cut out to farm," Derrick stated emphatically. "Think the Rangers will ever be more than part time work?" He looked toward Willis and Dave for an answer then to Captain Johnson.

Captain Johnson knew the answer. He had his doubts that they would be paid for this past month, much less for any future service. Times were tough. Texas owed a lot of money to the Federal government because of the war. The occupying army was in charge of keeping the peace. *What, if any, mission would be given to the Rangers?* William Johnson worried.

Derrick, not getting an answer from anyone, frowned. He didn't want to return to Smith County and bust sod for ten hours every day. His brother Darrell was doing that now. Derrick and Darrell had talked about their future. The only two ways they could see of getting away from farm work was to either ride with the Rangers or rob banks. The thought of Leroy Wiley coming after him made robbing banks a less than attractive career move.

Johnson looked away. His mind continued to dwell on what was about to happen between Leroy and the Yankee sergeant.

After attending to their horses, Lieutenant Penny gave the order for his men and the Rangers to rest. Leroy leaned against the trunk of an old Mesquite tree and began planning his next move. The easiest thing to do would be to walk up and give O'Connor a shot to his big fat belly. But that would be too obvious and O'Connor would be expecting him to do just that. Leroy thought about this for a moment then his face broke into a wide grin. *Hell, why not?*

He walked slowly over to O'Connor. The sergeant and two troopers stood there waiting for him to speak but Leroy didn't say a word. Seemingly without any fear of the consequences, he drew back his fist and hit O'Connor with a powerful right to the jaw. O'Connor staggered backward, but managed to catch himself before he fell. His face turned a furious red. He gathered himself for a few seconds, then let out a ferocious roar and charged at Leroy. Leroy reacted instinctively and side stepped the charging Union sergeant. The fight quickly drew the attention of the other soldiers and Rangers. They quickly formed a tight circle around the struggling men and cheered on their favorite. O'Connor was so angry, he was out of control. Most of his punches missed their mark. Leroy kept circling O'Connor while he peppered the sergeant's face with his fists. O'Connor finally landed a solid blow to the side of Leroy's head that momentarily stunned him. Luckily for Leroy, O'Connor was too exhausted to take advantage of the situation. As O'Connor stumbled forward, Leroy regained his footing and landed a hard right fist to his stomach. Just as the sergeant crumbled to the ground, Penny and Johnson shoved their way through the circle of men.

"Enough!" Penny shouted, furious at the apparent breakdown of discipline. "We have enough on our hands fighting the Comanche without fighting amongst ourselves."

Johnson spoke in a more even tone, "Step back, Leroy. Let him be." He then turned to Lieutenant Penny. "We can't let this go on." He gestured to the men who had by now had formed sides. "Lieutenant, I'm taking my men out of here. We will then proceed to deal with the savages who have been killing our fellow Texans."

Red-faced with anger, Penny jabbed his finger against Johnson's chest. "You'll do what I damn well tell you to do."

Johnson was taken aback by Penny's show of anger toward him in front of the men. The Rangers and cavalry troops froze. Men on both sides began to face off and reach for their weapons. Captain Johnson realized that it wouldn't take much to start a full fledged battle between the two sides. He glared at Penny before speaking, not bothering to hide his hostility. He chose his words very carefully while at the same time trying to regain his own composure.

"My men and I are riding out of here with or without your permission. We have our orders. You have yours. This has gotten off to a bad start. I'm sorry for that. I hope that in the future we will be able to work together. But it's going to take time. It won't be easy for your men or mine to put four years of killing and hatred behind us.

Penny took a deep breath trying to get his own emotions under control. "It's probably a good idea for you to take your men out of here before they cause any more trouble." He hesitated before giving the order Johnson was waiting to hear. "All right, on your way. But you understand this, I'm in command here and in the future, you and your men will do as I say."

Johnson nodded in agreement. There *would be more moments like this,* he thought. In the end, the Rangers would have to get used to the fact that they would be taking orders from an occupying army.

CHAPTER ∞ 7

It was a warm, cloudy day when Leroy reached the hill overlooking the family's farm near Tyler. *No one's out in the yard I guess they're having supper,* he thought as he rode towards his home. *Wonder what Mindy's going to say when she sees me?* He smiled as his mind pictured his pretty wife. Then he remembered his mother and father and the loss they had suffered.

"Nothing will bring Clayton back," Leroy sighed. "Even if I killed every Comanche in Texas. My brother would still be gone. I've gotta put that all behind me and take care of my family."

The dog, lying on the porch, started barking as Leroy slowly rode up to the house. *Damn,* Leroy thought. *That hound has been barking every time I come home for as long as I can remember.* The big hound, satisfied that he had alerted the family to Leroy's arrival, wagged his tail then curled it behind him.

Mindy opened the front door to see what was causing the dog to bark. She was wearing his favorite powder blue dress and had her pretty brown hair tied back with a blue ribbon. Leroy smiled and tried to take in everything about her. Riding closer, Leroy was surprised to see his brother Carter standing behind her. He waited for Mindy's reaction. *For a little gal, she's got a great big temper,* he reminded himself.

"You still mad at him?" Carter laughed as he watched Mindy frantically attempting to smooth her hair and pinch color into her cheeks.

"I was mad at him yesterday and I was still mad at him this morning but I'm not mad at him now," she laughed as she broke into a run toward Leroy. Her anger had vanished as soon as she realized that he was safe, and that once again, he had come home to her. Her heart pounded as she ran along the path that led to the love of her life. Leroy climbed down from the saddle and held out his arms. When she reached him, Mindy was unable to speak. She reached up to touch his cheeks.

Leroy winked at her and said, "I came back as soon as I could."

"I know," she murmured. She grabbed his hand and started pulling him toward the house.

Carter was joined on the porch by their parents and his wife. "Just like Leroy," he turned to his mother and laughed. "He's home in time for supper."

Nancy leaned against Carter and watched Leroy's happy homecoming. "Mindy's a saint to put up with him. He rides off with the Rangers for months at a time and then comes back whenever it suits him," she said.

Carter nodded in agreement. "No one here is going to argue with you."

Taylor and Verlinda Wiley were both thrilled with the safe return of their son. They led their two remaining sons and their wives back into the house so the family could sit back down to supper. Leroy could already smell supper cooking on the stove. He suddenly realized how hungry he was and how much he had missed his wife and family.

Leroy and Mindy had been repeatedly separated, first by the war, then by Leroy's commitment to the Texas Rangers, and now by the hard work entailed in just trying to survive and raise a family. Nevertheless, their life together had been what lovers long for, the joy of living each day given to them as man and wife. They were deeply in love, and this commitment enabled them to bridge the many gaps of separation that they were forced to endure during their married life. All

Mindy wanted was the security of Leroy's presence at the farm. But the burden of making ends meet fell to Leroy, and that burden was, more often than not, overwhelming. He had to ensure that the family could put the crop in every year, while at the same time feeding and clothing the family. Leroy had too much pride to borrow money from Carter. His father was not a young man anymore, and his ability to work the farm was now limited. Clayton, the true farmer in the family, was gone. It was up to Leroy to take care of his family, and he was determined to do that even if it meant leaving Mindy for months at a time. Mindy tried to understand his role as the family breadwinner, but it always upset her when he had to leave the farm to earn extra money.

Shortly after returning from west Texas and his encounter with the Comanche and Sergeant O'Connor, Leroy learned from Captain Johnson that the Rangers would be cutting back the number of men on active duty. It seemed that there wasn't enough money to pay for a full company of Rangers. In addition, the local military commander was of the opinion that his troops could handle things without any help from the Texas Rangers. In light of Leroy's problems with Sergeant O'Connor, Captain Johnson thought that it would be a good idea to keep Leroy away from the United States Cavalry, at least for the time being. Therefore, Leroy was one of the first Rangers to be asked to go on an unpaid leave of absence.

Enforcing the Yankee Reconstruction laws against his fellow Texans was definitely not something Leroy wanted to do. But still he was going to miss the camaraderie of the Rangers not to mention the extra money it put in his pocket. He couldn't help being somewhat melancholy as he rode back to his farm that early spring afternoon after his meeting with Captain Johnson.

"Sometime loving another person is hard work," Leroy spoke his mind. After all, no one was within hearing distance. "Life is full of problems and sometimes people expect too much from each other. Mindy forgets about all the responsibilities I have." He was trying to come up with the right words and decide when would be the best time to tell his wife what he had decided to do. His mind drifted back to a conversation he had with his brother after leaving Captain Johnson's office.

"One of the realities of life," Carter pointed out to his brother, "is that you have to make a living. There's not much work around here right now. You won't take money from me, and I can't see you robbing banks or rustling cattle. So what choices do you have left?"

"The cattle drives," Leroy had replied. "I plan on signing on with one of those cattle drives that are getting ready to head north to Kansas."

"Oh, my Lord," Carter exclaimed. "Mindy will be furious."

"That's for sure," Leroy leaned against the wall and looked out the window of Carter's law office toward the streets of Tyler. "But I got to do something and I ain't thought of nothing else." He turned back to look at Carter. "Willis is going with me."

"Oh, that will be a big help. When are you leaving?"

"In about a week,"

Carter raised his eyebrows. "You're a strong man, Leroy. But cattle drives are miserable in the best of times."

For a moment Leroy's face showed some concern, but then his grin returned, and he shrugged his shoulders. Carter had seen him do this time and again while they were boys growing up on the farm.

"Compared to four years in the Confederate Army, Carter," Leroy smirked. "It can't be that bad. I hear the chuck wagon cooks are pretty good. In any case, bad food is a lot better than no food. Besides, I'll draw enough pay in Kansas to keep the family going this winter and pay to put in next year's crop."

Carter was worried about Leroy's joining a cattle drive but he was reluctant to sat this to his brother. *What good would it do?* Carter asked himself as he watched Leroy pace back and forth across the room. He hesitated, then said in a thoughtful tone, said, "Send word when you can and try to stay out of trouble."

Leroy burst out laughing. "That's the problem, I'm going to be in trouble the minute I tell Mindy."

"We might as well have a last drink to your health before you face the wrath of Mindy," Carter smiled as he pictured Mindy giving Leroy hell.

Leroy gave a nervous chuckle and opened the office door. The two men made their way down the street to the saloon to have a drink together before Leroy left for the farm. Leroy noticed a soft breeze blowing in from the west. He took in a deep breath, then joined Carter in tipping their hats as they passed a plump woman carrying a basket of sewing notions.

CHAPTER ∞ 8

Mindy girl," Leroy smiled as he stepped up on the porch. "Let's plan a nice ride after church on Sunday."

Mindy reached up on tiptoes to give him a quick kiss on the cheek. "Remember this is Sunday Social day at church," she reminded him of the monthly covered dish dinner that the ladies the church put together once a month. "You know that Mama Wiley always wants to be the first one there and last one to leave. That doesn't leave much time for riding."

"Well," Leroy grinned. "Maybe we could hurry her along just a little bit. After the pies are served, of course."

Mindy's clear brown eyes gave him a suspicious look. "Just what are you up to, Leroy?"

Leroy laughed. "Is there something wrong with a man wanting to spend some time with his favorite girl?"

"No," she smiled. Although she suspected that Leroy was up to something, it was still nice to be asked to go for a ride, whatever his motive. Mindy passed Leroy and walked across the porch to sit in the swing. She had worked hard all week and was looking forward to Sunday, the Lord's day, when work was set aside and events such as the Sunday social filled her thoughts. When he sat down beside her, she lifted her arm and began to stroke the back of his head. He put his arm around her and they sat in the swing for the longest time, according to Mama Wiley who witnessed these sweet moments through the parlor window. It was one of those memories that she tucked away to share with her sister, Gladys.

While Leroy finished putting on his Sunday go-to-meeting clothes, Mindy cleared the breakfast dishes away from the table, handing each plate to Mama Wiley who then carefully dropped them into a tub of warm soapy water to soak.

Leroy saw his father packing jars of apple jelly and pear preserves into a box to take to the Social. There were limits to what Leroy thought should be taken to be shared with their neighbors. The cupboard, he reasoned, was not that well stocked. His father laughed when Leroy reached into the box and removed three jars.

"Leroy," his mother called out. "Put those preserves back in the box. We've got plenty."

Leroy turned to his father and asked, "Does she have eyes in the back of her head?"

"No," Verlinda said in a loud voice. "And there is nothing wrong with my hearing either."

Leroy looked at his father and made a funny face.

"She's a school teacher," Taylor whispered. "I knew I was in for trouble the day I married her. She knows too much, by golly."

Leroy laughed. He carefully placed the jars back in the box, except for one that he kept behind his back. Mindy had been watching all of this from the kitchen. Without saying a word, she casually walked to the table, smiled, then circled behind Leroy and took the jar of pear preserves from his hand. Leroy grinned when he saw her place the jar on the back shelf of the cupboard.

As they were getting ready to leave for church, Leroy noticed that his wife looked especially pretty in her Sunday dress. It was light gold with tiny blue flowers on the skirt and sleeves. His eyes never left her as she picked up her bonnet and walked over to the mirror that hung next to the gun cabinet by the front door. While adjusting her bonnet, she looked back at him through the mirror and said, "I feel awful about this Leroy, but I don't think we'll have time to go for that ride today." She paused while tying the bow under her chin then added, "I hope you aren't too disappointed."

"You can't plan anything else on Social Sunday days," Mama Wiley whisked by them, Bible in hand, bound and determined to get everyone to church on time. "Leroy knows that, so don't pay him no mind, Mindy." As she reached the door she turned and looked directly at Taylor. "Well, what are you waiting for? Bring the food and let's be on our way!"

Taylor motioned to Leroy to wait by the front door. After Mindy and Verlinda had stepped away from the porch, he offered his youngest son some fatherly advice. "If I were you," Taylor smiled. "I'd wait until the last minute before the start of the church service, then I'd take that pretty girl of yours and go for that ride you were talking about." He took a cautionary look out to where the ladies were waiting by the wagon before adding, "I'd just make sure I got back in time for the social. Maybe just a little early so folks can see you and Mindy helping the ladies set up."

Leroy laughed.

"Shush up," Taylor cautioned. "She's a school teacher; she'll get after both of us." He gestured toward his wife, who was getting more impatient by the minute.

How many times have I heard him say that, Leroy smiled to himself.

Leroy reached for his Dad's Sunday hat, handed it to him, then lifted his own black Stetson off of the coat hook, and followed his father out the front door and onto the porch.

It was a fine Sunday morning when Leroy stepped down from the wagon then lifted Mindy off the wagon seat and onto the ground. The congregation was already gathering at the steps of the church door. Taylor and Verlinda walked on ahead chatting with friends and neighbors. Leroy took his time pulling the box of food from under the wagon seat.

Mindy glanced across the church lawn then looked back at Leroy.

"We are going to be the last ones at church." She whispered. "Leroy, hurry up, they're about to close the doors."

Leroy waited.

"Leroy," Mindy sighed. "We'll be stuck on the back row with Willis."

"What would be so wrong with that?" he asked while pushing the box back under the seat.

"Not a thing except he starts snoring the moment Preacher Owings begins his sermon. "All the snorers sit on the back pew."

Suddenly, without any warning, Leroy grabbed Mindy by the waist and swung her back up onto the wagon seat. Before she could say a word he climbed up beside her and tapped the reins. The team started forward and Mindy suddenly realized she would not be attending church that day.

"You are a rascal, Leroy Wiley," She laughed. "Mama Wiley is going to be mad as she can be about us skipping church service."

Leroy tapped the reins again and looked down at Mindy's round face. In spite of her full cheeks, she was thin, with delicate features. Leroy thought she was beautiful. He was proud that after having their baby boy, she still had a flat belly.

Mindy glanced back at the church, made a helpless gesture with her hands, then smiled and said, "Let's go over by the lake." She slipped her arm through his and decided that this was turning out to be a very nice Sunday.

She's in such a good mood, he thought. *Wonder if I should let it wait until tomorrow?*

Scattered low hanging clouds below a pale blue sky made for a perfect ride in the country. Mindy leaned against Leroy as he drove the team toward a small lake almost a mile from the church.

Mindy noticed a few birds drifting down from the clouds. "Spring is finally here," she said cheerfully as they rode past hills already covered in light green foliage. "I love the color of the wildflowers."

"Not too many of 'em out yet," Leroy pointed to a few patches of color on the hillside they were passing. "Look, Mindy, there's a blue bird's nest."

"Blue birds?" she laughed. "Leroy, you know just about as much about birds as you do about farming."

"More, I hope," he responded with a chuckle. "At least I know a buzzard from a robin. That's more than I know about putting in a decent crop."

"Oh, you'll do just fine running the farm. You don't give yourself enough credit," Mindy frowned, then she leaned forward and turned in order to look directly into her husband's eyes before she asked the question that had been bothering her since they had left the church.

"Leroy, do you mind telling me why we are out here?"

Leroy gave her a quick glance before responding. She looked so happy, he decided not to tell her anything that would spoil her day. Leroy had no problem facing the Comanche or the Union Army, but Mindy was another matter. He hesitated, then deliberately hedged the truth, "I just needed some time alone with you, Mindy. I want to talk about a few problems that we, I mean I, have to work out."

Mindy looked closely at Leroy. He seemed tense. She mentally braced herself for the bad news that she knew was coming. She gripped his arm and closed her eyes for an instant, then opened them to meet his gaze.

"We need money to make ends meet. I don't know that we can depend on this year's crop to get through next winter, what with farm prices being so low," he explained. "Like before, I'm gonna have to work outside the farm."

"You're not going away with the Rangers again so soon are you?" She was suddenly conscious of the lump in her throat.

He winked and gave her arm a reassuring squeeze, "Nope, the Rangers have cut back for awhile. Just as well, the way things are right now with the Yanks running things here in Texas. I'd probably wind up in trouble for shooting blue bellies instead of the Comanche."

"Then what do you mean?" She looked up, relieved that he wasn't going off with the Rangers. She was still curious as to what had him so uptight.

Once again he lost his nerve. "Just that sometimes I might have to go where there's work." He nervously loosened the knot of his tie. *I hate Sunday clothes,* he thought to himself.

"But not anytime soon? Leroy, you just got back. JR and I both need you." Mindy shook her head.

Instead of answering, Leroy put his arms tightly around her and covered her lips with a tender kiss. She closed her eyes and felt her body relax. *He's not going anywhere,* she reassured herself. *He's staying right here with me.* She kissed him back with fierce passion.

Maybe we need to skip church more often, he thought.

A few moments later, Leroy lifted Mindy down from the wagon and they walked hand and hand to a quiet and peaceful crescent shaped lake. The water was almost clear and seemed to mirror the colors and shapes of the sky, clouds and the few trees that clustered around the far side off the lake. At moments such as this, Mindy realized how much she loved her husband.

CHAPTER ∞ 9

"When faithfully preached and obeyed, without addition or subtraction, the Bible, which is the inspired word of God, will keep man from sin!" Pastor Owings always tried to leave the members of his congregation with something to think about until the next service. He leaned forward over the pulpit and stood on his toes to drive his point home. Although the good pastor was a small man, he appeared much larger behind the raised pulpit. His glasses reflected the light coming through the large windows on each side of the altar, giving his eyes a sparkle. "And now, we will open the book of Hymns to page 42 and sing two verses of *Shall We Gather At The River.*"

The widow Mildred Sims plucked the keys of the harpsichord with all her might and music filled the air.

"The Bee-u-ti-ful, bee-u-ti-ful riv-er," sung by the worshipers could be heard almost a mile away from the country church.

"Leroy," a tone of panic filled Mindy's voice. "That's the closing hymn!" She reached up to the bodice of her dress and turned up the small round shaped gold watch pin to check the time. "We've got to get back to the church." She grabbed his hand and started to run towards the wagon. "If we hurry, maybe nobody will notice we've been gone."

Leroy, who could care less about appearances, didn't exactly race to the church social with the speed he had recently demonstrated while running from the Comanche.

As they approached the church Mindy caught a glimpse of the assembled ladies who were all glaring at the couple as their wagon came to a halt. *Oh, well, what do I care?* she smiled to herself. *The time I just spent with Leroy is worth the aggravation. If only Leroy would just behave himself, he might save us both a heap of trouble,* she thought. One glance at Leroy told her that wasn't going to happen.

"Leroy Wiley, I'd be much obliged if you'd tell me where the two of you have been?" Verlinda demanded in an angry tone of voice.

"Ma," he walked up to her and smiled, "The good book says that God isn't just inside the church. Mindy and I have been enjoying this pretty day the Lord has given us. And," he looked straight at his Aunt Gladys before finishing his explanation, "seems to me that God's more than preachin' and marryin' and buryin'."

Aunt Gladys smiled directly at her favorite nephew. *I was young once too, Leroy,* she thought. She realized Leroy was asking for her help so she stepped forward and reached for Mindy's hand.

"All right, Mindy," Aunt Gladys spoke as if issuing an order, "You and I need to help set the tables."

"I'm coming, Aunt Gladys," Mindy stammered as she rushed past her mother-in-law.

Leroy thought the whole uproar was funny.

After the meal, Mindy and Leroy were enjoying Preacher Owings' fiddle playing. Leroy didn't much care for his sermons, but Preacher Owings sure had a way with a fiddle. As the preacher was finishing one of his best Virginia Mountain tunes, Willis and Patsy began walking towards Mindy. Leroy realized that this could lead to trouble.

"Mindy," Leroy reached over and put his hand on his wife's shoulder. "We might better head on home," he said, while trying to catch Willis' eye.

Even though Mindy had a mind of her own, she still knew her place. Obviously disappointed, she turned to walk to the wagon with Leroy. Just as he thought he was in the clear, Leroy heard Willis speak his mind—a mind Carter had described on many occasions as being "uncluttered." Leroy wasn't entirely sure what Carter meant by that, but he knew from long experiences that thinking was not one of Willis' strong points.

"Mindy, you be sure and call on Patsy if you need anything while Leroy and I are gone."

Mindy stopped short and looked back at Willis, then glared at Leroy. "Whatever do you mean, Willis?" she asked in a sweet voice that Leroy knew was masking a fierce anger. "Leroy isn't going to be riding with the Rangers for awhile." She brushed her cheek with her sleeve. "Isn't that what you said, Leroy?"

Before Leroy could answer, Willis made sure that Leroy would spend the night sleeping on the front porch. "Didn't Leroy tell you that the two of us are headed down to south Texas to sign on with one of them big cattle drives?" Willis frowned, then twisted his lips for a brief moment until it finally occurred to him that Leroy hadn't told Mindy anything about the cattle drive.

"Leroy," Mindy's brown eyes grew even darker. "What exactly is Willis talking about?"

Leroy glared at Willis but didn't say a word.

"Leroy," Mindy felt exasperated. "Say it ain't so. Tell me that you wouldn't go off on a cattle drive without talking to me first."

She looked around her, first at Leroy, then at Willis and finally she met Patsy's sad face. Mindy was hurt, the baby that Leroy still didn't know about seemed to stir slightly within her, and she unconsciously placed her hand on the spot where she knew the baby rested. She lifted her chin defiantly and fought back tears.

"Take me home, Leroy," she said softly. She realized that she would probably have this baby alone. *Just like the last time,* she thought. *First there was the war, then the Rangers, now he's going off on some cattle drive. What's a body to do?* she asked herself.

"Thanks, Willis," Leroy hissed. "You sure set me up good this time."

"Hell, Leroy," Willis shook his head. "How was I supposed to know you ain't told her nothing 'bout the cattle drive?"

Patsy reached for Leroy's arm. "It ain't right that you didn't tell her."

Patsy was a pioneer woman used to hard times. Her face was lined from worry, while her hands were rough from daily chores. She was thin from "doing without" because Willis ate first, then the kids filled their plates in her kitchen. She ate last. Often as not, there wasn't much left. Patsy's one good Sunday dress had more patches than plain cloth. She worked as hard as most of the menfolk, yet there was a quiet strength about her that Leroy admired. He was not about to argue with Patsy. Leroy truly believed that next to Mindy and his mother, Patsy was the finest woman in Texas.

"I know, Patsy," he looked hurt. *What had Mindy done to deserve him treating her this way?* "I tried to tell her, but it's hard. I've had to leave her so many times."

Patsy touched her face and felt tears between her fingers. "Even so," she sighed. "It's harder on her than it is on you. She's the one being left behind."

Leroy leaned down and brushed her cheek. "I'll try to do better," he promised. His eyes followed Mindy as she walked straight to the wagon. *If only she knew how much I'm hurting,* he thought.

As they watched him follow his wife to the wagon, Patsy's heart went out to Mindy and Leroy. On the other hand, Willis' only concern was to make sure that Patsy wasn't angry with him. *It's one thing for Leroy to be in the doghouse,* he thought. *But I sure don't wanna join him.*

As the wagon carrying the young couple slowly rode away, Patsy's thoughts were about Mindy. She was worried about Mindy being upset while carrying the baby. She wished Mindy would go ahead and tell Leroy that she was with child.

Willis walked up behind Patsy and whispered in her ear,"How the hell was I supposed to know he hadn't told her nothin'. I don't read minds."

"Maybe you don't read 'em," Patsy jerked her head around toward Willis, her cheeks flushed with anger. "But you sure do speak yours!"

Willis grimaced, waiting for her to finish the lecture he knew was coming. He could tell that he wasn't off the hook yet. Patsy was seldom angry with him, but when she did get mad it was usually a barn burner.

"And," she pinched his arm as she spoke, "Don't use cuss words here on the Lord's property." She hurried back toward the church, leaving a confused Willis behind.

I kind of figure all property belongs to the Lord, he thought. *Ain't no matter where you say what. He's gonna hear it.*

CHAPTER ∞ 10

The day dawned with a bright blue sky and only a slight breeze, something that Leroy had learned to be thankful for when preparing for the trail. He took a deep breath and thought of Mindy. How sweet she had been last night pressing her face against his chest and asking him to promise that everything would be all right.

Taking slow, long strides, he walked past the old hound dog, who immediately began barking. That's when he saw Mindy standing on the porch in the early morning light, all wrapped up in a shawl looking small and frail.

She hiked up her skirt and walked toward him, shivering at the slight chill in the morning air. She wanted to beg him not to go, but bit her tongue. Instead, they hurried into the kitchen to share what would be their last breakfast together for the next several months.

While Leroy quietly cut the thin strips of bacon and mashed up the eggs on his plate, his mind was on the trail to south Texas. He heard his mother reassuring his wife that he would be all right. He looked up at Mindy. Their eyes met and she tried to smile. His wife would be all right, too, he heard his father say. Not to worry, they'd take care of Mindy. Leroy felt his chest tighten.

And then it was time to go. He watched Mindy throw a knitted shawl over her shoulders, carefully tie a bag of biscuits and ham, and briefly touch his shoulder. When she opened the door he saw the early morning sun pour into the parlor. None of this lightened his burden. No amount of sunshine would brighten his heavy heart. *How many times had they gone through this,* he asked himself.

A noise outside attracted his attention. Carter was there. Grim faced, silently waiting to see him off. *Why doesn't the darn hound bark at him?* Leroy asked himself. He noticed that Carter held a new blanket that was tightly wrapped and ready to be tied to the back of Leroy's saddle.

"I stopped at a farmhouse down the way," Carter pointed behind him. "And collected someone to ride shotgun for you."

Willis peered around Carter and managed a weak smile. "Patsy sent biscuits," was all he could say.

Leroy didn't speak. He walked over to his mother, held her for a brief moment then nodded toward his father.

"Time to move on," he heard Willis say.

As he passed Mindy, Willis spoke in a resigned tone of voice, "Bye, Mindy."

Mindy bit her lip. "Let Leroy finish his coffee," she was actually talking to Leroy, not to Willis.

The fact that she had cried until there were no more tears left gave her the strength to say goodbye in front of the little group gathered on the porch. Leroy's parents, his brother Carter and Willis made small talk about the cool morning and the wind blowing from the west. Leroy, his jaw set, said nothing and kept his eyes on Mindy.

"I'm so worried about you facing all those cattle rustlers and Indians," Mindy whispered. "Promise me that you're going to be careful."

"Who's been fillin' your pretty head with such silliness?" Leroy picked her up in his strong arms.

She hesitated, then whispered, "You'll mash the biscuits."

"They're gonna get mashed anyhow," he laughed.

Carter took the blanket roll and joined Willis who was waiting by the horses.

"The drives start all the way down in south Texas," Willis said to Carter.

"I know," Carter answered.

"There's not gonna be much grub, mostly corn meal and bacon with a few beans and biscuits thrown in." Willis paused for a moment. Carter remained in deep thought. "As long as they don't run out of coffee," Willis continued. "That bothered me a lot during the war, not having coffee."

Carter's attention turned to Willis' concerns about living on the trail. "You'll make it just fine, Willis," Carter gave him a pat on the back. "I'll bet you they have sweet breads just like Patsy makes."

Willis shook his head, "I'll bet they don't have no such thing, Carter." Willis swallowed hard. His thoughts returned to Patsy and their family. "Just so long as they don't run out of coffee. It don't have to be good tasting coffee, just coffee."

"I love you, Mindy-girl," Leroy whispered in her ear. "An', I promise you this, ain't no rustlers or Injuns gonna keep me from coming back to you."

Mindy touched his cheek.

He turned and confidently strode away.

As if reading Mindy's mind, Willis called out, "Don't worry about the Injuns, Mindy. It's them Mexican bandits we gotta watch out for."

Leroy heard Mindy's sharp intake of breath followed by a hushed cry. His shoulders sagged. *Damn fool,* thought Leroy. *I ought to shoot him now and put him out of his misery.*

Leroy walked back to hold Mindy for a moment and to reassure her once more that everything was going to be all right.

"Mindy," he lifted her chin. "Ain't no Mexican bandit born that I can't handle, so stop worrying. Just take care of yourself and the folks and I'll be back in a couple of months."

Mindy looked at him, relief showing on her face. "You'll be back before your birthday?"

"If I know an apple pie is waitin'."

She nodded. "I promise."

"Leroy," Carter called out. "You're taking longer to leave Mindy than the cattle drive will last."

"That's for sure," Willis turned his horse away from the house, "I'll wait for you down at the gate, Leroy."

Leroy gave Mindy a final hug, nudged Carter's arm, then climbed on his horse and caught up to Willis.

Mindy said a silent prayer and watched until they were out of sight. Then Carter took her arm, and the two of them walked silently back into the house.

CHAPTER ∞ 11

After the War Between the States, the combination of surplus cattle in Texas and the demand for beef in the northern and eastern markets led to the start of the "long drives" from just north of the Mexican border to the railhead in Abilene, Kansas. These cattle drives followed either the Shawnee, Great Western or Chisholm Trail. In 1866, Jesse Chisholm, a half-breed Cherokee Indian trader, drove a wagon through the Indian Territory to his trading post near Wichita, Kansas. The first cattle drives along the Chisholm Trail actually followed Jesse Chisholm's wagon ruts north through the flatlands.

Leroy was determined to sign onto a drive using the Chisholm Trail. He had spoken with several Rangers who had supplemented their income by driving cattle north to Abilene, and they all were of the opinion that the Chisholm Trail was by far the best route.

Leroy had heard all about the gambling halls and ladies of the evening in Abilene, but other than being a little curious, he really had no interest. In his mind, Abilene sounded like a place to lose your money and find more trouble than a man needed. According to what he had been told, more than one cowboy celebrating the end of the long drive had wound up planted in a cemetery known as Boot Hill.

Driving cattle meant living in the saddle, and that was difficult even in good weather. Leroy had lived in the saddle for weeks at a time both during the war and while serving with the Rangers, but not while driving a herd of cattle. The cattle had to be protected against attacks by Indian raiding parties and rustlers. They also had to be watched over during bad weather. Storms tended to spook the Longhorns, sometimes triggering a deadly stampede. Knowing the hazards of the drive weighed heavily on Leroy's mind.

"Willis, we gotta get us some sure-footed mounts. That might mean the difference whether we make the drive or fall out hurt." Leroy said as they rode along through the new prairie grass.

Willis thought for a moment before answering. "Won't they give us some good horses? I hear tell that the trail boss will carry four or five horses for each man if he's smart."

"Maybe so, but we still got to get us some chaps and a couple of quirts," Leroy continued making a mental list of necessary supplies.

"I need some socks and drawers," Willis frowned. "I need that more than I need a quirt."

Leroy ignored Willis as he rambled on about nothing for several hours. Just as the sun began to drop into the western sky, he noticed smoke coming from the chimney of a farmhouse up ahead. Leroy was hungry and tired. He swallowed his pride and decided to ask for a handout.

"Come on, Willis," he laughed. "All they can say is no."

"That," Willis replied. "And shoot us."

"Willis, you got no faith in your fellow man." Leroy laughed and tapped his spurs. He smiled as he galloped past a field of Mindy's beloved Bluebonnets mixed in with the dark green prairie grass.

The two men rode up to the farm house, dismounted, and were walking towards the front door when suddenly they were looking down the barrel of an old rifle held by a mean looking woman wearing a man's pants and boots.

"Just stop right there," the woman ordered.

"We don't mean you no harm. We're just trying to get some supper, Ma'am," Leroy held his hands out in a gesture of friendship. "We can pay for what we eat."

"I ain't got much and my man's sick," she made a slight motion with the rifle toward the house. "Better not come inside. I ain't too sure of what he's got, it's maybe catchin'."

Leroy realized that she must be alone. "That would probably be a good idea," he nodded in agreement. "Can we stay in the barn?"

"If you promise not to come near the house. I stay up all night watching Jesse so don't think you can sneak up on me."

"Don't plan to," Leroy slowly reached into his saddle bag. "I've got some money right here to pay for our keep. We're just passing through on our way down south to sign on to one of them cattle drives. We're family men and I promise you, we mean you no harm." Leroy would have offered to get a doctor for her husband, but from the looks of the farm, he was sure there was no one else in the house, sick or otherwise.

The woman shook her head. "I don't need your money but I sure could use some help with the chores." Lowering the rifle, she pointed toward the barn. "With my man being down, things ain't gettin' done."

"I can see that," Leroy pointed to a pile of wood needing to be chopped. "I'll get the wood chopped up for you and my friend here can draw some water from the well."

"We ain't got no well, but there's a cistern around back." She looked up at Willis and frowned. "I can draw my own water. There's more work for him to do out by the barn."

"Yes, Ma'am," Willis realized that she wanted to keep both strangers in one area of her farm. That way she could keep an eye on them. He started to slowly lead his horse to the water trough. "What do you want me to do?"

She pointed toward a shed attached to the barn. "That's my chicken coop. Go wring a couple of chicken necks for supper."

Willis turned towards the woman, a deep frown formed on his face, he slowly looked back toward the chicken coop. "Yes, Missie, if that's what you want me to do, I'll tend to 'em."

Leroy couldn't help but smile. Of all the jobs on a farm killing chickens was the worst. First you had to chase the chicken all over the yard, snap its neck when you caught it, and then watch it flop and twitch until it finally died. But that wasn't the worst part. The worst part of the job came after you plucked all the feathers out and chopped off the head. Then you had to clean out the bird's insides. Leroy hated the smell of dead chickens. After they were fried or mixed in with dumplings, well that was another matter.

After a while the woman seemed to accept the men for what they claimed to be, cowboys heading south to join on to a cattle drive. She checked to make sure they had the tools they needed, then went back inside the house and started making preparations for supper. But just in case, she kept the rifle by her side and the door bolted.

Leroy took off his shirt, pulled the ax out of a stump and started splitting the blocks of wood into kindling. After only a few chops, he heard an awful commotion coming from the barn. Leroy dropped the axe and walked over to the chicken coop. Willis was running back and forth trying to grab a pair of chickens. Eventually, without any help from Leroy, Willis was able to snap both of their necks. One head came completely off, splattering blood all over Willis. The chickens continued to flop and dance around in circles sending feathers and dirt everywhere. Leroy fell backward laughing. "Hey, Willis, I'll bet that's the hardest you ever had to work for a fried chicken supper," he called out as soon as he caught his breath.

"You get to milk the darn cows at daybreak," Willis answered. "I'm sleeping late."

Leroy finished chopping the wood and began stacking it neatly by the side of the house. He made sure to stack it so that no snakes could wiggle into the pile.

Willis finished plucking the feathers and cleaning out the innards then washed the fresh meat in cold water. When he was finished, he decided to risk getting shot by going around back to the cistern so he could clean up.

"Where's the chickens?" the woman yelled from inside the back door. She was obviously not happy to see Willis roaming around the back of her house.

"By the front door," then pointing to his bloody shirt, he added, "I wanna get cleaned up as best I can for supper."

"Soak 'em in the wash tub over by the cistern, then hang 'em over there. They'll be clean and dry by in the morning."

"Thanks, Ma'am but I ain't got no more clothes," Willis was ashamed of his appearance. A bath was out of the question but at least he could wash up if he had some soap and a wash rag.

"I got some extra clothes," she said in a matter of fact tone of voice. "You stay put and I'll leave 'em on the porch."

"Mighty grateful, Ma'am," Willis called out. But she had closed the back door before he finished speaking.

After stacking the wood, Leroy went to the barn to search for tools so he could fix the barn gate which had come off of it's hinges. He was surprised when Willis suddenly appeared in clean clothes.

"She gave 'em to me," Willis pointed toward the farm house. "Wonder who they belong to?"

Leroy shook his head, "Probably not anyone still alive. Nobody's been working this farm for at least a year."

Willis' expression darkened as he thought of Patsy trying to make do on their farm back in Smith County. "Let's do all we can, Leroy. She's a tough woman but she can't do the hard work." Leroy and Willis continued to work around the farm until after dusk.

The woman had seasoned the chicken, then cooked it with root vegetables and butter. She decided to put on a clean apron and set a nice table for the men. *No need trying to hide it,* she thought. *They must know I'm here by myself. Guess I gotta trust men sometimes. Still, it ain't a good habit to start.*

"You boys come inside and have some stew, you've earned it." She opened the door and motioned for them to come inside.

Leroy looked around the room as he walked through the door, it was clean but without much furniture or comfort items. He walked over and stood next to a pine bench by the dining table. She had covered the table with a white table cloth and set plates and spoons for three. Willis smiled and pointed at a basket filled with warm biscuits.

"I hope you're hungry, 'cause I've made plenty of stew for all of us and biscuits too. Come sit and I'll pour the coffee."

"We're thankful, Ma'am," Leroy said as he sat down on the bench. "Both of us are hungry and somethin' smells mighty good."

"Mary's my name," she smiled. "What's yours?"

During the course of the meal she told them that her first husband had died leaving her childless. Her second husband, a man named Seth Green, had run off before the war with the preacher's wife, leaving her with two small children. One caught a fever and died, the other was taken in an Indian raid. Mary dropped her head and touched her nose with a handkerchief when she spoke of the kidnapped child.

"She was only a baby," Mary said softly as she refilled the bowls with hot chicken and vegetable stew. "She'd be almost ten by now."

Her story brought back memories of Clayton's death at the hand of the Comanche. *Damn em',* Leroy thought. *The killing and stealing ain't gonna stop until we kill or run off every last one of them.*

Willis, not knowing what to say, silently broke his biscuit in half and dropped it into his bowl of stew.

The next morning the sky was completely covered in dark gray rain clouds. The horses were huddled together and none of the chickens were out of the coop. Leroy untied the slicker from the back of his saddle and got ready for the coming storm.

"The wind's coming from the north," Willis said. "Looks like rain for sure."

Leroy turned to Mary. "Wish we could stay and do more but we've got a long way to go and not much time. The cattle drives will be starting any day now."

Mary nodded then frowned at Willis. "Don't you have no slicker?" she asked.

"No Ma'am. I was hoping to buy a used one from somebody before starting on the drive."

"Well, I've got one," she motioned to Willis to stay put. "That no good second husband of mine was in such a hurry to get out of town with that Jezebel, he left behind his slicker and a few other things.

Let's see if you can use any of 'em."

"That's mighty generous of you, Mary," Willis exclaimed. "I sure could use some socks and," he cleared his throat and ducked his head, "you know, some drawers."

"Help yourself. His trunk is over there by the back door."

Leroy watched as Willis eagerly dismounted and ran back into the house.

After Leroy left for the cattle drive, Mindy watched the days slowly slip by. During the war years she learned that it was best to keep busy. She had plenty to do keeping the house and doing the chores that had to be done around the farm every day, come rain or shine. First came the early morning milking and baking, followed by washing, mending and caring for the small barnyard animals. Some days the list seemed endless, yet she was thankful to have her days filled. In the evenings she worked on her sewing and listened to Verlinda and Taylor tell the same stories over and over again. She never tired of hearing their stories about Leroy, Carter and Clayton as young boys growing up on the farm. Listening to their memories somehow made them belong to her too.

Mindy promised herself that when Leroy returned, she would speak to him about Papa Taylor. Taylor would go into town for supplies and more often than not return with very few, if any, of the needed items. Both she and Mama Wiley noticed that sometimes his conversation seemed confused, but at other times his memory was as sharp as a tack.

Although they were managing while he was away, Mindy told Mama Wiley that she would feel better when Leroy returned. She worried about Papa Taylor every time he went out to the fields by himself.

A week after Leroy had left for the cattle drive, she saw Papa Taylor sitting tall in the saddle out in the middle of the fields during the middle of a rainstorm. Mindy saddled her horse, rode out to bring him home and was surprised to hear him talking to himself seemingly oblivious to the torrents of rain falling all around him.

Shielding her face against the blowing rain, she called out, "Papa

Taylor, what are you doing out here?"

"Somebody's got to look out for this place," he said. "I can't find Clayton anywhere. He's supposed to be out here tending the stock."

Mindy drew in her breath when she heard Papa speaking of Clayton as if he were still alive. Tears began to stream down her face mixing with the cold drops of rain. "Let's go home, Papa Taylor," she said as she reached for the reins to lead the horse back to the barn.

Leroy was familiar enough with South Texas to have a general idea as to where the cattle ranches were joining their herds together for the long drive up the Chisholm Trail. After what seemed like an eternity of listening to Willis talk about anything and everything that was on his mind, they arrived in South Texas.

Resting their horses atop a gently rising hill, they looked down on a small town surrounded by pastures and homesteads. Leroy noticed that the river bottom stretched out almost as far as he could see, giving the countryside a peaceful setting. Only when he looked more closely, did he realize that the hills and pastures in the distance were covered with more cattle than he had seen in his entire life.

"That's why we're here, Willis," Leroy pointed toward the sprawling herds. "Ever see anything like 'em?"

Willis stared intently, "How many men would you say it takes to drive that many cattle north?"

"Probably more than any outfit will pay for," Leroy shook his head as he replied. "That's why we ain't signin' on with just any outfit. We're gonna check in with the nearest Ranger Headquarters and ask some hard questions."

"Like what?" Willis asked.

Leroy took a moment to look up into the clear blue sky before answering. "The first thing we need to know is which trail boss to sign on with. The captain at the Ranger Headquarters ought to be able to tell us who to go see about a job and give us a pretty good idea of what we're gonna be up against. From what I hear, cattle drives are tough enough when you got everything going for you."

"Leroy, them ranchers ain't gonna hire no inexperienced trail boss." Willis argued. "No matter who we sign on with he's gonna know his stuff."

Leroy frowned and lifted his eyebrows slightly. Over the years, Willis had become quite familiar with this expression. It meant that Leroy was getting irritated. When Leroy was really mad, his temper would get the best of him before he had time to raise his eyebrows.

Willis gritted his teeth and waited for Leroy to unload on him.

Damnit, Willis thought. *I didn't mean to get him all riled up this soon. I've got to put up with him for God knows how many more months.*

"Willis, I agree with you, them ranchers are gonna hire the best trail boss they can and probably the meanest. If I have a choice, I'd just as soon we avoid the meanest one of the bunch."

Willis shook his head and spat a wad of tobacco juice onto the ground. "To my way of thinking, we might not have much choice. It seems to me that since we ain't what you might call experienced in this line of work, we might have to sign on with whatever drive will take us."

"Not necessarily," Leroy grinned, his mood improving. "Remember, we'll have some help from the local Rangers. With any luck they'll line us up with the right trail boss."

Leroy tapped his boots against the sides of his horse and rode down the hill toward the town below, with Willis following. Both men picked up the smell of the cattle as soon as they were downwind from the Longhorns.

If the drive ain't gonna start for a while, thought Leroy. *Maybe we can find work in the breaking corral or doing range work.* Leroy had a way with horses and a healthy respect for these spirited animals. He believed that if a horse was worth his salt, he would try his best to break the man, rather than get broken himself. Handling horses took a whole lot of patience and a good deal of experience. Leroy liked to describe his own personal experience with horses as "lessons learned the hard way." He thought about what was involved in breaking horses and quickly decided to hold out for range work if he had a choice in the matter.

"Yes, sir. I think range work will do just fine until the drive starts," Leroy thought out loud.

"What are you talking about, Leroy?" Willis asked. "I didn't come all the way down here just to do range work. I got enough of that to do at home. I'm here to sign on to one of them cattle drives heading north to Kansas."

Leroy laughed. "The difference is that range work down here will put some Yankee dollars in your pocket." He reached over to give Willis a playful shove, "Don't worry, we won't have to hang around here for long. As soon as the drive starts, we'll be on our way to Kansas and some real money."

"I guess that's good news," came Willis' sullen reply. "I sure do miss my Patsy, and we ain't been gone from home that long."

At the mention of home and Patsy, Leroy felt a small lump in his throat. Given the chance, he would have gladly paid a month's wages to be able to hold Mindy in his arms.

The main street that ran through the small South Texas town of Rutersville looked a lot like Tyler. *Most towns this size look alike, no matter what part of Texas you're in,* thought Leroy.

He gestured toward the sheriff's office and nudged the reins slightly to turn the horse's head in the right direction.

"Ain't no Ranger Headquarters here, Leroy," Willis whined. "Let's go get something to eat. I've been hungry since we ran out of grub yesterday. Hell, a man can't live without biscuits and coffee. I gotta have something to eat."

Leroy slowly dismounted and stretched his aching muscles as best he could. He decided that Willis would only be a nuisance considering the mood he was in. He reached into his pocket and pulled out enough money for Willis to buy dinner for both of them while he went to speak with the town sheriff.

"I'll take whatever they got fixed," Leroy said, handing him a half dollar piece. Willis walked away with his head down after he took the money. It hurt his pride to take handouts, even from Leroy.

"Willis," Leroy called out as he tied his horse to the hitching post.

He waited until Willis turned around to face him. "Don't forget to ask for some pie. I favor some kind of berry or apple if they've got any."

Willis smiled and nodded, feeling better already. That sounded mighty good to him.

Leroy opened the door and stepped inside a small room lit only by the sunlight that seeped through two small dirty windows. He glanced around the room and tried to size up the man sitting behind a rough table that appeared to serve as a desk, filing cabinet and dinner table all rolled into one. The only other pieces of furniture in the room were a couple of worn out cane back chairs. Near the back of the office there was a cabinet containing two repeating rifles that Leroy was sure the sheriff had somehow managed to bring home from the war without the permission of their previous owners. The cartridge boxes sitting on the bottom shelf had "US Army" stamped on them for everyone to see.

Leroy smiled. *Hell, he ain't afraid of nobody. I like him already.*

"You have the look of a man wanting work," the sheriff, a balding man whose belly was beginning to thicken with middle age, looked up from a stack of papers.

Leroy noticed that the papers had what appeared to be old food and coffee stains on them. Obviously, the sheriff wanted to give the impression that he was a busy man, in case any of the town's leading citizens stopped by to check on him. It didn't take Leroy long to decide that this was probably not the case.

"You're right, Sheriff," Leroy approached the desk while making sure that he had a smile on his face. It didn't pay to get off on the wrong foot with any Texas lawman if you could avoid it.

"I'm here with my friend, Willis. We're looking to sign on with a cattle drive. My friend's over at the hotel right now buying dinner for the two of us." Leroy had mentioned that Willis was paying for the food to let the sheriff know that they were upstanding citizens.

"Where you boys from?" the sheriff asked, as he cast a wary eye toward Leroy. Roy Branson was a small town sheriff whose best gun handling days were behind him. He was, at that moment, a bit nervous. He had kept alive all these years by being a pretty good judge of character. The stranger appeared friendly enough and didn't act like a gunman. On the other hand, Branson had the feeling that the man standing in front of him was not someone you wanted to cross.

"East Texas," replied Leroy as he held out his hand. "Me and my friend are Texas Rangers. Not working much now though, what with the state police and the Yankee Army running things." Leroy's tone of voice let the sheriff know what he thought of both of those organizations. He had a feeling that the sheriff would agree with him on both counts.

The sheriff's manner changed completely. He stood up, held out his hand to Leroy and smiled. "The Texas Rangers are always welcome in Rutersville. Speaking of the state police and the Yankee Army, the way I see it they won't be around forever." Branson pointed toward the best of the wornout cane bottom chairs. "Sit a spell and let's visit. Then I'll buy you a drink over at the saloon."

"Much obliged," Leroy smiled and sat down as lightly as he could onto the rickety chair. "My name is Leroy Wiley. Like I said, I'm here along with another out of work Ranger hoping to sign on with one of the cattle drives headin' up the Chisholm Trail."

"Well," the sheriff chuckled. "I know you ain't plumb crazy. The Chisholm is the only one worth going on. Too much trouble trying to drive cattle up those other trails. Not that there ain't plenty of trouble on the Chisholm too, but it's about the best of the lot since they stopped letting us take our beef over to Sedalia. It seems them Missouri farmers claim that our fine Texas Longhorns make their stock sick."

"I heard about that," Leroy said. "Something about a Mexican tick infecting Missouri cattle."

"That's what they claim. They say that our Texas beef carries the tick with 'em. Now, the tick don't cause no trouble with our Longhorns but evidently, at least according to what them ranchers in Missouri say, the tick kills their cattle. There's probably a lot more to it than that."

The sheriff leaned back in his chair and laughed. "I hear that a few of our Texas cowboys raised so much hell in Sedalia that the ladies of the town don't want 'em back. I figure that plays some part in as to why the men who run Sedalia have put a stop to our cattle herds coming there." Sheriff Branson paused for the right effect before finishing his thought. "A man's gotta do whatever it takes to keep the womenfolk happy or he'll be sleeping out in the barn."

Leroy laughed heartily before adding, "Sheriff, I know exactly what you mean. I've had that kind of trouble on more than one occasion myself."

"Ain't we all?" The sheriff pointed to a worn map of Texas that was nailed securely to the wall. "Let me show you the Chisholm Trail. We've got a drive 'bout ready to start."

Leroy carefully climbed out of the chair and walked over to take a long hard look at the map. "Sheriff," Leroy turned and watched the man as he fumbled with a pair of reading glasses.

"Branson," the sheriff said as he joined Leroy and pointed to the start of the Chisholm Trail. "My name is Roy Branson."

"Know anything about the trail boss of that herd?" Leroy paused and looked Sheriff Branson right in the eye before asking the question that was foremost on his mind. "What kind of trail boss is he?"

"You mean what kind of man is he? A good man usually makes a good trail boss and in this case you've got the best."

Leroy gave a sigh of relief. "Do you think he's hiring?"

"Oh, I know he is. Came in here last week trying to get me to go along on the drive, but I'm too old. Trail driving is a young man's work."

"Some folks might say the same thing about being a lawman." Leroy nodded his head toward the cabinet containing the rifles. "What Yankee soldier donated those to peacekeeping effort of the state of Texas?"

Sheriff Branson laughed. "Actually a couple of 'em did." My brother and I hid six Henry rifles in Louisiana before we left Mansfield. We sneaked back across the Louisiana Red River after the war and found 'em right where we left 'em, along with twenty Yankee gold pieces that my brother found lying around someplace." The sheriff cleared his throat before adding. "Damn lucky weren't we?"

Leroy patted Sheriff Branson on the back and said in admiration,

"I wish I could have done the same thing after the surrender at Palmito Ranch."

"You were there?" The sheriff's expression became serious. He shook his head, then glanced at the map of Texas nailed to the office wall.

"Yep," Leroy let out a long breath and shook his head as he recalled the last battle of the Civil War. "Right after we won the battle we wound up having to surrender to our own prisoners. I tell you that was the damndest thing I ever had to do."

"I wish we could run all them varmints out of Texas, Mr. Wiley."

"Call me Leroy."

"No, sir. A Texas Ranger merits respect." Sheriff Branson took his hat from a rack fastened to the door and smiled at Leroy before finishing his thought. "Even if he is younger than me."

The sheriff laughed as he ushered Leroy out of the office and took a couple of slow, deliberate steps toward the saloon. "Let's go wet our whistles. Tomorrow, I'll take you out to the Bar S Ranch. That's where they're rounding up the cattle for the next big drive up the Chisholm."

Sheriff Branson led Leroy across the street toward the Short Grass Saloon. Leroy figured that the saloon was named for the type of grass that he had seen all across south central Texas. *No wonder the Longhorns are so skinny and bad tempered. They ain't got much to eat,* he thought.

The Short Grass saloon reminded Leroy of just about every other saloon he had managed to visit when he was away from Mindy's watchful eye. He would have preferred to have gone directly to the hotel and eaten his supper. Leroy knew from past experience that no matter how high the plates were heaped with food, Willis would eat every last crumb on his plate and then help himself to Leroy's food.

Liquor on an empty stomach didn't set well with Leroy, but he needed information from Sheriff Branson more than he needed the food.

Before the first drink was poured, the sheriff mentioned that Leroy, might also want to go over to LaGrange and check in at the Ranger Headquarters. Leroy didn't see much sense in this if there was a drive needing trail hands but after the sheriff explained about the problems the cattle drives had been having with rustlers and bandits coming up from Mexico, Leroy changed his mind.

The two men made arrangements to go out to the Bar S Ranch later the next day. After they finished their drinks, the sheriff offered to put Leroy and Willis up for the night, but Leroy politely declined the offer not wanting to impose on the sheriff any more than he had already. After thanking him for his hospitality, Leroy walked over to the hotel to see if Willis had left him anything to eat.

Leroy found Willis sound asleep at a table in the back of the hotel dining hall. He was leaning far to the right and looked as if he might fall out of his chair at any moment.

"Damn, Willis," Leroy muttered to himself when he realized that Willis had eaten half of his food. He sat down and quickly ate what was left, washing down the potatoes and red beans with a glass of water. He wrapped the only piece of ham that Willis hadn't eaten in a sliced biscuit.

He was untying his bandana from his neck and was about to wrap it around the biscuit when the serving girl walked up and offered a table napkin.

"Here, use this," she gave Leroy half of a smile. "It's a lot cleaner than that dirty old bandana of yours."

She was a plain girl, a little on the plump side, with curly brown hair and big brown eyes. Leroy appreciated kindness, especially from strangers who had no reason to help him.

"Why thank you, Missy," he smiled. "I'm most appreciative. You're right, my bandana ain't so clean."

"Then take the napkin and be done with it." She said in a curt tone of voice not wanting to start a conversation while she was busy tending to the other customers.

Leroy was surprised at her harsh tone. *After all,* he thought. *She was the one who offered the darn napkin, It's not like I asked for it.*

"Sorry, Ma'am," Leroy extended his hand to accept the offered table napkin. "Like I said, I'm mighty grateful for your kindness."

Her expression softened. "I'm sorry for being a bit short with you." She nodded toward Willis. "But your friend hasn't exactly been my favorite customer today."

"Sorry 'bout that," Leroy reached into his pocket for another fifty cents. He wasn't happy about spending the extra money but he felt obligated. Looking down at Willis, he said, "I'll get him out of here in just a minute."

He offered her the fifty cent piece.

"Oh, no," she held up her hand in protest. "I didn't mean to ask for any more money. He paid me when he ordered the meals." Pointing to Leroy's plate, she added, "I noticed he ate half of your ham, Mister. I can get you another slice."

Leroy held up the wrapped biscuit. "I've got enough right here, but thank you all the same."

"Well, then, what about some cookies?"

Leroy's face suddenly broke into a smile. "Ma'am, I'd be much obliged. To tell you the truth, I can't ever in my life remember turning down a cookie."

"I'll be right back," she reached over to shake his hand. "Carrie Sue is my name. You just passing through town?"

"Hoping to sign on to a cattle drive," he replied while holding her hand.

"Then you'll be heading out to the Bar S, that's where they've been rounding up the Longhorns."

"That's right, Ma'am. But first I, I mean we," he used his hat to point toward Willis, "got some business to tend to."

"Well, if they don't put you up at the Bar S, come back and see me. We've got plenty of rooms here at the hotel."

Leroy tipped his hat. Carrie Sue turned and walked back toward the kitchen. When she was gone, he reached over to wake up Willis.

Just as Leroy was giving Willis a not too gentle shove, Sheriff Branson walked through the doors of the dining hall.

"I see that you've met Carrie Sue," he smiled. "She's my daughter," he gestured around the room. "And this is my hotel. It belonged to my wife's family." His voice softened, "She died of consumption while I was fighting in Georgia. At least that's where I reckon I was when she passed away. May God rest her soul. Anyway, I sure do miss her. Carrie Sue takes care of things here and does a right fine job of it if I do say so myself."

"I'm sorry about your loss," Leroy said. "You sure do have a nice daughter and I agree she runs a good eating place."

"You're welcome to stay here and leave in the morning," Sheriff Branson smiled. "It's better than spending the night on the trail. You'll have enough of those in the next few months."

Leroy took a long look at Willis and decided to take the sheriff up on his offer. It would be nice to sleep in a real bed and have a chance to wash up.

Besides, Leroy thought. *Carrie Sue's breakfast is bound to be better than this cold biscuit and ham.*

"Sheriff," Leroy extended his hand in appreciation, "If it's not too much bother we'll take you up on your kind offer." Leroy put his hand on Willis' sweat stained hat and shoved it down over the sleeping man's eyes. "I believe that I can speak for both of us when I say that we are mighty grateful."

Sheriff Branson began to chuckle. "Carrie Sue might just put him out in the barn." He put his hands on his hips and shook his head before adding, "He's mighty dirty."

"Oh, I've seen him looking worse," Leroy grinned. "As for the barn, he's used to it and that sleeping arrangement would suit me just fine. I need a break from his snoring."

"You'll do no such thing,"said Carrie Sue as she came back from the kitchen. "I have Juanita heating a tub of water for the two of you right now. While you're washing up I'll have her clean your clothes." Noticing Leroy's expression, Carrie Sue added, "I've got some leftover clothes that should fit both of you. They belonged to some of Pa's visitors over at the jailhouse."

Leroy looked directly at Sheriff Branson. He wasn't about to wear clothes that had been taken off of a dead man.

The sheriff, reading Leroy's thoughts grinned. "She's talking about some clothes we found in the saddle bags of a couple of gunslingers who thought that I was too old to get the drop on 'em. I can promise you that them duds weren't taken off no hanged man."

Carrie Sue pointed her finger at her father. "You better not be planning to see how fast you still are, Pa. Not with all the hired guns coming through town nowadays."

Both Leroy and Roy Branson shared a laugh, but Leroy hoped that Sheriff Branson realized that his gun fighting days were behind him.

CHAPTER ∞ 12

After a good night's sleep Leroy and Willis had an early breakfast, then rode out of town on their way to the Texas Ranger headquarters in LaGrange. The Texas Rangers were still trying to rebuild their ranks and bring law and order back to Texas. Their job was made much more difficult than it should have been because of the constant interference from the Reconstruction government's arm of the law, the despised State Police. Realizing that the State Police would not be around forever, the Rangers worked hard to keep the peace while at the same time, not giving the occupying Union Army an excuse to disband the Texas Rangers.

Sheriff Branson caught up with them about four miles outside of town, just as they were about to cross the Colorado River.

A thin man wearing a wide brimmed hat with a high crown was riding with Branson. As the riders approached, Leroy and Willis began sizing the stranger up.

"Look at that fellow riding with Branson. See the Navy Colt in his gun belt? He ain't no cowboy, that's for sure," said Leroy.

"I think you're right. He's got one of them fancy lightweight military saddles. No, he sure don't look like no cowhand to me," Willis grumbled. "The way I see it, here comes trouble."

"You might be right," Leroy agreed. "But Branson is bringing him to us and we ain't done nothing to him. I think we're about to meet another lawman."

"We ain't done nothing to nobody," Willis shook his head. "But that don't mean much these days."

Leroy looked toward Willis and gave him a reassuring nod. "Don't worry, Willis. Ever' thing is gonna be all right."

Just as Sheriff Branson and the stranger rode up to them, the wind picked up and thunder echoed in the distance.

"That ain't a good sign," Willis said.

"Oh, hell, Willis. Stop acting like an old woman."

"Glad I caught up with you boys," Sheriff Branson called out. "I've saved you both a trip. This here fellow is Lieutenant Robbins. He heads the Ranger Company in these parts."

Leroy turned to Willis and grinned, "What did I tell you, Willis?"

The men waited for a reply from Willis. None came.

"Lieutenant," Leroy tipped his hat to show respect.

"Roy here tells me that you men are going to sign up with Corky Kell over at the Bar S, is that right?"

"Yes, sir," Willis spoke for the first time. "We got families to feed."

"We aim to sign up for their cattle drive, that is, if they'll have us," Leroy added.

"I can guarantee that they will," Robbins said with authority. "They got trouble ahead of 'em and they need men who can handle a gun as well as a rope and a quirt."

"Let's sit down for a spell over there by the river bank and let the horses get some water," Robbins straightened up in the saddle and gave a soft clicking sound with his tongue. The mustang lifted his head and began to trot toward the water.

The other men followed Lieutenant Robbins down the sloping knoll that led to the river.

Robbins took his horse to the edge of the river and watched the mustang drop his head down and begin to drink.

Leroy found himself looking at a clump of bushy trees that lined the riverbank. The trees were filled with grayish green leaves that look almost smoky from a distance. *Hell, those are the same kind of trees that hung over the river at Chickamauga. They were spooky then and they're spooky now,* thought Leroy. It took a nudge from Willis to bring him back to the present.

Sheriff Branson's paint had already joined the lieutenant's mustang at the river's edge by the time Leroy and Willis reached the water. After the men had dismounted, Leroy waited for Lieutenant Robbins to speak his mind. He didn't have long to wait.

"Men, I'm in a tough fix here. I'm doing my best to keep the peace but I've got my hands full. The ranchers want something done to protect their beef from the rustlers and bandits that are raiding their herds. By the time most of the herds get through to Abilene, more times than not they've lost half their cattle," Robbins paused for a moment before adding, "That's too much lost beef for the cattleman's liking."

Leroy nodded. Robbins continued speaking in a slow, matter of fact tone. "Here in Texas, before the herds even make it to the Red River, the trail boss probably has to deal with the Comanche, and you know what that's like. Once they're into the Indian Territory, the tribes up there just want to barter. Each tribe will have warriors waiting to see to if they can cut out part of the herd. They're all hungry because there's not enough agency beef to feed them."

Leroy's shoulders slumped for a moment. *Rustlers, Mexican bandits and hungry Indians,* he thought. *What in the hell have I got myself into?* He straightened up and looked at the two lawmen. "Lieutenant, if you don't mind me asking, why did you ride all the way out here just to tell us this?" he asked.

"When the sheriff sent word that there were a couple of Rangers looking to sign on with a drive, I thought I might put you two back on active duty," Robbins explained.

"For how long?" Leroy asked.

"For the duration of the cattle drive. Once the herd reaches Kansas, you can collect your wages like everybody else and go home."

"Wages for the drive and extra pay for Ranger duty? I think we can handle that," Leroy glanced at Willis, who nodded back in agreement.

The lieutenant smiled. "I'm sure the ranchers will ante up a few extra dollars. Not much though. They are, what we call down here, beef poor. They've got to get their herds to the railheads before they all go broke."

Leroy looked back at Willis. His friend noticed there was a definite twinkle in his eyes.

"We're glad to help, Lieutenant. And we can sure use any extra pay that we might get. But why us? Aren't there plenty of out of work Rangers 'round here?"

"Unfortunately, you're right about that," Robbins sighed. "We've had to cut back till there's almost no one on the payroll. But I don't want to hire someone from around here. I got a hunch that there is somebody tipping off the rustlers with information about the cattle drives. The two of you can blend in with the rest of the cowboys. That way the rustlers won't be expecting trouble. It should give you boys an edge and might help keep you alive."

Sheriff Branson spoke up. "We've already sent word to the trail boss who is gonna take the next herd up the Chisholm.

The Ranger lieutenant walked over to his horse, took a map out of his saddlebags and handed it to Leroy. "I've marked the usual trouble spots but the best advice I can give you is to keep your guard up and your gun ready."

Leroy walked over to a clearing and spread out the map.

Robbins knelt down and pointed out the marked areas on the map. With some effort, Sheriff Branson sat down on the soft grass. Willis didn't know how to read a map, so he decided to leave the planning to Leroy while he checked on the horses. When he was finished, he noticed a big sycamore tree near the riverbank. *I figure I have just enough time to sit down by that big ol' tree and spend a few minutes thinking about Patsy and the kids back in Starrville,* he thought.

"This is where the drive will get started," Lieutenant Robbins pointed to the exact location of the Bar S Ranch. He turned back towards Leroy and asked, "Are you familiar with old Jesse Chisholm's route to Kansas?"

"I've got a general idea," Leroy answered. "But it's mighty darn *general.* I'd be obliged for anything you could tell me about it."

"Well," Robbins began, "trouble follows any cattle drive 'til it gets clear up to Abilene." He turned back and pointed to his well-worn map. "The Chisholm and the Western Trails split about here, with the Chisholm heading straight north towards Austin. You have to worry about Mexican bandits till the herd gets past Waco. After that, they usually ain't much of a problem because they like to stay as close as possible to the Rio Grande so they can get back into Mexico in a hurry if they have to. Now up here when the Chisholm splits off from the Shawnee, that's where you're likely to run into rustlers."

"From the frying pan to the fire," Leroy shook his head and shrugged his shoulders as if he was trying to shake off an early morning chill. "First the Mexican bandits, then the rustlers. Hell, when can a man sleep without worrying about getting his throat cut?"

"If you want to be sure that you'll wake up alive, don't sleep too soundly until after you get paid and you're out of Abilene. Keep in mind, from what I hear, that cow town can be almost as dangerous as the trail."

"What about the Indians?" Leroy asked.

"As you might expect, the Comanche will be your main problem. Oh, you'll pass through parts of Caddo and Wichita country, but it's the Comanche you have to be wary of. The other tribes just want a few head so they can feed their squaws and old people some beef. The difference in these tribes and the Comanche is that the Comanche don't normally ask for the beef, they just take it along with a few scalps if they're in the mood."

"Once the drive crosses the Red River, then what?" Leroy looked closely at Robbins' map.

"First, you'll drive right through Choctaw country. Then after you cross the Canadian River up in the Territory, you'll see a few Cherokees. But like the Wichita and the Caddo tribes here in Texas, the tribes up in the Territory just want a few head in exchange for letting the herds cross their land," Robbins explained.

"Lieutenant, I've been fighting Indians ever since I joined the

Rangers. I gotta tell you, the Comanche will want more than a few head of beef. When they came into west Texas, they ran the Apaches out and that was no easy task. Right now the Comanche roam around just about anywhere they want in North Texas, which means they could hit the herd anytime after the drive passes Austin."

"Maybe before." Robbins nervously rubbed his chin.

Leroy nodded. "You get my point."

"Let's say that I understand your concern." Robbins said. "That's why I'm trying to put men on the drive who can handle a gun. Most of the cowboys who work these herds carry weapons so they can turn the herd in case of a stampede. If they have to, they'll shoot at bandits or rustlers. You notice I said shoot *at,* because most of these trail hands don't normally hit anything that they're aiming at, unless it's by accident. Oh, sure some of them fought in the war, but most of the cowboys you'll be riding with were too young to have served the Cause."

Leroy turned his attention back to the map. "Seems to me that most of the trouble takes place south of the Red River."

"Not necessarily. I remember what an old preacher said to me about the Indian Territory. The only white folks up there are either missionaries or running from the law," Robbins smiled. "The ones I've run into have definitely not been missionaries." He pointed to the Indian Territory on the map. "I wish I had a better map of the Territory but I haven't been able to find one. This map doesn't go all the way to Kansas.

Leroy grinned. "Lieutenant, I'll bring you back a map if they sell 'em in Kansas."

"The only way you can get any current maps nowadays is from the Yankees, and they're not about to part with one of their Army issued maps," Robbins shook his head.

"Oh, they have been known to part with things before that they were aiming to keep. I have a way of liberatin' stuff from the Yanks." Leroy turned to see if Willis was listening. He knew that Willis would remember all the times that Leroy had stolen Henry and Spencer rifles from the Union Army during the war. He wasn't surprised to see Willis leaning against a big tree, snoring peacefully, seemingly without a care in the world.

"Well, a better map of the Territory would be nice, but for now we'll have to make do with what we've got. This map shows you the route as far as the North Canadian River which is about midway through the Territory." Robbins began carefully folding his map. "The trail boss will handle the dealings with the tribes wanting beef. You won't have to worry about that. All you have to do is take care of the rustlers and Mexican bandits."

"You're not forgetting about the Comanche, are you Lieutenant?" Leroy asked as he stood up and put his hat back on, making sure that it was tipped at just the right angle.

Robbins smiled. "No, I just naturally figured that you'd keep them at the top of your list."

"Lieutenant, they make up about the first ten items on my list. I make a habit of keeping an eye out for the Comanch whenever I'm on the trail," Leroy grinned. "That's one reason I've managed to stay alive all these years."

Robbins turned to Sheriff Branson, "Let's head to the Bar S and introduce these men to Corky. I'll arrange for the extra pay to come from him."

"Considering the fact that the two of us don't have any money, that would probably be a good idea," Branson laughed.

Robbins didn't laugh. The lack of monetary support for the Texas Rangers from the Yankee controlled state government was a growing problem and a constant source of irritation.

The men led the horses away from the river and checked their girths. Leroy cinched his saddle a bit tighter. His saddle was the most expensive thing that he owned. He made a point of taking good care of it and the horse that he rode. Many times his horse was the only thing that had stood between himself and an early grave. When he was satisfied with the girth and the placement of the saddle, he walked over to wake Willis.

"Willis," Leroy said as he nudged the sleeping man with the toe of his boot. "Willis, wake up or I'm leaving you here."

"What?" Willis asked as he looked around. "Oh, it's you, Leroy."

"You ought to be damn glad it's me."

Willis looked up at Leroy and laughed. "I always sleep good when you're around, Leroy. Nobody's gonna sneak up on you."

"Well," Leroy reached down to offer Willis a helping hand. "I wouldn't be too sure of that when we're up in Comanch country. They got a way about them. I think they're part wolf. They can sneak up on a man without making a sound. 'Bout the only thing I can count on is smelling 'em. The one thing the Comanch can't do is get rid of that Indian smell." He pulled Willis to his feet, then turned and walked back to his horse.

CHAPTER ∞ 13

The Bar S Ranch was huge. Leroy couldn't believe the size of the spread. After passing through the gate the four lawmen rode for over an hour before they reached the ranch house. While they were riding they caught site of a group of cowboys watching over a large herd of grazing Longhorns.

"They're anxious to go," Branson pointed towards the cowboys circling the cattle. "After spending almost a month getting the cattle rounded up, they want to finish the job. All those cowboys can think of is getting to Abilene and spending some of their hard earned wages on women and whiskey."

Leroy nodded silently. Both he and Willis had a hard time believing the sight before them. There were no ranches like the Bar S anywhere near Tyler.

The four men gently nudged their horses forward and rode toward the big house. Branson rode ahead of the others.

"Corky!" Branson stretched up in the saddle and called out in a loud voice. He waved his hat in an effort to get the attention of a man standing by a corral full of horses. The man turned and returned the wave.

"Corky Kell, you ol' rascal, still trying to judge good horseflesh?" Branson joked.

Kell laughed. He had known Roy Branson since they were boys. Later, during the war, they had both served in the same cavalry regiment.

Leroy's first impression of the trail boss was not a good one. The man was tall with broad shoulders but looked more like a school teacher than a trail boss. *Hell, he's got gray hair,* Leroy thought. *Does somebody really believe that ol' grandpa is gonna drive this herd all the way to Kansas? Naahh.* He gave Willis a quick glance. Willis was staring intently at Kell. Although he was surprised at Kell's appearance, he decided to keep quiet and let Leroy handle things.

"Welcome to the Bar S," Kell smiled as he walked over to greet, first Branson, then Robbins. When his eyes turned to Leroy and Willis, his expression turned deadly serious.

Robbins picked up on Kell's uneasiness and spoke in a confident tone. "Corky, these two men are the Rangers that Sheriff Branson sent you the message about."

Kell pursed his lips, waiting for Robbins to finish. When Robbins didn't add anything more, there was an uneasy silence.

Sheriff Branson decided that it was up to him to move things along. "Corky, we've been talking about the trouble you and the other drives have been having. Lieutenant Robbins and I have been trying to figure out how to get you some help."

Kell nodded his head in agreement, all the while keeping his eyes on Leroy. Leroy had already formed his opinion of the trail boss. *Too old and too soft,* he thought.

"These men should help solve a few of your problems," Robbins said. "You still need men for the drive," he gestured toward Leroy and Willis before adding, "and their guns should come in handy along the trail."

"I've already got some good gunmen," Kell frowned. "There's enough of 'em out of work. Thank God."

"Now Corky, you're gonna need all the help you can get. Let's go inside and talk." Branson's arm pointed toward the big house. "The sun's beginning to get to me."

Kell's face melted into a big smile. "I must be forgetting my manners," he reached out to shake the men's hands. "I keep forgetting that our town sheriff is getting a bit long in the tooth. Let's go inside so we can quit talking in the wind."

"We're much obliged," Branson walked over and tied his horse to the post in front of the house. "It's been a long ride out here, we could all do with a glass or two of the Bar S special lemonade." He turned to Leroy and Willis, "Best stuff north of the Rio Grande."

Willis' ears perked up when he heard Sheriff Branson mention the lemonade. Leroy smiled and followed the other men, as they crossed the dusty, open area that served as the front yard for the owner's home.

Born and raised in south Texas around Longhorns, Corky Kell had been raising cattle and working on a ranch since he was a little boy. He was a big man, and although he looked older, He was only thirty-eight years old. His premature gray hair, thin from a lifetime of wearing heavy Stetsons, was freshly cut in preparation for the long drive to Kansas.

Kell stepped up on the broad porch and rested his arm against one of the whitewashed posts attached to the railing. Then he stepped aside and motioned for the men to walk through the double doors leading to the parlor of the big house.

"As I said before, welcome to the Bar S, gentlemen. Mr. Hamilton's in town so I'll be the one talking business with you."

Branson turned to Leroy and Willis, "Corky always does the hiring anyhow. Mr. Hamilton is the owner of the Bar S, but he's what you might call semi-retired."

Suits me, thought Leroy. *I don't care what rich folks do to pass the time. Anybody who lives in a house this size has too much money anyhow.*

The men stepped into a broad welcoming parlor where two Mexican women were waiting to take the men's hats. Leroy noticed that the hat racks were made of deer antlers and lined one entire wall of the parlor. He shook his head at the thought that it took two Mexican women to hang hats that could have been hung up by the people wearing them.

Corky Kell led the way into a large square room that was built around the biggest stone fireplace that Leroy had ever seen. Most of the chairs and couches were covered in cowhides. The wooden tables were made from expensive hard woods, not from soft pine like the furniture that the Wileys owned. The lace curtains that hung on each window seemed out of place. This was a man's room.

Kell sat down easily at a large wooden roll top desk that rested against the far wall. With a wave of his hand, the Mexican women disappeared, only to return a few minutes later with trays of lemonade and sandwiches. Leroy smiled at the younger of the two women, who held out a tray filled with sandwiches. She had eyes as black as any squaw and hair that shined in the sunlight. Leroy noticed that she never lifted her eyes long enough to make eye contact with any of the men. After they had eaten the sandwiches and drunk the lemonade, an elderly Mexican man walked into the room carrying a pot of hot coffee. Leroy thought it was the best coffee he had ever tasted. During the war and while riding with the Rangers he had become used to drinking a broad range of liquid described as coffee. He had come to believe that anything that turned hot water brown or black could be called coffee.

Finally, another Mexican man entered the room carrying a box of large cigars. Willis thought that he had died and gone to heaven.

"Manuel, bring out Mr. Hamilton's maps, please." Corky Kell's soft and refined voice didn't sound like any of the trail bosses' that Leroy had always heard about.

"We went over the trail with that 1850's map that I carry around with me," Robbins spoke up.

"I'd still like to go over the route once again if you don't mind. I want to point out some areas where we had some trouble on the last drive. But first, while Manuel is getting the map, we need to attend to some business," Kell carefully put on a pair of spectacles, curling the ends over his ears. He then took out a thick ledger type book and turned to face Leroy and Willis.

"If I hire you, we've got to have an understanding right here and now. I usually get to know the men who will be working for me before I take them on a cattle drive. But this is special circumstances. You men are Texas Rangers. That means that I can trust you. It also means that you won't back down from any trouble. No man can be a Texas Ranger and also be a coward. Can the two of you read and write?" Kell asked as he handed the ledger to Leroy. "If so, sign your name. I also want you to list your next of kin and where they live. That way I can send them your wages if, God forbid, something happens and you don't make it all the way to Kansas."

Willis frowned.

Kell continued. "If you can't write, make your mark and tell me where to send the pay to your family. Trail driving is a dangerous business. I always ask my men to take care of their kinfolk. I don't want any man's wages left unclaimed."

Leroy glared at the trail boss. *There ain't no way we're not gonna make it, old man, Leroy thought. You might ought to give me your next of kin's name so I can send 'em your pay if you drop dead on the trail.*

Leroy signed his name, then glanced at Willis. He realized that Willis was to embarrassed to admit that he couldn't read and write and didn't want to make his mark in front of the other men. He spoke without looking up from the ledger. "Willis, if you don't mind, I'll just fill in your name while I'm at it."

"Have them send my pay to Mindy, Leroy," Willis said softly. "I don't want no stranger breaking any bad news to Patsy. Mindy can tell her whatever needs to be said."

Leroy nodded in agreement and carefully wrote, in his best penmanship, *Arminda Elizabeth Wiley, Starrville, Texas.* Then he added another line. *In case of death, send word to my brother, Carter W. Wiley, Esq. Lawyer, Tyler, Texas.*

He handed the ledger back to Kell. Kell placed the ledger on one of the shelves in the roll top desk, then walked over to sit in a big easy chair that was covered in soft brown leather.

"I'm sure that Lieutenant Robbins and Sheriff Branson told you some of the problems that we'll be facing on the drive. Now, I want to tell you about the real trouble."

Leroy stared at the trail boss and asked himself. What *could be worse than the Comanch?*

"Even if you took away all the trouble, we'd still have our hands full just trying to walk the cattle north. The Chisholm is the best trail out there because it's mostly flat without many trees and it stays clear of most of the settlements. But we still have to cross a bunch of rivers and worry about the weather." Kell leaned back and lifted his feet. Immediately, a Mexican woman hurried into the room and shoved a padded footstool under his legs.

Leroy wondered how Corky Kell would do away from all this soft living. *There won't be any footstools on the trail,* he thought.

Kell continued, "Over the past twenty years I have found that cattle tend to be light sleepers. The least little unfamiliar noise can spook the whole herd and start 'em running. We can't have that. Despite what you might think, stampedes are our worst enemy, not a bunch of Godforsaken savages."

Leroy wasn't buying everything that Kell was saying. He had never seen stampeding cattle cut out a man's tongue, then stake him out on top of an ant hill just for the fun of it. Leroy figured that if Kell had spent anytime fighting the Comanche, he'd know just how dumb the words he had just spoken sounded to a Texas Ranger.

As if reading Leroy's thoughts, Corky Kell added a few more words of warning. Leroy felt a nudge from Willis. Immediately, his attention was drawn back to the trail boss. He glanced at Willis, wondering if he had missed something important.

"I'm assuming that you boys haven't been on a cattle drive before. If you have, stop me right here and it'll save us both some time. I want both of you to have a clear understanding of what you are getting yourself into." He paused and waited for a reply. None came, so he continued. "Remember what I said about cattle being light sleepers. Anything can get them riled up. I've been on drives when something as silly as a coyote's howl or the rattle of the chuck wagon would trigger a stampede. Storms are the worst. Anytime you have lightning in a flat, open area and loud thunder to boot, you can bet you're going to have a stampede. And that, boys, can kill you faster than any Indian or rustler."

Leroy had to stifle a chuckle. *There he goes again,* thought Leroy. *This man ain't never seen Comanche coming at him like the wind itself, rid-*

ing right through men firing at 'em.

"How do you stop the Longhorns when they do stampede, Mr. Kell?" Willis asked. Everyone turned their attention to Willis. This was the first time he had spoken since they had arrived at the Bar S.

"My top hand will tell you all about driving a herd," Kell reassured Willis. "He'll also give you instructions as to what to do in case of a stampede and what's even more important, how to prevent one. But to answer your question, if the herd bolts, everyone mounts their night horses immediately and takes off after the herd. The cattle have to be turned or we could lose half the herd. Mostly, it takes pure luck to be able stop 'em. My best riders will draw up alongside of the lead cattle, firing their pistols close to the cattle's ears. That's not easy, I can tell you, what with the animals scared out of their wits. Turning 'em is the key because if they stop sudden, it'll cause a pile up that will kill more of 'em than if we just let 'em run. The worst thing that can happen during the stampede is that I lose some of my men. I don't like calling on widows after the drive is over."

Leroy suddenly realized why Corky Kell was so respected by Sheriff Branson and Lieutenant Robbins. The man not only knew his business but he also cared about the men who worked for him. *During tough and dangerous times, men such as Kell are the ones you want to have on your side,* thought Leroy. *Maybe I've misjudged the man.*

"Now that you know what you're up against, if you still want to sign on, we'll go over the maps once more. Then I'll turn you over to my top hand, Jimmy Flanagin. If you have changed your minds and don't think this is what you want to do, I'll hire you both to work here at the Bar S while I'm on the drive. I only leave behind men that I know can handle a gun and take care of any trouble that come up. Everyone on both sides of the Rio Grande will know when we start driving the herd. It makes me nervous leaving the ranch unprotected and I don't like being nervous about Mr. Hamilton's property." He looked closely at Leroy and then Willis. "Of course, if you stay here, I can't pay you what I would if you were on the drive, but Mr. Hamilton allows me to pay fair wages to anyone who works for the Bar S. Fair wages are good wages. It's probably still more than what you've been used to working for the Rangers." He turned to Lieutenant Robbins and smiled.

Robbins did not return his smile.

Leroy and Willis walked slowly across the yard toward the corral. Flanagin saw them approaching and motioned for them to follow him into a the bunkhouse. The unpainted wooden bunk house stood in marked contrast to the main house, which had been built using limestone and painted white oak.

As the men walked towards the bunkhouse, Willis whispered to Leroy, "He ain't nothing but a kid."

Flanagin turned, his smile broadened into a mischievous grin.

Leroy frowned at Willis and elbowed him in the ribs. Willis knew to keep his mouth shut.

"I'm older than you think," Flanagin said as he stepped up onto the porch of the bunkhouse and turned to face the two Rangers.

"You'll have to pardon my friend, Willis." Leroy felt like more than elbowing Willis. "He's quick to talk and slow to think sometimes."

Willis felt terrible. *There I go again,* he thought. *When am I gonna learn to keep my big mouth shut?*

"But he's a hard worker and a darn good man," Leroy added. "No one will cover your back better than Willis."

Flanagin made a point of reaching past Leroy to shake Willis' hand. "I'll take those traits anytime. My name's Jimmy Flanagin. You'll be answering to me during the drive and I'll answer to Corky. He's the trail boss and a darn good one." He turned and extended his hand to Leroy. "Let's go inside and talk business."

Willis followed the two men into the darkened bunkhouse. *Maybe he ain't a kid after all,* he thought.

Jimmy Flanagin was a brawny young man with sandy colored hair that seemed to be in a constant state of disarray. Not quite as tall as Leroy, he had broad shoulders and muscled forearms. He had clear blue eyes; a square jaw and a face that gave the impression of an easy going manner. Nothing could have been further from the truth. If

Corky Kell had trouble with one of the hands, Flanagin took care of the problem, usually with his fists. Unlike most cowboys, he enjoyed driving the cattle north to Kansas. On the previous drive, the cook had to be left behind at Red River Station after he fell and broke his leg. During the remainder of the drive, the food was horrible, yet Flanagin thrived. One of seven children in a poor immigrant Irish family, he had known hard times while he was growing up. As a boy, Jimmy usually left the table hungry. He could eat most anything and get by with less than most men. He was an honest, hardworking man, and when the going got tough, Kell knew that he could always depend on him. He ran the cattle drive the same way he had commanded a company of Confederate scouts during the war. Over the years quite a few slackers and troublemakers had quickly learned that Flanagin was a hard man.

Willis stopped to look at the long row of bunks lining both sides of the room. At the far end stood a large stone fireplace with black pots and pans hanging from hooks that were fastened to a round black piece of wrought iron. Tables and chairs made of heavy pieces of oak were arranged in tight circles near the middle of the room.

As they walked through the bunkhouse, Leroy noticed that the ceiling was slanted upward toward a point. *Strange way to build a ceiling,* he thought. *Wonder why they built the roof like this?* Leroy had grown up working part time as a carpenter. He knew how to build a bunkhouse, and someone had wasted a lot of time and money when they built this one for the Bar S.

Flanagin led the way to a small office set apart from the main room of the bunkhouse. The cluttered office appeared to also serve as his living quarters. On the desk was a photograph of a pretty girl whose face was ringed with soft brown curls. Leroy pointed toward at it. "Mighty pretty lady," he smiled. "I've got a pretty gal waiting for me back home in Tyler."

Flanagin's expression softened as he reached over and lightly touched the frame that held the photograph. "My wife works at the bank, so I live in town whenever I can get away."

"She must be pretty smart," Leroy smiled. "My Mindy could teach school if she wanted to, but she stays out at the farm with my folks."

"I assume Corky went over the pay with you. My job is to go over the rules that everyone has to follow. If you do what you're told, then chances are that you'll get to Abilene in one piece. He turned to a bookcase that was nailed to the wall of the small office and pulled out a green ledger book. First, I want you to write your name or make your mark here in my ledger."

"The name is Leroy Wiley," Leroy motioned with his thumb back to the doorway where Willis stood quietly listening to what Flanagin had to say. "My friend's name is Willis. We've already written down our names and next of kin for Mr. Kell. As for keeping the drive safe, that's going to be part of our job. We're both Texas Rangers."

Flanagin paused for a moment before speaking. "I wasn't told about any Rangers going with us." He turned and looked out the window toward the big house. "Corky usually tells me about things like that beforehand. Still, it's a darn good idea." He paused again and looked directly at Leroy, then to Willis. "You boys will still have to pull your share of the load. We ain't got enough cowboys as it is." Flanagin pointed to the ledger. "If you don't mind, Corky's got his record book, and I've got mine. I like to know who's on the drive with me."

Both Leroy and Willis nodded in agreement. Flanagin sat down and opened the ledger before continuing. "Ever work on a drive before?" He looked up at Leroy, waiting for an answer.

Leroy tugged on his hat, "Nope, but we've both taken care of stock most of our lives. You might say the only break we took was when we fought the Yanks during the war."

"Flanagin stopped turning pages in the ledger book, "What outfit? Terry's Texas Rangers?"

Leroy smiled. Obviously, Flanagin was a former Rebel. "Nope, most of us from Smith County were in the 28th Texas Cavalry."

Flanagin shook his head, "Our paths probably crossed. Toward the end of the war our outfit joined up with the 28th Texas Cavalry. By that time we were in an infantry outfit, the 14th."

"Yeah," Leroy turned to Willis. "We met up with the 14th Texas

Infantry outside Chattanooga. We stopped being a cavalry regiment when we ran out of horses."

Flanagin took a deep breath and shook his head. "Sad days."

"Sad days still," Willis spoke for the first time. He was leaning against the rough lumber that served as a frame for the doorway. "That's why we're here. Leroy and I need money to take care of our families back in Tyler."

Flanagin nodded in agreement. "Well, we all have to make the best of things." He looked up at Leroy, and then added. "You said that you've had some experience handling stock. I can tell you now that handling cattle and driving a herd of cattle is two different things. Making Longhorns go where they don't necessarily want to go is hard work and at times it can be mighty dangerous."

"We'll do our share of the work," Leroy assured Flanagin.

"I'm sure you will." Flanagin watched as Leroy filled out several lines in the ledger. He noticed that Willis didn't move forward to sign the book. "What about you?"

"I've signed for him," Leroy said. He continued writing without looking up at either Willis or Flanagin. "Not much room to move around in here so I'll save Willis the trouble."

Willis was relieved. *One of these days I've got to figure out how to write my name,* he thought.

If Flanagin realized Willis' embarrassment, he didn't show it. When Leroy was finished writing, Flanagin opened a cabinet that took up most of the space in the small room. Turning to Leroy and Willis, he gestured toward the racks of folded clothes. "Help yourself to whatever you need."

"How much you chargin' for these duds?" Willis asked.

"Nothing," came the reply. "The Mexican women here at the ranch make what we need for the trail drive, and Mr. Hamilton pays for it. You'll find shirts and pants and drawers to fit most any man. Small stuff is on the bottom shelf because short fellows can't reach very high." Flanagin laughed out loud. "Big stuff is up on the top shelf."

"I like the colors," Willis smiled. "And you sure can't beat the price."

"What do we need?" Leroy asked, not wanting to take advantage.

"There's a list nailed to the wall over there by the fireplace," Flanagin said as he walked past Willis. "I put it up there for the greenhorns so they'll know what to pack for the drive. I'll check on you boys later. Right now I've got a few things to attend to."

Willis watched Flanagin walk out the door of the bunkhouse before speaking. "Leroy, I ain't never seen nothing like this before. Do you think I can take some stuff from the bottom shelf that might fit my kids? My older boys could sure use some clothes. The younger ones can wear hand-me-downs, but the older ones ain't got no one to hand down things to them."

"Willis, we can't be loading ourselves down with stuff like that. We'll have enough trouble carrying what we need on the drive. Besides, it wouldn't be right."

Seeing the disappointed expression on Willis' face, Leroy added, "Bet we can find some mighty nice duds in Kansas for your kids, and just think, we'll have money. Kell says he'll settle up with us in Abilene."

Willis nodded and thought for a moment before he spoke. "Greenhorns, is that what Flanagin called us?"

"Yep," Leroy laughed. "I guess we are greenhorns to fellows like him."

Leroy and Willis found everything they needed. They picked out pants, drawers, socks, shirts and chaps. The chaps protected both a cowboy's pants and his legs.

Before they could carry their new clothes to their bunks, Flanagin walked back through the door. He was followed by two Mexican men.

"Let's see what you fellows picked out," Flanagin pointed to the closest bunk beds.

Willis shot a frown at Leroy. He thought that Flanagin was checking to make sure they hadn't taken too much. He was wrong. Jimmy wanted to make sure that they had all the equipment they would need for the drive.

The Mexican men began to rummage through the two stacks of clothes. Every once in awhile, one of them would speak to Flanagin in Spanish. The Mexican man didn't have a smile on his face when he spoke. Leroy wished that he could understand what was being said.

"He says that you didn't get any gloves and that your boots won't do for the drive. You need higher heels to help keep you in the saddle in case of a stampede. This is Juan; he'll find what you need. We'll have to charge you for the boots but you'll pay just what it costs the Bar S to buy 'em. Corky will take the charge out of your wages when we get to Abilene."

"Fair enough," Leroy nodded. "We want to have the right gear to do our job."

Willis frowned. He wanted to take all of his wages home to Patsy and the kids. It didn't make sense to him, having to buy a new pair of boots when his were just fine. Maybe they were a bit worn, and granted, water did come in through the holes in the soles when it rained, but he had worn worse boots during the war.

Shortly after Flanagin left, Leroy and Willis were wearing new boots and new hats with extra wide brims and high crowns. They had also been given brand new ropes and quirts. They might still be green horns, but at least now they looked the part.

CHAPTER ∞ 14

The cattle drive began at daybreak on a very windy spring day. The supplies had been loaded the night before and the chuck wagon was already on it's way to set up the first campsite. It was time to head for Kansas. Corky Kell looked around to make sure everyone was ready, then he raised his arm and waved his hat to signal Flanagin to begin the cattle drive. Flanagin, in turn, rose up in his stirrups and yelled in a loud voice, "Head 'em up and move 'em out!"

Leroy and Willis were like most of the other cowboys, excited to start out on the long drive to Kansas where they'd be able to collect their wages. The Bar S paid thirty dollars a month, which was good money for these hard times. Willis and Leroy were each being paid an extra twenty dollars a month for providing security during the drive.

The early part of the route seemed flat enough, but Kell had warned them that in a few days the ground would get a lot rougher. The trail boss expected the herd to cover twelve miles during good days and eight to ten miles on a average day.

"How many Longhorns you figure are in this herd?" Willis asked Leroy. "They must have half the cattle in Texas mixed in with the Bar S herd."

Leroy laughed. "I heard Flanagin say that there are over two thousand head of cattle on this drive, and that they're all from the Bar S Ranch."

"Gawd almighty," Willis sighed. "How does a man get that many cattle?"

"Probably got 'em like everybody else after the war. Just claimed 'em." Leroy pointed to several Longhorns slowly prodding along ahead of them. "They ran wild for four years during the war 'cause nobody was here to tend to 'em. That's what makes 'em so hard to handle now."

Willis seemed to think about this for a few minutes then asked, "Leroy, how come we gotta ride back here and eat all of this dust?"

Leroy frowned and hesitated a moment before answering, "I plan to change that as soon as I get a chance to talk to Kell. Things should settle down once we're off the ranch. Right now, we're like any other cowhand. We ride drag 'cause we're the new drovers. The boys that have ridden with this outfit before are all riding up front."

"Well, all I know is I'm sick of eating dust," Willis complained. "And did you say we ain't even off of the Bar S yet?"

Leroy nodded. "Yep. This here is one heck of a spread." He reached over to give Willis a friendly shove. "Hey, Willis, listen to me. At least while we're back here we won't have to drive 'em into the water. I'll bet you that getting these Longhorns to swim across a river ain't easy."

Willis ignored the shove. He took his hat off and wiped his brow with his shirt sleeve. "What time do you think they stop to eat?" He looked up at the rising sun. "I get mighty hungry 'round dinner time."

"They have to stop around mid-day and let the cattle graze."

"Then we can rest up a bit," Willis sighed.

"Nope," Leroy grinned. "That's when we start our other job, earning that extra twenty dollars a month. I figure that's the time somebody might try to pull something."

Willis took a deep breath and blew it out through his lips. "I'm sick of this already and we ain't even started. By the time I get to Kansas, I may never eat beef again."

Leroy threw his head back and laughed.

The first few days on the trail passed without incident. Then late one afternoon, when both the herd and the cowboys were exhausted, a group of riders approached from the north. The men appeared to be ranchers, as they rode toward the herd waving their hats.

"Mighty friendly fellows," Willis laughed. "What do you think they want from us?"

"I ain't sure, Willis. But be ready in case we got trouble." Leroy looked around and spotted a cluster of trees on the right. *That's not too far away,* he thought. "Let's see if we can sneak over there and watch what happens."

"Why?" Willis asked, puzzled at Leroy's concern. "There's only six of them and we've got over twenty hands working the herd."

"Yeah, that's the problem. These boys are cowhands, not gunmen." Leroy began easing his horse away from the herd. "I figure we've got just enough beef in front of us that they won't notice if we move over yonder by them trees." He glanced at Willis, then toward the approaching riders. "There's something funny about the way they're acting. I can't figure it out, but I don't like the looks of things. Those fellows are spaced just far enough apart to draw down on both Kell and Flanagin without getting in each other's way. They may be trying to look friendly, but I got a feeling they're up to no good."

Leroy was right. As Kell and Flanagin rode forward, several of the riders drew their pistols.

"What do we do now?" Willis asked. "Looks like they mean business, and they've got the drop on Kell."

Leroy grinned. "You are right, as usual, Willis. However, the problem them rustlers have is they've got the drop on a bunch of cow punchers, not us."

"You mean we're gonna take on six of 'em?" Willis shook his head. One glance at Leroy and he knew the answer to his question.

"Let's have some fun, Willis." Leroy dismounted and tied his horse to a tree branch. "If I can get in with them Longhorns and they don't gore the hell out of me, I think I can sneak up on those buzzards. As soon as I draw, you fire a shot over their heads."

"Why not just blast 'em?"

"In good time, Willis," Leroy grinned. "In good time."

"Leroy, didn't you hear Flanagin's talk about how easy it is to stampede a bunch of cattle?"

"I think that was Kell warning us about that, Willis. Flanagin talked about other stuff, like doing our share of the work on top of providing security for the drive."

Willis shook his head, leaning down low, he pleaded. "What difference does it make? If you spook them cattle, we're gonna be in a heap of trouble."

"Looks like we're in trouble already. What's a little more?" Leroy said as he started making his way toward the herd. He kept low, moving slowly just as Willis had seen him move many times during the war.

He ain't changed one bit, Willis thought. *He's still a damn fool.* Willis couldn't resist a smile. *But he ain't dead yet. No matter what he does, Leroy always lands on his feet.*

Leroy had a way with animals, and although Longhorns tended not to like any man, Leroy showed no fear, and the cattle didn't seem to be bothered much as he slowly walked toward them. One big steer gave Leroy a curious look, then dropped his head and continued to graze. Leroy made his way carefully through the herd until he was close enough to hear the leader of the rustlers order Kell, Flanagin, and several of the cowhands to throw down their guns and leave the herd.

"If you want to stay healthy, you'll throw down your gun belts and be on your way." Leroy heard the rustler shout. "If not, we'll drop you all right here."

"I don't think we're going to do that." Kell said in a matter of fact tone of voice.

Leroy was impressed with Kell's calm manner. It wasn't that he was arrogant, just sure of what was the right thing to do.

"Then you'll die here and now," the bearded rustler motioned his men to spread out.

Leroy stood up, gun drawn and said, "I wouldn't move if I was you. If anyone is going to die right here and now, it's gonna be you."

The rustler laughed. "Says you, Mister?" You aim to take on all six of us by yourself?"

At that moment a bullet whizzed by his head. The rustler turned in the direction of the shot. "What the hell?" he yelled, just as Leroy shot him in the chest. The other rustlers were momentarily stunned by the unexpected turn of events. Before they could recover, four more of them were dead and the other one had dropped his weapon and raised his hands.

"Just let me go," the rustler hollered. "I ain't meaning no harm."

Leroy shook his head, "Too bad," he called out to the rustler. "Looks like you found religion a bit too late."

Kell rode up to the man and yanked him off of his horse. "You can start walking back to whatever hole in the ground you came out of." Kell motioned to Flanagin. "Take the man's mount."

As Flanagin climbed down from his horse and moved toward the rustler, the man spoke in a voice filled with panic. "I won't make it without my horse. You know that."

"If you get back to civilization, maybe you will have learned a mighty important lesson in life." Kell watched as Flanagin took the man's Colt and rifle.

"You're lucky," Leroy grinned. "If we were the Comanch, we'd strip off the bottom of your feet before we let you go."

"I'll be lucky if I don't' run into some of them devils." the rustler snarled.

"Who's calling who a devil?" Willis rode up and looked down at the man. "I don't see that you're any better than the Comanch. You and your friends were ready to kill a bunch of cowboys who are just trying to make an honest living."

Kell turned to Flanagin, "Get the herd moving, Jimmy."

Flanagin nodded and turned to Leroy.

"Looks like you just earned your extra pay," Flanagin said. "I'm grateful."

"You were doing all right without me," Leroy said as he climbed up on the rustler's horse. "Willis, let's go get my Mustang. Then we'll take these horses over to the wranglers."

A short while later as the herd started moving, Leroy watched as Kell rode over to the wranglers and told them to leave the saddle on the rustler's horse. "I'm not going to be responsible for the death of any man if I can help it." Kell said as he watched the wranglers cut the horse out from the horses used for the drive. With a slap on the horses hip, Kell sent the horse galloping back toward the startled rustler.

"He's a good man," Willis remarked. "Not many like him."

"That kind of good man will get your ass shot off one day," Leroy said in anger. "That rustler just might be waiting for us down the trail."

"I hope not," Willis sighed.

Leroy pointed his finger toward the departing rustler as he spoke. "If he is, I hope I'm not the one that takes a bullet for Kell's mistake."

Leroy tapped his spurs against the Mustang's ribs and rode forward intending to have a few words with Flanagin.

Jimmy was busy getting the herd moving again. Kell still hoped to make his planned twelve miles today, but the delay caused by the band of rustlers had made that goal almost impossible. Kell knew that making twelve miles each day depended on grazing time, river crossings and other factors beyond his control, but he was determined to make at least ten miles each day, twelve if there wasn't good grass and water. The dry spell that had hit south Texas after the round up was taking its toll on the Longhorns. The Longhorns had to have water, and water was in short supply. Already both men and cattle were showing signs of thirst.

The lead drovers had finally gotten the herd moving forward. Their main job was to keep the cattle pointed in the right direction. Leroy decided not to bother Flanagin until the herd was settled into its usual pace. He moved to the side and watched the cowhands working the herd. Behind the point riders rode the swing men. They helped turn the cattle if the point men signaled the need for them to move closer together or to turn in one direction or another. The rest of the herd usually followed in the steps of the lead cattle. Leroy noticed that the swing men were joining the flankers riding up and down the length of the herd. He was so engrossed in watching the drovers work that he didn't notice Kell riding over to join him. Kell pulled his big stallion next to Leroy and offered him a drink from his canteen.

"No, thanks," Leroy smiled. "Mine is almost full."

"Make sure you empty it before sunset, and by that I mean drink it all. A man needs lots of water while driving cattle. I've seen tougher and stronger men than you pass out from lack of water." Kell made a sweeping gesture while pointing to the herd of Longhorns. "The drover's job is to keep the herd together in as narrow a line as possible. If they do their job, we won't lose too many strays."

Leroy nodded. "I'm trying to learn as much as I can."

"Don't worry about it," Kell's tone was serious. "Despite what Flanagin says, I've hired enough men to handle the drive. Your job is to watch out for trouble. You can bet there's plenty more waiting for us between here and Abilene. After what you did back there, I'm wondering why we didn't hire Rangers before to guard the drives. It's a darn good idea, and I'm glad that Robbins and Branson talked me into hiring you."

"Willis and I will try to earn our keep," Leroy grinned. "If you don't mind, we'll ride up ahead now and then so we can scout things out."

"Ride wherever you please," Kell replied. "I consider you and Willis the eyes and ears of my herd, my cavalry so to speak."

"Agreed," Leroy pulled up the reins and started the Mustang back toward Willis, who was still riding drag. Before he had gone very far, he stopped and rode back to speak his mind to Kell. "During the war I had to hang a man who needed hanging. I've never regretted it. Just now you didn't hang a man who damn sure deserved hanging. I hope the day doesn't come that we all regret you letting that rustler go free."

"My call," Kell replied while looking at the herd, not at Leroy. "Not yours."

"Agreed," Leroy nodded his head. "I ain't arguing the point."

Kell watched Leroy turn and ride back toward Willis. *He's a hard man,* he thought. *But a good man. I'd have liked to have had him in my regiment during the war.*

CHAPTER ∞ 15

Later that afternoon, the drovers had the Longhorns moving along at their usual slow pace when they spotted the chuckwagon near a stretch of tall green grass and a nearby stream. Cookie had stopped the chuck wagon and already had supper cooking. The chuck wagon was always a welcome site to the tired and hungry cowboys. When it came to picking out a campsite, Cookie knew his business. He had chosen a stretch of flat ground to bed down the Longhorns. After working for Corky during the last two drives, he could almost read his mind. Good grazing grass was hard to find, so whenever they happened upon some particularly fine grass, Kell would allow the herd time to rest and graze.

Cookie set up the campsite and started preparing sourdough biscuits and bean stew. Before the start of the drive, he had put a mixture of flour, sugar and water in a large sourdough barrel. After a few days on the trail, the mixture would begin to ferment naturally. During the drive, Cookie would scoop out the dough and mix it with some more flour and water to form the sourdough.

When the day's work was done, the cowboys would enjoy their main meal of the day, then settle the cattle down for the night. The cowboys would circle the herd slowly, making sure they didn't frighten the cattle, until they had the Longhorns bunched tightly together. By the end of the day the cattle were as tired as the drovers, so it didn't take long to bed them down. All that remained was posting guards around the herd. All night long the cowboys took turns watching the cattle. Leroy could hear the men singing to the cattle each night when he fell asleep.

By the time the cowboys had finished breakfast, packed up their bedrolls and saddled fresh mounts, Cookie had cleaned and stored away the mess utensils and tidied up the chuck wagon. He was careful to tie everything down so that nothing could rattle and spook the herd.

It didn't take Leroy and Willis long to become accustomed to the routine of the cattle drive. Each morning, before dawn, Cookie would call out in a calm but stern voice, "Grub pile. Don't make me roust you out of them bedrolls. I ain't about to be the cause of no stampede, so git your sorry butts up!"

Kell was always the first man up. He made a point of walking around the campsite pouring coffee for his cowhands. He visited with the men, listened to their complaints and offered encouragement whenever they needed it.

"Not too many trail bosses help the cook out." Flanagin said to Leroy. "He's always looking out for his men and trying his best to keep ol' Cookie happy. I guarantee you the food tastes a heck of a lot better when the cook's in a good mood."

"Have you worked for him a long time?" Leroy asked as he carefully placed the blanket on his Mustang.

"Yep, since the war ended. I knew Corky before the war and worked for him off and on while I was growing up. One of these days I'll tell you about serving under Corky during the war. He was the best officer I ever knew." Jimmy shrugged his shoulders as if trying to shake off the bad memories. "I've trusted him with my life more times than I can count and I'm still alive."

"Well," Leroy grinned as he cinched the saddle tight around the Mustang's belly. "It's part of my job to keep you alive now."

Jimmy laughed. "You seem to be doing a pretty fair job of it, at least this far." He watched Leroy climb up on the Mustang's back. "I could tell that you didn't approve of Corky letting that rustler off easy, but that's his way. He bends over backward to be fair."

"We should have left the sonofabitch swinging from a tree limb to let the rest of his kind know that stealing cattle ain't such a good idea," Leroy said as he rode toward Willis.

The next day the drovers and the herd faced their first river crossing. There would be a lot more rivers to cross en route to Abilene, but the first river crossing was usually the most difficult. Persuading the Longhorns to wade into the river and swim to the other side wasn't going to be an easy task for the cowboys. The lead cattle arrived at the river just before noon, which meant that the sun light was reflecting off of the water and into the eyes of the cattle. When the Longhorns reached the river they refused to get into the water and instead began milling about aimlessly. After over a hour of hard work and little success, Leroy was so frustrated he was ready to start shooting beef for supper.

"What in the hell is the matter with 'em?" he asked one of the drovers.

"Nothin'," came the reply. "There doesn't' have to be nothin' wrong for the herd to decide that they ain't getting in that water."

"Well, how long do we wait?" Leroy leaned on the saddle horn. He was tired down to his bones and the mosquitoes were like swarming hornets around his head and neck.

"We wait as long as Kell and Flanagin tells us to wait," the young cowhand said in a slow drawl. "I hear the boss has picked out a place where there's solid footing on each side of the river. The trouble now just might be the sun. Cattle don't like to head into the water if the sun's glaring in their eyes."

Leroy watched as one of the young drovers, Travis Lindsey, rode his horse into the water to show the lead cattle the way. "The currents not bad at all," Travis shouted at Flanagin.

"Keep 'em moving," Flanagin called out. He rode up to the lead steer and began to gently tap him with his rope. The cowboys began riding among the cattle trying to coax them into the river. "Keep 'em bunched up so they'll cross together."

"Hell, what's the matter with them? It ain't that deep," Leroy said.

"Don't matter," the drover said in a resigned tone. "Like I said, sometimes they just ain't gonna get wet."

Finally, the first Longhorns waded into the muddy river.

"Don't let 'em break the line," Kell called out to the swing men.

"What does he mean?" Leroy asked.

"If the line of cattle gets broken, then we gotta start all over again making them get into the river."

A few moments later Leroy watched as the cattle began to separate.

"To hell with that," Leroy pointed to the widening gap between the Longhorns. "Them darn Longhorns have had their way long enough."

"Stay here, man. You ain't got no idea what you're getting into," the cowboy warned. But Leroy ignored the warning and rode down the river bank.

Leroy rode confidently into the herd of Longhorns and began helping the drovers close the gap that had started to develop. Eventually, the herd was packed so closely together that their backsides almost touched. Just when it seemed that things were going well, all hell broke loose. For no apparent reason, the Longhorns seemed to panic in midstream and began wading around in circles. Leroy and several other cowboys rode as close to the cattle as they could in an effort to lead them to the far bank of the river. The Longhorns slammed against each other, their eyes bulging and nostrils flaring. Several of them began throwing their fearsome horns in all directions. No matter what the cowboys did, nothing seemed to help. The situation was quickly getting out of control.

No! thought Leroy, as he watched the cattle begin to panic.

He rode alongside the cattle, while the other drovers worked to get the frightened herd to the far bank of the river. In the midst of all the noise and confusion, Jimmy Flanagin shouted a warning to Leroy that he was too close to the cattle. Before Leroy could move away, one of the Longhorns whirled it's head around, raking it's horns across the side of Leroy's Mustang. The horse reared and bucked, throwing Leroy into the mass of stomping cattle. He tried to stand, but was immediately knocked back down by one of the steers. Kell saw what was happening and charged into the middle of the herd. He circled around, and made his way toward Leroy. By this time, Leroy had regained his footing and was struggling to keep from being either gored or trampled by the Longhorns. Suddenly, he felt a strong hand grab ahold of his arm and pull him part way out of the water. Leroy reached over, grabbed the saddle horn and held on as if his life depended on it, which it probably did. The added weight caused the big Appaloosa to stumble nearly throwing Kell off the saddle. Leroy lost his grip on the saddle horn and fell back into the river, but by this time, he was clear of the Longhorns. Corky Kell had saved his life.

The near stampede had only lasted for only a few a short minutes, yet the cowhands were physically and emotionally exhausted by the time they got the herd across the river. It then took several more hours before the herd was settled down and put to bed.

That night Leroy fell asleep before Cookie could serve up a cold supper. Later he woke up with terrible stomach cramps. He stumbled over to a small cluster of trees away from the campsite and vomited until he had nothing left in his stomach. The next morning after breakfast, Kell gathered his trail hands around the campfire and gave them a no nonsense talking to.

"This time we got off easy," he began. "The next river crossing will not be handled like this one was. We lost a few Longhorns but no one was injured. That, I can tell you, was a miracle. Jimmy will give you your assignment and make it crystal clear to each and every one of you where you will be when we make our next river crossing."

The men listened intently. When Kell finished, Jimmy Flanagin stood up and read off the names of the cowboys and their assignment. When he was finished, he still had not mentioned either Leroy or Willis.

Leroy could not remember feeling so low. He glanced at Willis who had his chin dropped to his chest. After the meeting, Leroy turned and walked away to gather his thoughts.

Corky Kell followed at a respectful distance. He waited until Leroy was ready to talk. As the Texas Ranger started walking towards his horse, Kell caught up with him and put a hand on his arm. "You did fine out there today, Leroy," he said.

Leroy shook his head. "Thanks for saying so, but I don't believe you. I've never in my life messed up like that. Men have always depended on me. This time I let everyone down, especially you."

"Not really," Kell said in a low voice. "Although, I can see where you might feel that way but it's because you don't know any better. You showed some real courage back there at the river, the same kind of courage that I'm sure you must have demonstrated during the war. You have my respect and my trust and I can assure you it takes a lot for me to say that."

"What about Flanagin? How does he feel about all of this?"

"He feels the same way I do."

"I doubt that," Leroy paused and leaned a weary arm against a tree.

"It's true or I wouldn't say it."

"If I did such a fine job, how come Jimmy didn't call my name out? Everybody noticed that Willis and I were the only two left off the duty list. We're both feeling mighty low right now."

Kell took a deep breath. "Leroy, you expect too much of yourself. Jimmy didn't call out your name because I told him not to."

"I probably know the answer but I have to ask why." The hurt showed on Leroy's wrinkled brow.

"It's not what you think," Kell smiled. "The truth is that both you and Willis are too valuable to me. I can't afford to have either of you trampled in a stampede. I'll need both of you if I'm going to get this herd through to Kansas. We've got plenty of trouble ahead. You know that as well as I do. Forget about cowhand duty. Like I told you before, I've got enough men to handle the drive. I need both of you to act as my scouts and to keep your guns ready in case we run into trouble."

Leroy's face showed obvious relief. He nodded, but didn't speak. Kell gave him a pat on the shoulder then began to walk away. He had only gone a few feet when he heard Leroy call his name.

"Mr. Kell," Leroy spoke with a voice choked with emotion. "I just want to thank you for saving my life."

"Leroy, you would have done the same for me," Kell replied.

"I know, but that's different," said Leroy. "I was wrong about you from the start. Now I understand why Jimmy and the other cowboys feel the way they do about you."

CHAPTER ∞ 16

Anybody heard from Leroy?" Carter asked as he walked through the door and sat down at his parent's kitchen table.

"Keep your voice down, Mama and Papa Wiley are taking their afternoon nap. As for your wayward brother, no, darn him," Mindy said. Her voice softened. "Even if he could write letters on the trail, he never was much of a letter writer."

Carter laughed. "You're right about that, Mindy. But he does have other talents."

"Well," Mindy handed Carter a plate of apple pie as she spoke. "I'm going to be real happy when this darn cattle drive is over."

"They only make about ten miles each day. Even with good weather, it's going to be a long time before he makes it home from Abilene."

"As long as he makes it back in one piece I won't complain." Mindy looked around to make sure that Leroy's parents didn't hear what she was about to say. "Carter, is there anyway to get word to Leroy, I mean, in case of an emergency?"

"No, not that I can think of, Mindy. Not unless someone rode over to the Chisholm Trail and caught up with him. I'm not sure exactly when he left on the cattle drive, so there's no way to tell how far he's gone. Unless we hear from Leroy, and both you and I know that's not likely to happen, we can't be sure of where he is."

Carter watched Mindy closely. He decided to wait until she felt like talking. He took a moment to look around the warm kitchen with its odor of simmering stew. Carter sniffed the good smell of home baked bread that was cooling on a rack near the table where he sat. He felt completely at home. *I still belong here,* he thought, suddenly moved by memories. *After all these years and a home of my own, I still belong here.*

Mindy busied herself pouring water from a brass teapot. She finally turned back to him. "Carter," she hesitated. "I was just worryin' a little bit, that's all."

Carter had practiced law long enough to know when he was being lied to. He ignored Mindy's last remarks. "What emergency are you talking about? Are the folks all right?"

"Oh, yes," Mindy reassured him. "They're fine and dandy. It's just that I was wondering if I would be able to get ahold of Leroy if I needed him." She looked up and saw Carter frowning at her. "Never mind, Carter."

Carter took a deep breath, stood up and slowly walked over to put his hands on Mindy's shoulders. "Mindy, the time has come to be honest with me." He leaned down and looked her square in the eye before asking, "What's the matter?"

Mindy turned her face away and nervously ran her hand through her hair. "I'm going to have a baby and I didn't tell Leroy before he left. Now, I'm not so sure that I did the right thing. I know I should have told him, but I didn't want him to worry. I'd rather Leroy keep his wits about him."

Carter gently reached his arm around her and held her close. "Frightened?" he asked.

"A little. I'd sure like to have him here with me this time."

"Well, depending on when the baby comes, he might make it back in time."

Mindy touched her waist, "No one can tell yet, but I'm almost four months along. I wanted to tell somebody besides Patsy."

Carter frowned. "I'm glad that you decided to tell me, but you really should have told him."

Mindy started to cry. "I had planned to tell him, but suddenly he left to go off on this cattle drive. I got mad at your brother and didn't tell him."

"Well he definitely should know about this, Mindy. If you want me to, I'll ride to the Red River Station and wait for him. I seriously doubt that he's made it that far." Carter reached into his waistcoat to pull out a handkerchief.

"How do you know that he'll pass through Red River Station?" Mindy took the offered handkerchief and began to lightly touch the corners of her her eyes.

"He has to. Before he left, Leroy told me that he was going to sign on with a drive going up the Chisholm Trail. For a moment, I had forgotten that every cattle drive the uses the Chisholm Trail has to pass through Red River Station."

Mindy sighed, then looked up at Carter. Her large brown eyes became misty. "If I start to feel poorly, I mean really poorly, I might ask you to do just that."

"Don't hesitate to send Papa to town if you have any problems, and I promise I'll find Leroy for you."

"Carter, knowing that I can depend on you means so much to me."

"But Mindy," Carter frowned. "Don't wait too long. It's not going to be easy to find him, and it's going to take time to get him back here." He kept his arm around her as he started walking toward the door. "Have you seen Doc McKinley yet?"

She shook her head. "No, not yet."

"I'll see that he calls on you tomorrow. Meanwhile, take care of yourself." He leaned down and kissed her cheek. "I'll send someone from Tyler to help with the chores."

"Carter," Mindy's dark brown eyes became even darker. "You know that we don't have the money to pay someone, and Leroy won't take charity."

"Right now, Leroy isn't here to say no, is he? If Leroy has any complaints, he can take them up with me when he gets back."

She giggled, "He'll probably do just that. He has an independent streak, you know."

Carter laughed as he climbed up into his saddle. "That, Mindy, is the understatement of the year."

He took a moment to look around the farm. He glanced at the barn which was badly in need of repair, and made a mental note to get someone to fix it. Then he kicked his horse into a gallop, rode past the sandy creek and up the gentle slope of the hill toward Tyler.

Carter Wiley was a practical man. As he rode back to his law office, he tried to sort things out in his mind. He passed a sparkling lake surrounded by beautiful wildflowers, but for once, he didn't take notice of its natural beauty. His mind was on other things. *No sense wasting time,* he thought. *I'll send a rider in the morning to Red River Station and leave a message for Leroy. Mindy's only four months along, so he should be able to finish the drive and get home before she has the baby. But what if something goes wrong? He wasn't here when JR was born, but that was during the war. He needs to be here for Mindy this time.*

CHAPTER 17

Leroy and Willis were saddle sore and covered from hat to boot with a gritty dust that had turned their clothes to a light tan color. Neither man had slept much due to the warm, humid weather which had kept them and the Longhorns awake most of the night.

"Let's go, Willis," Leroy picked up his breakfast pan and tin coffee cup. "I'll take yours too." He reached over to stack Willis' breakfast utensils on top of his own.

"Another day, and we're still a hell of a long way from Kansas," Willis moaned. "They all seem to be running together just like they did at the end of the war."

"Nope, this one's gonna be different. Look at them rain clouds." Leroy grinned as he motioned with his hat toward the dark clouds that were approaching from the West.

"Rain?" Willis groaned. "That's all we need."

"Unroll the slickers while I put this stuff away."

Willis got up slowly and walked toward the horses. "Rain, that means I'll be eating mud instead of dust."

"Oh, come on, Willis. Things ain't that bad. I don't want to hear you whining just because there ain't no place to hide out here under the big sky when the lightning hits. We'll just have to tough it out like we always do. After four years in the Confederate Army, and more years than that in the Texas Rangers, you ain't gonna let a little rain get you down."

Thunder rumbled across a dark sky, and in the distance the drovers saw flashes of lightning coming out of the dark storm clouds. Cattle and cowboys continued their slow trek across a rolling plain with a growing sense of dread.

Flanagin felt the first drops of rain begin to hit his hat and slicker. Soon water began to cascade from the brim of his hat. "Think we ought to hold 'em up here awhile?" he asked Corky.

"The only cover around these parts is behind us," Kell answered. "That storm is heading our way, and it's moving fast."

"Well, we damn sure can't outrun a storm while we're driving a herd of Longhorns." Flanagin spoke with a tinge of apprehension in his voice. "I'll tell the drovers to bunch 'em up tight. Maybe they'll lie down."

Kell shook his head. "Maybe if they'd walked twelve miles instead of the five or six that we covered yesterday." His expression was one of concern. "Those cattle are ready to run. It won't take much thunder and lightning to spook 'em, then we'll have a stampede on our hands."

Flanagin remained quiet waiting for orders. Kell took a deep breath. "Get the men ready, Jimmy."

"I've already done that." Flanagin said in a resigned tone of voice. "They're waiting for us."

"Send word to Cookie. Tell him to find whatever shelter he can up ahead."

Flanagin nodded and quickly rode away. Kell looked around until he saw Brian Pemberton.

Brian Pemberton was the youngest cowboy signed on to the drive, yet he was without a doubt one of the best men in the saddle that Corky Kell has ever seen. It was to Brian that Corky turned to now.

"Brian," Kell softly called out to the young cowboy. "Get to the front of the herd. Take Travis and Clint with you. Be ready. I think they're gonna stampede."

Brian nodded, then galloped off to find his two friends. Brian rode a small, quick two year old horse that reminded Kell of an Indian pony.

Brian was a slender young man with a sixth sense when it came to cattle. He always seemed to know how they were going to react in various situations. Brian had been too young to serve with his brothers in Colonel Kell's cavalry regiment, but near the end of the war, he had run away from home and enlisted in his brother's regiment. His mother, a widow, had written a letter to Colonel Kell requesting that her youngest son be sent home. Upon receiving the letter, Kell had issued the order and Brian was returned to his mother. Of the four Pemberton boys who fought for the Confederacy, only Brian survived the war. After the war, Brian became like a son to Kell. Although he worried about giving the boy such a dangerous assignment, he felt that he didn't have a choice. Next to Flanagin, Brian was the best cowboy on the drive.

When the thunderstorm broke, the cattle began bawling and pawing at the ground. The drovers rode around the herd, singing and trying their best to keep the animals calm. Willis and Leroy joined in and followed the lead of the other cowboys.

Suddenly there was a nearby flash of lightning, followed by a tremendous boom of thunder. Immediately, the herd was up and charging into the early morning light in a full fledged stampede. The roar of the hoofs was as loud and frightening as any Yankee artillery barrage that Leroy had faced during the war.

It's like they've gone mad, he thought.

The lightning continued to streak through the sky all around them, while the booming thunder added to the roar of the stampede. At times the lightning seemed to light the darkened sky. First came sheets of lightning, followed a short time later by forked lightning. Rain stung Leroy's face as he rode as fast as his horse could run towards the front of the stampeding herd. Longhorns were everywhere. The cattle tripped and trampled over each other during their mad dash across the plains. Only the lightning enabled Leroy to see the horrible sight ahead of him.

Brian and Travis were at the head of the herd of Longhorns. Brian rode as close as he could to the big steers that were leading the herd, at times almost touching their horns. He fired his pistol close to their heads trying desperately to turn them. He knew that if the cattle continued to run, like this they could lose half the herd.

Brian emptied his pistol and still the Longhorns refused to turn. It was then that he realized that stopping this stampede would take more than skill. They needed luck, and right now luck seemed to have deserted them.

Just as Brian was giving up any hope of turning the herd, he saw Travis race ahead of him. Travis was riding at a furious pace, turned almost sideways in his saddle while using his rope and pistol in a desperate effort to turn the Longhorns. Suddenly, Brian saw Travis' horse go down. Both rider and horse went head over heels. Brian thought that the horse must have stepped in a hole to have gone down so quickly. If Travis screamed, no one heard him. He disappeared under the thundering hoofs. Brian rode on; soon Jimmy and several other men, including Leroy and Willis, joined him.

Finally, the other cowboys were able to draw alongside the lead cattle and begin to gradually turn them into a circle. As more and more cattle joined the circle, the stampede slowly ground to a halt.

An hour later, Kell and Flanagin tried to come up with a head count. Three men were missing.

"God help them," Kell sighed. "I know they're back there."

"They're pounded into dust if you ask me, Leroy whispered to Willis. "The way I figure it, ain't nothing gonna be left of 'em."

Willis flinched. "Don't tell me no more, Leroy."

"I'll find them Corky. Stay here in case you're needed." Flanagin tried to find the strength to climb back on an exhausted horse and begin his sad task.

"No! The cattle are down. They're spent. My job now is to find my boys and do what has to be done." Kell staggered toward a horse. *So little can be done,* he thought. *Pick up what's left of those boys and put them in the ground. Oh, I'll say a few words, mostly for those of us left alive and then we've got to move on.* He wiped tears from his dirt-crusted face and pulled himself up into the saddle.

Leroy followed. He wanted to help. As he climbed back into the saddle, he heard Willis say, "I'm staying here, if it's all the same to you, Leroy. I don't wanna see what's left of 'em."

Leroy nodded but said nothing.

Jimmy Flanagin found Travis beside the remains of his dead horse. The horse's insides had been torn out and spread across a large area. All of Travis' ribs had been broken and scraped bare of flesh. Both Travis and his horse had been smashed into the ground. Although the remains were flat and nearly void of blood, they were still a horrible sight. Flanagin picked up a mud caked rag that was oncc part of Travis' familiar blue checked shirt. Next to the cloth was part of a six-shooter. Leroy thought that he had seen every possible way for a man to die during the war, but this had to be the worst thing that he could imagine happening to a man. *Even the damn Comanche couldn't do this,* he thought. *God help us all.*

They used one of Cookie's shovels to bury what little they found of Travis. They never found the other two missing cowboys.

As they buried the remains, Willis slipped up behind Leroy and whispered, "There wasn't much left to bury."

"Hell," Leroy responded in anger. "For all I know we might have just buried part of the horse."

"Leroy," Willis swallowed, then managed to speak in a shaky voice. "Promise me that if something like that happens to me, you won't tell Patsy anything about it."

"Willis," Leroy glared at him. "What do you take me for, a damn fool? Of course, I wouldn't say nothing to her. But don't you fret none cause that ain't gonna happen to either of us. I'm learning all about this here cattle driving business, and I'm learning fast."

"You've got to, if we're gonna stay alive," Willis shivered. He couldn't shake the images of the trampled young drover. "God darn it, what's next?"

The question posed by Willis gave Leroy an opportunity to get his mind off of burying the young cowboy. "The Comanche and maybe a few Mexican bandits, that's what's next. We ain't about to get away this easy."

"I'm ready to go home," Willis looked around to make sure that no one else could hear what he had to say before speaking his mind. He whispered to Leroy, "The way things are going, we ain't gonna live long enough to get paid our wages."

Leroy grinned. "There's no way we're going back now, Willis. Not empty handed. We are on our way to the Yankee lovin' state of Kansas, and we ain't turning back."

"That's real cheerful news, Leroy. Real cheerful news." Willis dropped his bedroll on the wet ground, propped his head against his saddle and covered his head with his hat.

Leroy did the same thing. He didn't remember falling asleep. He slept soundly until he woke up in the middle of the night shivering from the cold.

In the morning the drive moved on toward Red River Station. Before saddling his horse after breakfast, Leroy made sure his Colt revolver was loaded and ready for action. Although the gun had its drawbacks, the Colt was Leroy's favorite weapon. The revolver weighed over two pounds and had an eight-inch barrel. It was designed for fast shooting at close range. It was not a weapon for gunfights but Leroy was not a gunfighter. He knew that the Colt was accurate for only about seventy-five feet. For that reason, Leroy kept a Henry rifle strapped to his saddle.

When the herd reached north central Texas, they encountered their first Indians. A group of ten Comanches rode along side the herd for several miles, keeping their distance, but making their presence known. Leroy caught up with Kell and gave him the bad news.

"They're Comanch all right. And there's more of 'em waiting up ahead of us. What I'm telling you, Mr. Kell, is that there's enough of 'em to do us in if that's what they want to do."

Kell shook his head. "They're wanting beef. They'll ask for a few dozen head. I'll try to get them to settle for less."

"They may want more than beef."

"I doubt it," Kell said. "They've got a good thing what with the drives going through here. I don't think they'd want to ruin everything for the sake of a few scalps."

"I hope you're right." Leroy shook his head.

"Should we ride out to meet the chief?" Kell asked.

"No, let 'em come to us. We'll have to deal with 'em soon enough."

"We'll play this your way, Leroy. You have a lot more experience dealing with the Comanche then I do." Kell motioned for Flanagin to join him at the front of the herd. "Stay close, Leroy. I may need you."

Leroy nodded and kept his Mustang even with Kell's big roan. After a few minutes, Flanagin caught up with them.

"Jimmy, pass the word to the men to remain calm. We don't want to stir them up."

"Yes, sir," Flanagin frowned. "I've picked out ten head, think we can settle for that?"

A slight smile crossed Kell's face. "I'll do my best. They'll probably ask for more. I figure about twenty head."

"No way I'm handing over twenty head to a bunch of damn Indians," Flanagin answered.

"Jimmy," Leroy lifted his hat. "How much is your hair worth? Mine's worth a lot more than a few Longhorns."

Flanagin smiled and removed his big Stetson. "I'm losing it anyway. But I guess you're right. I'd sure rather lose my hair naturally and not have a Comanche hair cut."

"We'll know soon enough," Leroy tilted his head toward the east. "Here they come."

"Jimmy, ride back and talk to the men. Hurry. I don't want an incident."

Incident? Leroy thought. *Is this what he calls getting killed by the Comanch? I wonder how Kell has managed to live this long out here on the trail?*

Five Comanche warriors and a young chief rode up to the front of the herd. They spread out slightly, rifles in hand and waited. They looked fierce, even without their war paint. Their leader, wearing a short headdress by Indian standards, spoke in chopped, but clear English when approached by Kell. Leroy kept his Mustang slightly behind Kell. He never took his eyes off of the Comanche chief. The young chief returned his glare, then turned his attention to Corky Kell. "Twenty cattle, no less. Then you cross Comanche land."

Kell was right on the money, thought Leroy. *If he's as smart as I think he is, he'll tell Jimmy to cut out a few more Longhorns.*

"Ten," Kell answered.

"Twenty. No less or the cattle with horns will walk north alone." The men surrounding the chief nodded in agreement.

"Ten and some flour from my supply wagon," Kell pointed to the rear of the herd. Leroy smiled, knowing that the chuck wagon was sent ahead of the herd hours ago.

The chief looked at one of the warriors, then smiled at Kell. "I can take you to wagon filled with food. Wagon waits with my people. If you want wagon and man with much hair; you give us twenty cattle with horns. If you say no, I keep wagon and add five horses."

Leroy chuckled out loud and shook his head. *We ain't gonna get no supplies back and probably no cook either,* Leroy thought. *Them Comanche squaws are going to be making sourdough biscuits tonight.*

The Comanches glared at Leroy. Kell also shot Leroy a disapproving look. *Hell,* thought Leroy. *The damn Comanch can read my mind.*

"If the wagon and my cook are all right, and if you'll promise safe passage until we cross the Red River, you can have your twenty cattle."

The Comanche chief nodded and he continued to glare at Leroy.

"Go tell Jimmy to cut out ten more head, Leroy." Kell said. "And make it fast."

Leroy backed the Mustang up, a move that impressed the Comanche chief, then he quickly rode off to find Jimmy Flanagin.

The Comanche pointed his finger at his chest and then at Kell. "I pick cattle with horns. Only then will you get wagon and man who cooks."

"Where is the wagon?" Kell asked.

"With fifty of my warriors. They wait at the Sandy Creek watering hole."

Kell took a deep breath. "I'll take you to my foreman. You can help him pick out the cattle."

The other Comanche rode behind Kell and their chief toward the rear of the herd. Leroy had already told Flanagin to get ten more Longhorns cut out of the herd. Flanagin was in the process of separating the cattle when Kell and the Comanche rode up. The Chief seemed satisfied with the cattle that Flanagin had picked out. He sat on his horse beside Kell and waited for Flanagin and two of the drovers to finish the job.

An hour later, the Bar S drovers caught up with Cookie, who was still shaking from his encounter with the Comanche.

"We're gonna get one hell of a supper tonight," Leroy grinned at Willis. "Ol' Cookie is still shaking in his boots."

"Who can blame him?" Willis stared at the horizon. "How many more Comanche do you think are out there?"

"Oh, probably enough to wipe us out anytime they damn well please, but I think we're gonna be just fine 'cause the Comanch enjoys doing business with our trail boss. They got their twenty head. That's what's important to them right now. Willis, they'll use every bit of that beef. There won't be one square inch left of any of those Longhorns when the squaws are finished." He chuckled. "I can see that Comanche chief wearing a pair of Longhorns on his head and thinkin' that he looks mighty handsome."

"Who cares as long as we get out of here in one piece," Willis said as he continued to look in every direction.

"Agreed," Leroy grinned. "Just think, Willis, we've only got another two or three tribes to go through before we meet up with those Yankee loving Kansas farmers that I told you about."

Willis spat out a big wad of tobacco. He decided not to comment.

CHAPTER ∞ 18

As the name suggests, Red River Station was located on the banks of the Red River which separates Texas from the Indian Territory. In addition to serving as an important source of supplies for the cattle drives heading north, the trading post offered one of the few chances the cowboys had to post a hastily written letter to let their families know where they were and that they were safe.

During the war Carter's letters were of great comfort to her and the rest of the family. Leroy wasn't much for writing letters. Mindy knew and accepted that, although she didn't like it.

The Bar S men halted the cattle along the bank of the Red River to allow them to drink their fill and rest for a few hours. Because many herds stopped in the area, the grass was so thin it was almost nonexistent. Still, the Longhorns were more than ready to rest.

"Leroy, will you write my Patsy a letter? But send it to Mindy. I don't want Patsy upset 'cause somebody came to the house while I'm on the cattle drive. Mindy can read my words to Patsy when she sees her at church on Sunday."

"I hadn't planned to write to Mindy, Willis. It's hard for me to say what I want to when I have to write down the words. But if you want me to, I'll write down a few words for Mindy to read to Patsy."

"Mindy's gonna be real mad if you write to Patsy for me and don't' write to her about how you are and how you're missing her."

Leroy threw his head back and laughed. "Now, Willis, how would you know whether or not I'm missing Mindy? I ain't said a word about her since we left Tyler."

"Leroy, you ain't fooling me," Willis pulled out a piece of paper and a stub of a pencil from his saddlebags. "Now write what I say to Patsy, then I'll sit here and watch while you write a note to Mindy."

"Anything you say, Willis," Leroy sighed. "You're the boss."

Slowly, Leroy began to compose his letter.

Dear Mindy,

I take pen in hand to write you some words to say to Patsy for Willis and also to tell you that I miss you more than I can say. We have reached the Red River. Tomorrow we will cross over into the Indian Territory. We have already met up with a hungry bunch of Comanche but they didn't make no trouble. The trail boss gave them twenty head of cattle so they went away happy. Well, I wouldn't say they were happy but they did go away which was all I wanted them to do. I ain't much on worrying about whether the Comanche are happy or not. I have been told that the Indians on the other side of the river won't cause us no trouble either. They just want beef to keep them alive during the winter. The man who runs this outfit gives the Injuns what they want so don't you worry your pretty little head about me. The Comanche walked away with twenty Longhorns and we rode away with all of our hair. I guess that was a pretty good trade after all.

Willis wants me to tell you to tell Patsy that he is very sad without her and the kids but he is in good health and otherwise good spirits. He says that he never wants to spend another day away from Patsy and his kids but that he is doing this for their good. Willis says that knowing that he has Patsy waiting for him back home lets him be away from Patsy and the kids without going crazy. Mindy, you know that I ain't much for writing words on paper so I will say in closing that you know how I feel about you. I can't make this too silly in case somebody reads the letter before it gets to you.

God bless you and my family,
Your husband,
Leroy W. Wiley

Willis has started talking again about what he wants to say to Patsy but I'm tired of writing all these words down so I'm going to say goodbye sweetheart and you can say whatever you want to say to Patsy. You can remind her that Willis snores louder than a bunkhouse full of cowhands.

"Jimmy, get 'em moving!" Corky Kell stretched up high in the saddle and waved his hat at Flanagin.

Flanagin responded by putting his fingers in his mouth and sending out a high-pitched whistle. Leroy thought that Flanagin's whistle was almost as irritating as the thunderstorm they encountered back on the Texas prairie. He had wondered why that noise didn't start a stampede until Corky explained that Flanagin had made that same whistling noise around the cattle during the round up.

If I was them Longhorns, I'd run just to make Flanagin stop whistlin', Leroy thought.

After a night's rest the drovers once again got the Longhorns headed north to Kansas. They crossed the Red River without incident and moved on into the Indian Territory. They hadn't gone far when they were met by a band of Choctaw Indians, waiting patiently to collect their fee.

"Look at them Choctaws, Willis," Leroy grinned. "They look peaceful enough."

"Says you," Willis growled. "The only thing I can say that's good about 'em is that they ain't Comanche."

"Agreed," Leroy laughed. "If you don't mind, I'm gonna ride up front and listen to Corky try to strike a deal."

"As long as they ain't shootin' at us, any deal that he makes will be fine with me. It ain't my cattle he's giving away." Willis watched Leroy ride away. *Wonder why he's so interested?* Willis thought. *I wished I had asked him to read to me what he wrote to Patsy. She ain't much for jokes and Leroy sometimes gets people all riled up without realizing it. Then he remembered that pretty day back at the Sunday Social when he had told Mindy about the cattle drive. I guess I ain't perfect either.* Willis sighed. *But Patsy loves me anyhow.*

Leroy rode toward the front of the herd. He watched as Corky and Jimmy rode ahead of the herd to meet the waiting Choctaws. He was surprised to see Corky dismount and greet the Choctaws like they were old friends. *I ain't never gonna trust no Indian that much,* he thought. *I don't care what tribe they belong to.*

Kell and Jimmy may trust 'em, but I know better. I would have stayed on my horse, just in case.

While Kell and the Indians were fussing over each other, Leroy took a moment to look all around the green river valley. It was a pretty sight. The valley was full of wild flowers and blooming trees. The area reminded him of northern Mississippi.

Suddenly, he began to frown. *Northern Mississippi,* his thoughts drifted back to the war. *That little town, what was it called? Water Valley? That was the name, Water Valley, Mississippi. We passed through there on our way to Shiloh.* He felt a cold chill run through his body causing his shoulders to tremble slightly. Leroy shook his head as if to clear his mind of sad memories. "Forget what is too painful to remember," Leroy reminded himself of what Mindy had said.

"Sure appears to be a friendly conversation between Corky and the Choctaws," said Brian Pemberton as he halted his Mustang next to Leroy.

"Looks that way, don't it," Leroy leaned over toward Brian and chuckled. "Kell drives a hard bargain with the Indians. They tell him what they want and he gives it to 'em. Of course, in his defense, he ain't in a real good bargaining position. Still, he could try to bargain just a little bit."

Brian slowly removed his hat and wiped his brow with his shirt sleeve before answering. "That's his way. He likes to get along if he can." He looked at Leroy and grinned. "Saves time and trouble if you ask me."

"Well, I didn't, Mr. Pemberton," Leroy reached over to give Brian a friendly punch to his shoulder. "But next time, I'll remember to ask you, considering your advancin' years and wealth of experience."

Brian laughed. "I can't imagine a Texas Ranger asking me nothin', Mr. Wiley." As he watched two of the new drovers ride by, his mood abruptly changed. "There's a few men on this drive that I don't trust and there goes two of 'em."

"Hiring and firing is way above my pay grade," Leroy said. "Kell hired 'em, I'm sure he knows what he's doing. If not, Flanagin will take care of 'em. I wouldn't want to tangle with Jimmy unless I had to."

"Jimmy ain't happy with 'em being along either. You and Willis ain't the only new men on the drive. One reason Kell agreed to hire you and Willis, what with you two being inexperienced and all, was that he had just hired some men that he didn't know. Kell didn't want to leave them working on the Bar S while most of the hands were on the drive, so he brought them along with us."

"I haven't noticed anyone acting suspicious," Leroy frowned. "Who are you talking about?"

"Mostly the men who just rode past us. The big fellow who calls himself Charlie Wilson and that sneaky red haired fellow that hangs out with him. Haven't you notice that they stay together all the time?"

Leroy shook his head, "Brian, the same thing could be said about me and Willis."

"You and Willis are different," Brian argued. "Charlie Wilson and his friend are up to no good, I tell you. Jimmy had me and Travis watchin' Wilson and his sidekick, what's his name?" Brian thought for a moment. "Bright, Tom Bright. Well, Travis and I were supposed to watch both of them and report what we saw to Jimmy, but now Travis is gone," Brian paused and dropped his head.

"Travis was a friend of yours?"

Brian nodded. "The best friend I ever had."

Leroy couldn't think of anything to say to comfort the young cowboy so he went back to the subject that concerned him. "I was under the impression that Kell only hired men that he knew from previous drives or drovers who had recommendations from other trail bosses."

"Usually that's the case, 'cept this time, we were in need of hands. Didn't you hear about the last drive?"

"No," Leroy answered. "No one ever mentioned any other Bar S drive to me."

"During the last drive Corky lost four drovers. Some of the men that he counted on to go with us on this drive decided to stay at the Bar S and pass up the extra money. Corky knew that the trail hands he was leaving behind couldn't protect the ranch against the likes of Wilson and Bright, so he talked it over with Jimmy and they decided to take both of them along on the drive so they could keep an eye on 'em. I tell you the two of 'em look like shady characters to me."

Leroy leaned over on the saddle horn to relax and think about what Brian had told him. *How come Flanagin ain't said nothing to me?* Leroy thought. *I think I'll have a word with the top hand on the Bar S.* "Brian, I'm going to go talk to Willis. Thanks for filling me in on this. I'll keep an eye out."

"I'd do more than that, Mr. Wiley," Brian leaned over and spoke almost in a whisper. "I'd watch my back. They know now that you're a Texas Ranger. I heard 'em talking about you and Willis."

Leroy nodded.

"Mr. Wiley," Brian said. "Just so you know that you can count on me. I ain't no greenhorn. I was just over sixteen years old when I signed on for my first drive. That drive went up the Shawnee Trail and that was a big mistake but I learned a lot. The Choctaws didn't like our herd being driven across their land. That's when Kell struck a deal with them and he's lived up to it. So have they."

"How many Longhorns did it take to strike the deal?"

Brain shook his head, "It's not the beef. Oh, we gave the Choctaws a few head, but it was the supplies that he promised to bring to the Choctaws on his way back from Kansas. The Choctaws are big on keeping their word and they respect Mr. Kell because he kept his word and brought back the supplies that he promised."

"What kind of supplies?"

"Corn meal, flour, stuff like that," Brian answered.

Leroy nodded and tapped the Mustang with the reins. "I'll have a talk with Jimmy as soon as he and Corky are finished with the Choctaws."

"I think that would be a good idea, Mr. Wiley," Brian added.

Leroy sent the Mustang off in a gallop toward the front of the herd.

Back at Red River Station, the station manager opened his cash box to count the money he had earned from the cattle herd that had just past through. After removing the script, he noticed a plain white envelope laying in the box. It was from a lawyer over in Tyler and it was addressed to one of the cowhands on the Bar S cattle drive.

"Hey, Ben," the station manager called out. "Wasn't that the Bar S drive that just went through?"

"Yes, sir," Ben replied.

The station manager frowned and tapped the envelope against the metal cash box. "Oh, well, maybe some of them Bar S cowboys will stop by on the way back from Kansas. Remind me to give this to one of 'em. Maybe they'll take the letter to South Texas and give it to the Bar S trail boss." He put the letter back in the cash box. *Hope it wasn't too important,* he thought. *It looks like some kind of legal business.*

"You have trouble ahead," the Choctaw Indian warned Corky Kell. "Rivers have too much water for the cattle to cross."

"I know," Corky said as he put his hands on his hips and looked north across the Indian Territory. "I hear that both the Washita and the North Canadian Rivers are going to be difficult."

The Choctaw nodded. "Cimarron River too. Maybe you should go east toward Fort Gibson." He joined Kell and looked out across the grassy plains which formed a rolling prairie.

"No," Corky shook his head. "That's too far out of the way and besides, I've driven cattle on the Shawnee Trail between here and Fort

Gibson, and that's not a good route. I'll have to take my chances going straight north through the Territory to Kansas."

Kell waited for a reply. When the Choctaw remained silent, he turned and asked, "How can I help your people?"

"I need several of your cattle to feed my women and children. It has been a very long winter. When you go back to Texas, bring us food so I may feed my people next winter."

"Consider it done," Corky smiled. "I'll bring you the supplies on my way back to Red River Station."

The Choctaw reached over to clasp Corky's arm. Then he turned to signal his braves to bring his horse.

"I heard him," Leroy said as Kell and Flanagin approached. "If the Indian's right, and I'm betting that he is, we're gonna have an interesting time getting this herd through the Territory. Did I hear him say there are three rivers between us and Kansas?"

"Actually, there are four," Kell said as he climbed up on his horse. "The Washita and the Canadian, followed by the North Canadian and the Cimarron, with the North Canadian being the most difficult one to cross."

Leroy looked at Kell then glanced at Flanagin. Jimmy's expression told Leroy just how tough the rest of the drive was going to be.

As the herd began to move forward through flat land covered with tall grass, Leroy and Willis joined the other cowboys riding slowly around and through the herd. The next few weeks were long and hard. Willis said more than once that driving cattle was the hardest work he had ever done. By this time, the food had become so monotonous that Leroy went off on his own several times to hunt for wild game. Other than a few prairie dogs, he returned empty handed. He helped Cookie slaughter a steer but the meat was so tough that Willis only ate half of the piece that was placed on his plate. In all the years that he had known him, Leroy had never seen Willis leave a plate half full.

"What's wrong, Willis?" he asked.

"The more I chew the bigger the the bite gets," Willis complained. "It's like the horse meat we had to eat during the war."

"You got horse meat?" Leroy asked, pretending to be serious. "I never got any horse meat. You had it easy, Willis."

Willis was not in the mood to put up with Leroy's attempt at humor. His lips were cracked open. The rest of his face and hands were so chapped he hardly noticed his sore back and legs. "You ate the same thing I did, Leroy. We were together every day during the war except when you and Carter went off looking for your brother."

"That's when you must have gotten the horse meat because I darn sure don't remember getting any meat at all." Leroy reached over to shove Willis' hat down over his eyes. Willis grunted and turned away.

Leroy decided it was best to leave him alone. He walked over to the edge of the campsite to look at the trail ahead. Wildflowers added splashes of yellow, orange, red and a touch of purple to the light green grass that covered the land as far as he could see. The flowers reminded him of home and Mindy. *How she loves those little flowers,* he thought. *Don't matter what color, she loves 'em all.* He promised himself that when he got home he would bring her wildflowers every night for the supper table. He felt a gentle wind touch his face. *As soon as we cross those darn rivers,* he thought, *we'll put these godforsaken Indians and the rest of our trouble behind us.* Leroy had no way of knowing that the real trouble would come after they had forded the last of the four rivers and crossed the Kansas state line.

CHAPTER ∞ 19

As the Bar S herd made its way North to Kansas, most residents of the state still harbored hard feelings towards Texas and Texans. This hatred of all things to do with the state of Texas had its roots in the passions generated by the Civil War. Even before the war began at Fort Sumter, there had been violent clashes throughout Kansas between Confederate and Union sympathizers.

By the end of the war quite a few people had moved away from the state, including most of it's pro-Confederate residents. Those that remained despised and feared the Texas drovers, many of whom had served in the Confederate Army. The cowboys from Texas, on the other hand, were suspicious of anyone from Kansas and hated the former Jayhawkers, as they called the Union guerrilla bands who rode roughshod across the Kansas-Missouri frontier. Leroy considered the Jayhawkers nothing but a bunch of no good looters, arsonists and murderers.

"As soon as we see the cloud of dust, we'll go out and stop 'em right here at the border," Jacob Wilkerson said, as he raised his fist in the air. "Each and every cowboy that comes up here from Texas is nothing but trouble."

The men who had gathered in front of the general store nodded their heads in agreement. Most of the men were carrying pitch forks and clubs. Only a few of them were armed with either pistols or shotguns.

"They was all in the Rebel Army, no question about that," one of the farmers called out. "Some of them are still wearing their gray jackets and pants."

"We don't want them here, that's for sure. This ain't Abilene. They think they can drive their cattle through here, tearing up good farm land, and still not pay us a penny for the trouble they cause."

"It's time we take a stand against the next herd that comes our way," Jacob said, his voice full of anger. The crowd of farmers roared their approval. After the demonstration Jacob led several of the men into the general store to see how many guns he and the others could buy on credit. It was going to take more than pitch forks and clubs to stop a bunch of Texas cowboys from driving their cattle across the border into Kansas.

Luck was on their side when the Bar S herd crossed the Washita and Canadian Rivers. The flood waters had receded and the cattle were able to cross without too much difficulty. They crossed the Washita at Rock Crossing, which allowed the Longhorns to walk across on a firm river bottom, which as the name suggests, was made of rock. After crossing the Canadian River, with its muddy water and steep banks, Kell found a nearby campsite that had plenty of grass for grazing, so he rested the herd for the remainder of the day. Other than the river crossing, the men of the Bar S Ranch ran into very few problems as they made their way across the southern half of the Indian Territory. The lack of firewood did cause Cookie to use up what little kindling he was able to carry in the back of the chuck wagon. Eventually, he had to resort to burning buffalo chips as the herd moved across the open prairies. The buffalo chips produced enough of a fire to cook the food and heat the coffee, but the smell did nothing to improve the cowhand's appetite. While the weather held, the herd was usually able to make Kell's targeted twelve miles before bedding down for the night.

When they reached the northern part of the Indian Territory, the Bar S cowboys found that it wasn't the swollen North Canadian and Cimarron Rivers that slowed down the drive, but the vast herds of buffaloes. While they were moving the Longhorns between the Red Fork and the Salt Fork of the Arkansas River, Kell was forced to halt the herd for almost an entire day while thousands of buffaloes crossed the trail ahead of them. Both Kell and Flanagin were afraid the buffaloes would spook the cattle and trigger a stampede.

"Have you ever seen so many buffaloes?" Willis asked. "Somehow I didn't figure there were that many left."

"Don't worry," Leroy answered. "The buffalo hunters will get up here before long, and by the time they're finished there won't be nothing left but dead carcasses lying all across the Territory."

"Kind of sad," Willis said. "Somehow it don't seem right that all those buffaloes are gonna be killed just for their hides. He twisted his face up to the cloudy sky and let out a deep breath. "I was hoping that we wouldn't have no more thunder and lightning, but I don't like the looks of those clouds coming out of the west."

"Just rain clouds, Willis." Leroy looked at his friend and had to laugh at his appearance. Willis had grown a droopy mustache and long hair while on the trail.

Willis continued to look at the dark clouds, while Leroy rode over to the chuck wagon. He wanted to find out what time Cookie was planning supper.

As he approached the chuck wagon, Leroy heard Flanagin arguing with two of the drovers. Leroy was not surprised to see the two men Brian had warned him about squared off and looking as if they were going to jump Flanagin at any minute.

Never needing an invitation to join a fight, Leroy quickly dismounted and walked toward the three men.

"Any trouble here, Jimmy?" he asked as he let go of the Mustang's reins and dropped his arms to his side. The Mustang stopped, just as Leroy had taught him to do while on the trail drive.

"Keep out of this, Leroy," one of the men snarled. "We ain't got no trouble with you."

Leroy looked toward Flanagin, then back to the two drovers. "I was talking to Jimmy. I ain't interested in what you got to say."

The man stirred uneasily, recalling the last time he had tangled with a Texas Ranger. He gave Leroy a sharp look. "Ain't no reason for you to butt in. This don't concern you."

"I'm still waiting to hear from Jimmy. If he says it don't concern me, then maybe, just maybe, I'll move on."

"It seems that these two no accounts want to draw their pay now and cut out," Flanagin said. "That wasn't part of the deal when they signed on and they know it."

Leroy shuffled his feet, planting them just wide enough apart to appear as if he was about to draw his Colt sidearm. "You agree to the same thing I did?" he asked.

Tom Bright, the drover with the bushy red hair, spoke for the first time. "We've had our fill of Indians and stampedes. Now I hear a bunch of them Kansas farmers plan on tangling with us when we cross the border."

"There's nothing to keep you from leaving," Flanagin said. "But no one gets paid until we reach Abilene and sell the stock."

"I ain't got no time for credit. Kell's got the money right here and now to pay us and you know it."

"You can stop wasting your breath," Flanagin pointed to the waiting horses. "Mount up and get back to where you're supposed to be or ride on out of here. Either way you ain't getting paid until the herd gets to Abilene."

Bright made a move for his gun but before it was halfway out of the holster Leroy had drawn his Colt revolver and had it pointed at the two drovers. "You heard the foreman. Not git while the gittin's good."

The big drover, named Charlie Wilson, laughed. "You ain't gonna shoot us, not with the Longhorns already spooked by them buffalo." He looked at Jimmy and spoke in a threatening tone of voice. "Like I said before, Flanagin, you better go tell your boss to get the cash box out of the chuck wagon. We mean to draw our pay and draw it now."

Flanagin suddenly threw himself at Wilson slamming his shoulder into the man's chest. Both men fell backwards and crashed into a pile of rocks. Leroy dropped his gun and charged the other drover. The man was much larger than Leroy and was already drawing back his fist as Leroy ran forward. Before he could land a punch, Bright hit him square in the jaw. Leroy was knocked to the ground and momentarily stunned. As he struggled to get to his feet, the cowboy began wildly swinging both fists against his head and chest. Leroy managed to grab hold of the drover and pull him down into the dirt. The two men rolled around in the dirt for several moments until Leroy found himself flat on his back looking up into a pair of huge fists that pounded his face relentlessly. He tried without success to roll over and take Bright with him. Nothing seemed to work. He glanced over at Flanagin, hoping for some help, but a quick look told him that Jimmy had his hands full. Leroy's unexpected turn of his head caused the cowboy's right fist to miss his face and smash into a rock behind his head. The man cried out, arched his back and began cradling his obviously broken wrist. That was all that Leroy needed. *I've got you now, you sonofabitch,* Leroy thought. He reached up and grabbed the man's broken wrist and twisted it with all his might. The man screamed out in pain, fell to the side and began rolling in the dirt. Leroy got to his feet and reached down with one hand to grab the man by the scruff of his neck. With his other hand he grabbed a hand full of red hair and yanked.

"Ain't no doubt in my mind that the two of you are wanted in Kansas. I've got a mind to take both of you into Abilene and turn you over to the Marshall. But to save me the trouble of looking after you until we get there, I'm telling you one last time to git out of here now before I string up the two of you. We don't need your kind around here causing trouble. We've got enough to do without stopping to hang buzzards like you."

The man's foot slipped while he was trying to stand. Agonizing pains shot up his arm. He cradled his arm while he tucked his head deep into his shoulders and moaned. "I've busted my arm. I need help."

"To hell with you and your arm," Leroy stepped forward and gave him a shove. "Get help from the Indians. Maybe they won't see you for what you are and scalp you first."

Satisfied that Bright was no longer a threat, Leroy turned his attention to Jimmy who was still fighting with the other cowboy. Leroy watched as Jimmy dodged a blow then landed a powerful right hand to the left side of the man's head. Wilson staggered for a second, then his eyes seemed to roll back in his head as he crumbled to the ground. Jimmy kicked the cowboy once in the ribs, then reached down and grabbed the unconscious man under his arms and dragged him over to Leroy.

"Help me get these two no accounts up on their horses and out of here," Jimmy was so out of breath he barely got the words out.

Leroy nodded. When they had finished lifting the two battered cowhands up onto their horses, Leroy and Jimmy both collapsed onto the ground, both of them too exhausted to do anything more. About this time, Brian rode up and spotted the two drovers slumped over their saddle horns. He immediately realized what must have happened. With two slaps of his hand, Brian sent the two horses on their way with their riders hanging on for dear life.

"I knew they were no good," Brian spit out the words in anger. "I just didn't want to say nothing to Mr. Kell. It would have been disrespectful for me to tell him his business."

Leroy shook his head as he slowly got to his feet. "Everybody needs to be told now and then, no matter who you are. Ain't nobody right all of the time."

Jimmy reached up and gingerly touched his jaw. "I've got a couple of loose teeth. I hope Cookie has made soup for supper tonight."

Leroy laughed. "I know how you feel."

Willis joined them at the chuck wagon and stared at Leroy's swollen face. "What happened to you, Leroy?"

"Oh, I took a fall when my Mustang stepped in a prairie dog hole," he replied.

Glancing at Jimmy, Willis shook his head. "Did Jimmy's horse step in the same hole?"

Brian began to laugh. Willis looked around and asked, "Did I miss something?"

CHAPTER ∞ 20

Strong winds and and a hard rain greeted the Bar S cowboys as they approached the Kansas border. Kell signaled Flanagin to keep the herd moving in spite of the weather. He knew that if they were going to run into anymore trouble, this was where it was most likely to happen.

Just before the herd passed by the town of Caldwell, Kansas, they were met by an angry mob of farmers armed with pistols, rifles, clubs and pitchforks.

"You'll stop right there and go no farther!" Jacob Wilkerson stepped forward, rifle in hand. He planted his boots firmly in the mud and struck what he must have thought was a defiant pose.

Corky Kell looked over his shoulder at Flanagin. "Get the Rangers up here now, Jimmy." Flanagin nodded then rode back to find Leroy and Willis. Kell silently counted the farmers. *Twenty of 'em,* he thought. *All armed and looking for trouble.*

"You hearing me, Texas cowhand?" Jacob yelled at Kell through the rain and the wind.

Kell nodded. "We're not looking for trouble. We're just trying to get our beef to Abilene."

Jacob looked at the men on either side of him, then laughed. "You're a long way from Abilene and a damn long way from Texas, but that's where you're going back to."

"I don't think so, Mister," Kell replied. "These Longhorns are going to the stockyards in Abilene. I've got a contract to deliver my herd to Joseph McCoy, and that's what I intend to do. I also plan on spending some money in Caldwell at Mr. Stone's store. Our chuck wagon is about out of supplies."

"And liquor?" one of the farmers shouted. He was a big, husky man with a booming voice. "Maybe Abilene wants a bunch of drunken cowboys taking over their town, but not us. We're God-fearing people here in Caldwell."

"We won't be stopping long enough to cause you any problems," Kell motioned to the farmers. "Get out of our way and I guarantee you there won't be any trouble."

Jacob raised his rifle. "Trouble? I'll show you some trouble. I'll shoot the first Texas steer that crosses my land."

"And I'll shoot the first damn fool that tries to do that," Leroy rode up next to Kell. Willis, Jimmy and Brian rode forward and joined them. All of them holding rifles in their hands.

"Well, what do we have here? Leftovers from Quantrill's Raiders?"

"Nope," Leroy shouted as the wind began blowing harder. "But I promise you we've faced Jawhawkers down before."

"We're driving this herd through here with or without your permission," Kell said. "Either make your move or get out of the way."

In the past, Jacob and the other farmers had set fire to the prairie grass causing the frightened cattle to stampede. The rainstorm had made lighting a fire impossible. This left the farmers with a dilemma.

"Jacob, they've got gunmen with 'em this time," one of the farmers turned and spoke to Wilkerson with a hint of fear in his voice. "We won't be able to start a fire in this weather, and we can't scare 'em off with a few rifles and pitchforks. Get what you can and let 'em pass."

Jacob didn't reply.

"Jacob, be reasonable," the man pleaded. "We're not going to be able to stop 'em."

The other farmers looked at one another, then slowly began to back away from Kell and the other cowboys.

"You're all a bunch of sorry no accounts cowards," Jacob shouted angrily. "You can't be trusted to stand up for what's right."

Leroy managed a grin despite the tense situation. He tapped the Mustang's ribs and rode slowly toward Jacob Wilkerson, ignoring the rain blowing in his face. He called out, "This your land?"

"You bet it is, you sonofabitch," came the reply.

"Well," Leroy lifted his rifle and propped it on the saddle horn. "If you don't move your ass right now, the only land that you're gonna own will be about six feet under."

Jacob shook his fist at Leroy. "We'll meet again, you no good Texas cowhand, and when that times comes I'll personally take care of you."

"Better get in line," Leroy laughed. "There's a couple of Yanks and a whole lot of Comanch ahead of you."

"Get money for the cattle to cross, Jacob!" shouted one of the retreating farmers.

Jacob looked back at him in disgust and shouted. "If you want their damn money, you come up here and collect it yourself!"

Leroy looked back at Kell and motioned him to get the herd moving. There were only a few of hours of daylight left, and he knew they had to get the cattle as far away from Caldwell as possible just to be safe. Kell had told him about how these Kansas farmers would, if given the chance, try to stampede the cattle in the middle of the night.

Brian's eyes picked up movement from behind a cluster of rocks and trees to his left. He whirled and pointed his rifle toward a farmer hiding behind the rocks. He hesitated and those few seconds cost him his life. The farmer's shotgun blast lifted him off his horse. His chest exploded in red.

"I got one of 'em!" shouted the farmer.

Corky Kell quickly dismounted, half falling from his horse. "God, no!" he cried out as he reached Brian. "Please God, no."

Leroy and Willis immediately opened fire, their shots ricocheting off the rocks. The two Rangers separated, closing in on the farmer from two sides. Just as Brian Pemberton was taking his last breaths and before the farmer could reload his shotgun, Leroy rode up to him and shot him twice in the abdomen. White hot pain seared through the farmer's stomach. He dropped the shotgun, grabbed at the gaping wounds in his abdomen with both hands, moaning and struggling to say something. Realizing that the man was dying and no longer a threat, Leroy turned the Mustang around and rode back to see how the other farmers were going to react. Leroy glared at the men as they continued backing up slowly. When he started to ride towards them, to a man they all turned and began running. It seemed to Leroy that they were trying to disappear into the blinding rain.

Kell bent over Brian, trying to shield him from the pounding rain. Brian lay still for a few moments, then, he reached up and grabbed Corky's shirt. He opened his mouth as if to speak, but not a sound was heard. Suddenly, he began to shake violently. This lasted a few seconds, then he closed his eyes and stopped breathing.

Jimmy touched Brian's neck and felt for any sign of life. He looked up at Corky and shook his head, "He's gone."

The cowboys gathered around waiting for Kell to let Brian go. Kell bent over the young man's lifeless body and held him until Jimmy motioned for two of the cowboys to take the body away.

"God damn sodbusters," Leroy roared. "They're first on my list now. They just passed the Comanche."

"I'd like to kill 'em all," Willis said.

"Me, too," Leroy said. "If we ever get the chance, we'll do just that."

It was just after dawn when they buried Brian. The ground was soggy. Leroy grimaced when they put the body, wrapped in a single blanket, into the muddy hole.

"He deserved better," Kell choked out the words through tears. "But he's in a better place now."

At least the sonofabitch that shot him is dead, Leroy thought. *You can bet he ain't in a better place.*

That morning no one touched Cookie's biscuits and beans. The cowboys drank their coffee, then climbed up on their saddles and silently went about their duties to get the herd moving once again toward Abilene.

Leroy and Willis rode ahead of the herd scouting the trail for any further signs of trouble. Willis glanced at Leroy. He was grim-faced.

Just let one of those Jayhawkers get in my way, Leroy thought. *Please let one of 'em show up asking for money to let this herd pass. I'll blow a hole in 'em so fast they won't know what t hit 'em.*

The next day the sky finally cleared, and a bright yellow sun appeared. Leroy was tired to the bone. He had only eaten bits of food for two days. *In just a few more days,* he thought, *we'll be in Abilene. I can put all this behind me and go home to Mindy and my boy.*

CHAPTER ∞ 21

The name Abilene, meaning "city of the plains," was chosen from the Bible by the first residents of this Kansas prairie town. Before the cattle herds began arriving, the town was made up of twelve buildings constructed from mud and logs with dirt covered roofs. A cattle dealer from Chicago named Joseph McCoy was credited with turning Abilene into a center for the cattle industry. He did this by persuading the Kansas Pacific Railroad to begin shipping cattle from Abilene to the large meat packing city of Chicago. From there the meat could be easily shipped to markets in the meat starved northeast. McCoy had chosen Abilene for two reasons. First it was a railroad junction with an abundance of good grass around it. This allowed the cattle to keep their weight up before being loaded into cattle cars and transported to the slaughtering house. And second, the town was outside the reach of the angry Kansas farmers who resisted their lands being "invaded" by the cattle drives from Texas.

Joseph McCoy purchased land, arranged for lumber to be brought in by train and hired a small army of workers and carpenters to rebuild the town. Although the streets remained unpaved, and the sidewalks were made from wooden boards, Abilene began to grow. A three story hotel named Drovers' Cottage was built, along with stockyards, loading chutes, offices, barns and of course, saloons. At one point McCoy hired three cowboys and a Mexican to put on a wild west show featuring a large Buffalo in order to entertain the cowboys. He even hung a banner across Main Street proclaiming in bold letters, *Abilene, Kansas, The Market For Texas Cattle.* It didn't take long for the cattle and the cattle buyers to begin arriving in Abilene. During cattle driving season, the section of Abilene located south of the railroad became known as Texas-Abilene.

Jimmy Flanagin smiled for the first time since Brian Pemberton's death when he saw the pastures where the Bar S cattle would graze until the day they would be sold and shipped to Chicago. The spring rains had left the pastures around Abilene in good condition. He rode back to Corky Kell and gave his report. Kell nodded, but said nothing. Jimmy knew what to do. He gave the drovers their orders and the Longhorns began walking the last of their thousand mile journey. They would ride to market the rest of trip. It had been a long journey for both the cowboys and the Longhorns.

Just north of Abilene the Bar S cowboys had settled the cattle down for the night. Even though they were all anxious to get into town, Corky had insisted they rest that first night. Most of the men got little, if any, sleep. The drovers had been on the trail for almost three months, wearing the same dirty clothes. A hot bath, a good meal and clean clothes were high on most of the Cowboys' list of things to do once they got to Abilene. A few of the men had women and whiskey at the top of their list.

The spring rains had brought cooler than usual weather to Abilene. Leroy spent most of the night shivering in the chilly air and thinking of home and Mindy. He promised himself that he would make sure to have at least three of his mother's quilts covering his bed from now on.

The cold air didn't appear to bother Willis. Leroy could hear his snoring from the other side of the campfire. *Damn Willis and his snoring,* he thought. *I swear his snoring has gotten worse since we started this drive.*

Early the next morning Leroy and Willis enjoyed one of Cookie's best breakfasts before getting ready to head straight into town. They planned on first visiting a barber, followed by a trip to one of Abilene's famous bathhouses. The only thing left to do was to draw lots to see who had to stay and guard the cattle. Leroy knew that Willis had lost when he heard his friend complaining in a loud voice. "It ain't fair," Willis said. "I mean, I know the drawin' was fair, but it ain't fair that I have to stay out here while most everbody else is going to town. Darn my luck, if I didn't have bad luck, I wouldn't have no luck at all."

"Don't worry, Willis," Leroy called back to him as he climbed on his Mustang and headed toward Abilene. "I'll be thinkin' about ya."

"Thanks, Leroy," Willis muttered. "I sure do appreciate your thinking about me."

CHAPTER ∞ 22

I can't wait to get a bath and shave," Leroy rubbed his wind burned face.

"You'll pay $1.25 for that, Leroy, maybe more," Flanagin laughed.

Leroy whistled and shook his head. "Nah, Jimmy. No bath and shave could cost that much unless a pretty lady is doing the shaving."

Jimmy laughed again. "If that's the case, the shave will cost you a hell of a lot more than that."

"Tell me about Abilene."

"It's hard to describe. The town changes every time I see it, which has only been a couple of times, mind you. After the first drive, the place had a few shops, a couple of saloons and a big fancy hotel none of us could afford to stay in. We stayed out by the cattle and came into town when we could. The next time I saw it, the town was ankle-deep in cow and horse shit and had a lot more saloons and stores and such. I just remember the smell. It was pretty strong. Once I picked up a glass of water and saw pieces of cow shit floating around in it. From then on I didn't drink nothing that didn't come out of a bottle, mostly whiskey or beer."

Leroy smiled. "I can tell Mindy that for once, I had a good excuse for having a drink or two. My Mindy, she doesn't approve of me drinking spirits."

"Speaking of the ladies," Jimmy raised his head and let out a low whistle. "You've never seen anything like it. They're all dressed up in low cut shiny dresses with black lace stockings. They wear a bunch of colored jewelry, and their hair is all curled up around their heads. But I warn you, they cost a lot of money. The sportin' ladies, as the towns-folk call 'em, will take your money faster than the gamblin' tables."

Leroy begin to laugh. "I can't wait to see Willis' face when he runs into some of them sportin' ladies."

"Best place to hang out is the Alamo saloon," Jimmy grinned.

"I like the name of that place."

"Oh any place where you might spend your money has something about Texas written on it. They like our money, and we like Texas."

"Well, they ain't gettin' mine. I intend to take every dime I've earned back to my family so they won't go hungry this winter." A frown crossed Leroy's brow. "I can't let that happen, Jimmy."

"I know what you mean. Most of the drovers we came up here with are in the same tough shape. They'll need all they've earned during the drive and the money the Bar S gives them for the trip back home just to keep their families going."

"Let's see," Leroy begin to figure in his head. "Thirty dollars a month plus twenty dollars for protecting the herd and another thirty dollars for the month Corky pays me to get back home to Tyler - why, that's more money than I ever thought I'd see at one time."

Jimmy pulled up the reins to stop his horse. "There it is, Leroy. There's the town of Abilene."

The two cowboys rode past the shops that lined the main street. Jimmy pointed out that the prices listed on freshly painted signs were probably higher than normal because the cowboys were in town. Jimmy called it the "Texas discount." While they were in the haber-dasher's shop buying new clothes, Kell walked in. His first stop had been the office of the town sheriff.

"Looks like Abilene doesn't have a Sheriff," Kell explained. "Seems that the man who had the job has passed away."

"By natural or unnatural causes?" Jimmy asked. "He looked pretty healthy the last time we were here."

"That," Kell laughed, "was two sheriffs ago."

"I guess that means we have to look out for ourselves," Leroy said. "I don't trust any of these Kansas Jayhawkers."

Both Kell and Flanagin nodded in agreement.

With parcels tucked under their arms, Jimmy and Leroy headed for the nearest bath house. Leroy had no intention of putting his brand new clothes on his dirty body. For the price of twenty-five cents, he rented a tub full of hot water. The barber told him that he could soak as long as he wished. After two rinses, Leroy finally felt clean enough to soak in, what he would later describe to his family and friends as the "finest tub ever to come out of Kansas City." Meanwhile, Kell had gone to the Metropolitan Hotel where he met with Joseph McCoy. Earlier that day he had given the men an advance on their wages so they could enjoy the entertainment in Abilene while he made sure the cattle were counted and the agreed upon price collected from the cattle buyers.

Several of the cowboys were having their photographs made while wearing their new store bought clothes. After haircuts, shaves and baths, the men looked entirely different from the rugged trail hands who had arrived in Abilene the day before. Leroy decided to wait and have his photograph made with Willis.

He intended to stay out of trouble, save his money and go home to Tyler with enough money to keep his family in food and supplies through the next winter. He stood back and watched as other men from the drive paid a lot of money for dances with ladies dressed as Jimmy had described them, all painted up and smelling sweet. The younger drovers, those without families, crowded around the card tables and threw away their money as if their pockets would never be empty.

The next day Leroy gave Willis a tour of the town. By this time another herd had arrived, and Abilene was in full of excitement. Leroy took him first to the habadasher's, where Willis bought his first ever suit of new clothes, then to the bath house, and finally, the two of them stopped at the photographer's store where they had their photographs taken for Mindy and Patsy. Afterwards they wandered over to the

Alamo Saloon where Leroy decided to try his luck in a draw poker game. Willis said he wasn't about to risk any of his money gambling and would rather just walk around town while Leroy was playing cards. Leroy decided that no matter what happened, he would only risk five dollars from his hard earned wages. After a few hours of draw poker, Leroy was a happy man, he had walked in with five dollars and left with eleven dollars and fifty cents. According to Jimmy, who sat in on a couple of hands, he was one of the few men to ever leave the Alamo Saloon with more money in his pocket than he had when he first walked through its swinging doors.

Meanwhile, Willis couldn't believe his eyes as he walked down the streets of Abilene. Sidewalks eight feet wide and shops full of every fancy thing imaginable. He couldn't wait to tell Patsy about all that he had seen. After window shopping, he crossed the street and headed to the south side of town where Leroy had told him the saloons were located. *Might as well get a drink or two,* he thought. *I guess I've earned it during these past three months. Never seen so many saloons.* He walked past the Last Chance and the Lone Star saloons before stopping at a place called the Lady-In-Lace. He picked the Lady-In-Lace because when he looked through the saloon's swinging doors he saw a crowd of men and women dancing with some fine fiddling in the background. That's when he heard a fellow talking about Texas toast, which was supposed to be the specialty of the house. Whatever Texas toast was, it sounded good to Willis.

Willis dusted off his new clothes and walked into the cool, dark room. A bar, at least thirty feet long stretched across the entire back wall of the saloon. A mirror stretched behind the bar and made the place look twice as big as it actually was but Willis hardly noticed the bar or the mirror. His attention was drawn to the other walls. They were covered in life size oil paintings of ladies with very little clothes on. *Mostly feathers,* Willis thought. That's *about all there is covering them gals up.* In the midst of all the talking and laughter mingling with the clinking of glasses and fiddle playing, Willis felt something tickling his ear. He reached back to swat away the fly or whatever bug was lighting on him, when he realized it was a feather, just like one of those in the pictures on the wall, and it was held by one of the prettiest girls Willis had ever seen. At least he thought she was probably pretty. The room was dark, and he was busy looking at her fancy curls and the shiny low cut dress that didn't leave much to the imagination.

"Excuse me, Ma'am," Willis smiled as he removed his sweaty hat. "I didn't mean to bump into ya'."

"How about a drink, Cowboy?" she said in a sweet voice.

Willis cleared his throat and tried to clear his mind of the picture of Patsy standing over his body with a shotgun pointed at his face. "Don't mind if I do, Ma'am. I better have just one though."

"We'll start with one," she laughed and reached her arm through his. "And some meat and potatoes and just maybe a piece of mincemeat pie. How does that sound, Cowboy?"

Of all the things to eat in this world, Willis probably liked mincemeat pie more than just about anything. "How did you know I like mincemeat pie?" he asked. He gave her a big wink as they reached the bar. She winked right back at him.

"Oh, just a guess," she smiled. "I'll bet you like other things too."

"Sure do," Willis leaned over the bar and asked the barkeep for a shot of whiskey. "I like those other things what you mentioned, meat and taters and such. But mincemeat pie is one of my favorites."

"What's your name, Texas?" she asked.

There goes that sweet voice again, Willis thought. *She sure is special.*

"Willis."

"Well," she turned to the barkeep. "Andy, pour my friend Willis here a double and make it the good stuff.

The big, dark haired, heavily bearded bartender poured a drink for Willis into a large glass then poured the lady a drink in a much smaller shot glass. The light brown whiskey tasted like velvet as it traveled down Willis' throat. It burned a little bit when it hit his stomach, but by then Andy was pouring Willis another glassful.

Not to be ungracious, Willis emptied the second glass of whiskey, then wiped his mouth with his sleeve. "The Lady-In-Lace sure is a friendly place," Willis smiled.

"You ain't seen nothin' yet," Andy leaned over and whispered. "Wait 'til the dancin' starts."

Willis was beginning to feel a little light headed, but he thought dancing with this pretty lady might be fun. "What's your name, Ma'am? If you don't mind my asking, that is."

"Paulette," she tilted her head as she spoke.

"Paulette sure is a mighty pretty name," Willis looked down at her and smiled.

The piano player and fiddler started playing "The Yellow Rose of Texas." The next thing Willis knew, Paulette had pulled him out onto the dance floor and was whirling around him kicking her feet up in the air showing off her black silk stockings and the white lace that was fastened under her skirt. Willis tapped his boot in time with the music and clapped his hands.

"Wheee-doggies," he yelled as Paulette circled her arms around him and tapped the toes of her shiny black shoes against the sawdust covered floor of the Lady-In-Lace Saloon, Dance Hall & Eatery.

After a few dances the room seemed to swirl around Willis even when he wasn't moving. He found himself leaning on Paulette. "I better find a chair," he said. "I ain't used to all this dancin'."

"Come on over here with me, Cowboy," Paulette said. Willis could barely hear her above the noise of the saloon. As soon as the fiddler began playing "Cotton Eyed Joe," the entire room full of cowhands began clapping their hands to the music.

When he finally made it to a table. Paulette told him that what he needed was a thick steak, some potatoes and a big slice of buttered Texas toast. Within minutes, Andy placed a new glass of whiskey and a heaping plate of food on the table in front of his glassy eyes. By this time, the whiskey had taken on a copper color that made him wonder how the liquor could have changed colors in the same glass.

Willis finished half of the steak and most of the potatoes, but he decided to leave the whiskey alone, at least for now. *I'll get me some water as soon as I can get up,* he thought.

When he tried to stand, his legs began to shake. He sat back down hard in the chair and almost fell over backwards. Paulette caught the chair and kept him from falling. "You need to lay down! Honey and I've got just the place," she said. "I'll take you to a cot I have in the back where you can rest until you feel better."

"I don't know what's wrong with me, Paulette," Willis said as he rubbed his hand against his forehead.

"You just need to let your supper settle a bit, that's all," Paulette slowly helped him up from the chair.

She led him to the stairs in the back of the saloon. He stumbled a couple of times, but eventually made it up to the landing at the top of the steep staircase. "I think I'm drunk, Missy, I mean, Paulette."

"Oh, no, Cowboy," she said. "I've seen drunks before, and you're sure not drunk." *Not yet,* she thought.

She opened the first door and helped Willis into the room. "You can lie down here." She walked over and began to turn down the covers on a big feather bed.

"That don't look like no cot I've ever seen," Willis managed a chuckle. "Looks plum too nice to lay on."

"Don't you worry about nothing. Just lie down and get yourself comfortable," Paulette said.

Willis looked around for a chair, but there wasn't any other furniture in the room. Just a bed and a small washbasin. He sat down, and Paulette helped him take off his spurs and boots. Paulette's taking off his boots was the last thing he remembered before waking up in the feather bed with her arms draped over him.

Good Gawd Almighty, Willis thought. *If Patsy ever finds out about this I'm a dead man.!* He quickly began to plan his escape. *Patsy ain't never gonna know nothing about this. I wouldn't tell Patsy about Paulette on her dying day. She'd kill me even then. I gotta get out of here before Leroy finds me. He'd never let me forget that I spent all this time at the Lady-In-Lace., with,* his thoughts momentarily froze, *Paulette.*

"Where's my clothes?" Willis shook Paulette awake after looking around the room for his clothes.

"Don't worry. They're getting washed," she answered sleepily. "I got up early this morning, so I decided to take a little nap with you."

"Getting washed?" he asked in an exasperated tone of voice. " My duds were brand new. They won't need washin' for at least another two weeks."

"You should have told me those clothes were new. I wouldn't have gone to the trouble to have 'em washed up."

Willis sat up and put his hand on his head. "Good God Almighty! I'm in a whole lot of trouble," he muttered to himself before turning back to Paulette. "My head's still swimin'. I guess I'm still a little drunk."

Paulette rolled out of the other side of the bed, reached for a satin robe, and walked to the door. Willis looked away. After all, he hardly knew the lady.

"Here they are. I told you not to worry," she said as she peeked out the door. "Your clothes are already cleaned and pressed."

How long have I been lying here in this bed with Paulette? Willis asked himself. *By now Leroy must be looking for me all over Abilene.*

She brought the clothes over and placed them on the foot of the bed. "I'll be dressed by the time you've put your pants on, Honey," she giggled.

While Willis dressed. Paulette poured cold water from a china pitcher into a washbasin for him to wash his face. Then she slipped on her shiny red dress. Willis watched while she arranged her curls over one ear and tied a red ribbon around them. In all his life, Willis had never seen a woman dress in such clothes. She sat down and took her time pulling on a pair of black silk stockings before reaching for a long red boa and draping it around her shoulders.

"What good will that do?" Willis asked, pointing at the feather boa. "It sure won't keep out the cold."

She smiled. "Honey, don't you worry about it," she said as she opened the door. "Let's go have one last dance then we'll see Andy and let him total up your bill."

Willis winced. *Wonder how much I owe?* he asked himself. *Shouldn't be more than a dollar or two. I can't spend no more of Patsy's money.*

The fiddle player was still playing a lively version of "Cotton Eyed Joe" when Willis and Paulette came down the stairs. When the fiddler finished, he turned to the piano player and waited for his cue. Several cowhands called out the names of their favorite tunes but the piano player ignored the requests and went back to, "The Yellow Rose of Texas." *Wonder if he knows any other tunes?* Willis thought.

"One more dance, cowboy," Paulette said as she pulled Willis out onto the dance floor.

"Maybe just one," Willis smiled. "I don't know when I'll have the chance to dance with such a pretty gal again."

CHAPTER ∞ 23

After leaving the saloon, Leroy went hunting for Willis. Several hours later, he finally found him in, of all places, a dancing hall. Leroy stood by the front door and watched as Willis danced with a pretty lady dressed in a bright red dress with a large bustle. *If I only had that photographer now,* he thought. *I'd have Willis doing chores around my farm for free for the rest of his life just to keep me from showing that picture to Patsy.*

When Willis saw Leroy, he quickly walked away from Paulette.

"I was only gonna have one or two dances,' Willis explained to Leroy. "Them dances cost a lot of money."

"I bet they do!" Leroy's grin covered his entire face.

I sure am in trouble, now, Willis thought.

"Well thank you, Miss Paulette," Willis smiled. "I had a real nice time. I hope I didn't bother you none with my snoring? Ever-body says I snore."

"Your snoring?" Leroy's eyes grew as wide as his grin.

"Hush, Leroy," Willis said. "I'm trying to settle up my bill. I'll explain ever-thing later."

Leroy held his hands up, "Willis," he said with a chuckle. "I'm not the one you have to do the explaining to."

Willis frowned at Leroy.

"Andy will have your tab all figured up in a minute, Honey," Paulette smiled. "Come back and see me sometime." She motioned for the big bartender. Leroy figured that old Andy weighed at least two hundred and fifty pounds and none of it was fat.

"That'll be twenty-two dollars, Mister," Andy said emphatically.

Willis looked at Leroy with a stunned expression on his face. His mouth dropped open and he stared at Paulette. "I may be drunk, but I ain't that drunk."

The big bartender folded his arms across his massive chest and moved toward Willis. "I said," he paused for effect. "Twenty-two dollars."

"Leroy," Willis whispered, his voice strained. "Do I have to pay this?"

Leroy looked at Andy. "Will you settle for five dollars?" he asked.

The bartender shook his head and pounded the top of the bar with his fist. "I said twenty-two."

"Ten, and not a dollar more," Leroy offered while he nonchalantly slipped his gun hand from his belt down next to his pistol.

"Twenty-two and not a dollar less," Andy moved closer.

"That's almost a month's pay," Willis said. "I got a family to feed."

"And I've got a business to run. It'll cost you more if you get arrested and have to spend a few nights in jail."

"If Abilene had a sheriff, which it doesn't have at the moment, that might be a problem," Leroy said, as he stepped between Willis and the huge bartender.

The bartender's expression changed. "I'll take fifteen dollars."

"You'll take five," Leroy said, never taking his eyes off the bartender he tilted his head toward Willis. "Give him five dollars and let's get out of here."

"Leroy," Willis argued. "That's a lot of money."

"Things cost more here," Leroy said. "Pay the man and be done with it."

Willis reached for his money belt. A look of panic covered his face. "It was in my clothes," he whispered.

"I take it you weren't in the clothes when your money belt disappeared?"

Willis gave Leroy a stricken look, then looked helplessly at Paulette. She shrugged her shoulders and looked away.

"Give him his money," Leroy said to the bartender. "Now!" The other customers, anticipating trouble, began to back away from the bar.

"If he doesn't get his money back, we're outta here," a big Texan stepped forward and faced the bartender. "It ain't right."

Murmurs of agreement could be heard all around the room. Andy motioned to Paulette. She frowned and looked down at the floor before speaking.

"He didn't have much, Mister," Paulette said. "I'll get his money belt and take out five dollars, he can have the rest."

Leroy nodded but said nothing. Paulette ran up the stairs and threw the money belt down from the top of the stairs.

"She sure was a pretty gal, Willis. Didn't remind me none of Patsy though." Leroy said as they walked out onto the street.

"Darn her for taking my money," Willis snarled, then he reached over and grabbed Leroy's arm. "I wasn't thinking straight. I should have been thinking 'bout my Patsy. So, Leroy, since Patsy ain't here and she never did see me dancing with that Kansas City Belle, can you see your way clear not to ever tell her nothin' 'bout it?"

"There's only two ways she'll find out," Leroy grinned.

"Oh, I ain't never gonna tell her, Leroy. You know what a terrible temper Patsy has." Willis had a terrified expression on his face. Leroy had never seen his friend this afraid, not even when the two of them were facing the Comanche.

Leroy pursed his lips and pretended to be in serious thought. "Well, if I don't say nothing, I guess she'll never know."

"Now, Leroy," Willis warned, "That wouldn't be a good idea for you or for me. Mindy would probably want to know what you were doing in this here dance hall while I was dancing with that pretty gal from Kansas City."

Leroy's thoughts actually turned serious. *He's right, Mindy wouldn't be happy if she heard that I was spending my time visiting dance halls here in Abilene.*

"Rest easy, Willis. Your secret is safe with me. You can go back to your expensive dancing."

"No, thanks. I ain't interested no more." Willis said as the two of them walked away from the Lady-In-Lace Saloon, Dance Hall & Eatery.

CHAPTER ∞ 24

Kell and Flanagin walked out of the dining hall of Drover's Cottage after collecting the final payment for the Longhorns and the extra horses from McCoy. With their saddle bags full of cash, they went straight to the hitching post where they had left their horses. Both men were surprised to see that someone had moved their mounts across the street.

"That's strange," Corky turned to Jimmy. "I wonder who moved the horses are over there?"

Before Jimmy could answer, he felt a gun in his ribs.

The two drovers that Leroy and Jimmy had fought and the rustler that Kell had let go free, had their six-shooters pointed at the Bar S trail boss and his top hand.

Kell and Flanagin were shoved in the direction of the livery stable. Flanagin knew immediately that it was unlikely that either of them would ever walk away from this alive.

"You can't keep us from taking the money," Tom Bright said to Kell.

"I damn sure intend to try," Kell answered. He abruptly stopped in the middle of the street and confronted the three robbers. It was only then that he recognized the cattle rustler. He shook his head and spoke in a resigned tone of voice, "Leroy was right. I should have strung you up back there on the trail."

Kell looked over and saw the grim look on Jimmy's face. His expression told Kell everything that he wanted to know.

Gotta try for 'em before they get us inside, Jimmy thought. *Be ready Corky, I'm going to need you.*

Just as they reached the big double doors of the livery stable, Jimmy whirled around and caught one of the drovers with his elbow.

Leroy and Willis were sitting in chairs outside the Alamo Saloon when they heard several gun shots fired in rapid succession.

Leroy turned to Willis and said, "Sounds like those shots came from over near the livery stable."

"Leroy, whatever it is, it's probably none of our business?"

Leroy pointed down the street at Kell's and Jimmy's horses tied to a hitching post near the stable. "See them horses? Looks to me like this just might be our business."

Willis sighed, "I was just getting comfortable, but let's go see what's going on."

"Willis, look!" Leroy touched Willis' arm. "There's three men running out of the stable and they're carrying Kell's saddle bags."

Without waiting for a reply, Leroy drew his Colt pistol and fired off several shots in the direction of the fleeing men. One of the men stumbled and fell to the ground. He quickly got to his feet with the help of one of the other men. The two Texas Rangers crouched down low and started to run towards the livery stable.

"Nice shooting, Leroy," Willis said. "I think you hit one of them."

"Hitting anything at this range is pure luck and you know it. I was just lettin' them know that we're on to them." Leroy kept running toward the door of the livery stable. "We need to find Kell and Flanagin. We'll deal with those crooks later."

They stopped at the door of the stable. Leroy motioned to Willis, who nodded and went to one side of the door. Leroy went to the other side and carefully looked inside. In the darkened entrance, he saw immediately that Corky and Jimmy had both been shot. Jimmy was shot in the chest and Corky had been shot in the middle of his back.

Leroy bent over Corky, then turned his attention to Jimmy Flanagin.

"It was that sorry pair that skipped out on us back in the Territory," Jimmy struggled to speak while coughing up blood.

"I saw 'em, Jimmy," Leroy said, "I promise we'll git 'em for you."

Jimmy gave a slight nod of his head. "You'll have to, 'cause I'm finished."

Willis bent over Kell and lifted his head. "Mr. Kell, Leroy and I are gonna git your money back for you. You can count on us."

"Take me back to Texas if you can," Kell whispered. "And tell Leroy he was right. I should have hung that rustler. He was with those two no account drovers. I'm so sorry Jimmy had to pay for my mistake."

Before Willis could answer, Corky Kell's head fell to one side. Willis gently closed the trail boss's eyes and let him lie on the hay covered floor of the stable.

"Kell's had it," Willis whispered, not wanting Jimmy to hear.

"Jimmy's gone too," Leroy said, his voice void of emotion. "Go find some of the men from the Bar S to help us with the bodies, then me and you have some work to do."

Willis sighed, "I figured you'd say something like that. We'll need cartridges and some supplies."

"Cartridges, yes, but I don't intend to load up on supplies, cause I plan on running down those sorry bushwhackers before they get very far. Hell, they might still be here in town."

Willis found Bobby and Eli Gilbert, two brothers from the Bar S who had worked for Jimmy and Corky for a number of years. Leroy told the men to have the town's undertaker get the bodies ready for the trip back to Texas so that both men could be buried near their home. He told Bobby to send a telegraph to Mr. Hamilton at the Bar S, telling him what had happened to Corky Kell and the money, and to tell the other drovers that if he found the killers and the money, he would see that the money was sent to the Bar S. When he was finished giving the Gilbert brothers their instructions, Leroy turned to Willis and said, "Let's go earn our extra pay."

CHAPTER ∞ 25

That cattle drive has to be over by now, Mama Wiley," Mindy frowned as she looked out into the summer garden. "Leroy would have told me if he was going to be gone this long."

"Maybe he didn't want to worry you," Mindy's mother-in-law continued working the butter churn without looking up. "You know how he is. He keeps himself to himself, as the old saying goes."

"Well, Carter said that he was sending word to Leroy about the baby."

"Maybe Leroy didn't get the letter. Are you sure Carter knew where to send it?"

"He told me that Leroy had to pass through some place called Red River Station. Carter promised that he was going to send word to Leroy about the baby and tell him that he ought to come home."

"Has Carter said anything more to you about it?"

"He sure has," Mindy put her hands on her hips and turned to face Mama Wiley. "He said that he sent the letter right after we talked. He also said that Leroy couldn't have crossed the Red River without going through Red River Station. That tells him that Leroy got the letter and still went on to Kansas."

Verlinda Wiley stopped churning butter and looked up at Mindy. "Knowing that boy as well as I do, I have to admit that sounds like something he would do."

Mindy nodded. "Carter also told me that the Rangers want Leroy to report as soon as he gets back to Tyler—something about trouble with the Comanche out in West Texas. So help me, if Leroy leaves again to go fight Indians, I'll never forgive him. He left us to put in the spring crop. If he goes off with the Rangers you know he won't be here to help with the harvest either."

Verlinda knew how upset Mindy was about Leroy's absence so she tried to take Mindy's mind off the subject of Leroy and the cattle drive. With this in mind, she walked over to the front door, looked out and turned to her daughter-in-law, "Look, Mindy, a summer storm is coming our way. The wind is starting to blow trees up in the hills," she pointed to the gentle hills rising in the distance. "Soon we'll see thunder and maybe even a bit of lightning from the heavens."

Mindy joined her on the front porch. "When that darn fool husband of mine gets home you're going to see the biggest storm ever to hit Smith County and it isn't going to come from heaven, I can tell you that."

Mama Wiley put her arms around Mindy's shoulders and started to laugh. "I'll be glad to throw in some thunder and lightning of my own if you need me to."

Mindy leaned against Verlinda. *How good she is to me,* Mindy thought. *Still,* she frowned, *her son is a different matter.* Suddenly a pain ripped through her lower abdomen causing her to cry out and bend forward at the waist.

A look of panic crossed Verlinda's face. "What's the matter, child?"

The pain seemed to come in waves. Verlinda took hold of Mindy and helped her to a bed where she could rest. It was only then the Verlinda saw that Mindy's dress was covered in blood. While Mindy lay there moaning, Verlinda ran to the front porch and called to her husband. "Taylor! Saddle a horse and hurry into town. Bring the doctor back with you. Mindy's losing the baby."

Willis filled the saddle bags with all the supplies he could carry. *Stayin' around here my foot,* he thought. *Them killers rode out of here as if the devil himself was after them,* he thought. *We'll be lucky if we catch up to 'em down in the Territory.* He climbed on his horse and led Leroy's Mustang across the street.

"If there was a sheriff here we'd get some men deputized to help us," Willis said as he handed Leroy the reins.

"Well, there ain't no sheriff, so we're on our own," Leroy felt like cussing as he climbed into the saddle. "I figure they're headed south toward the Territory."

"Probably the same way we came, that is, unless they head over to Missouri."

Leroy paused and looked at Willis. "What makes you think they'd do that?"

"I don't know, just figuring what I would do in their place. Something unexpected."

"Nope," Leroy said as he tapped the Mustang with the edge of the reins. "They'll go where they think there's no law to catch up with 'em. That means they'll go straight down into the Territory."

Willis nodded, pulled his hat down low and rode beside Leroy as they headed back toward Caldwell, Kansas.

Ten days later the two exhausted Texas Rangers sat down by the North Canadian River bank to gather their thoughts.

"Leroy, we ain't gonna find 'em. They could be anywhere by now."

Leroy looked at Willis, pointed to the south and said, "Maybe the Indians can help us."

"How?" Willis spit out a wad of tobacco juice in frustration. "They ain't got no trail to follow."

"We can tell them what they looked like, especially the big fellow with the red hair. Maybe that will be enough."

Willis thought for a moment. "Where are we gonna find these Indians? And if we do find 'em, why would they help us track them varmints down?"

"Because Kell was friends with the Choctaws. Remember, I told you I heard him promise to being them grain and supplies on his way back to Texas."

"I don't know, Leroy," Willis shook his head. "Them Choctaws just might shoot us for not bringing the supplies that Kell promised. They might think this is a trick and we're out to cheat 'em."

"The way I see it, that's our only shot at catching those sonsofbitches. We'll ride south and see if we can find some Choctaws to talk to."

"I ain't got nothing better to do," Willis moaned. "It's not like I can go home to Patsy with what little money Kell advanced us back in Abilene."

By the time Willis had mounted his horse, Leroy already was already wading across the river on his Mustang headed South.

After they entered Choctaw country, Leroy passed a number of landmarks that he remembered from the drive north. So much had happened since then. The images of Corky Kell, Jimmy Flanagin and Brian Pemberton flashed before his eyes. Remembering those faces caused Leroy to utter a few cuss words and push his Mustang a little harder.

After checking with several farmers, Leroy determined they needed to ride east of the Chisholm Trail toward Durant if they were going to find the Choctaws who had met with Kell on the drive north.

Just before sunset they rode up to an Indian village. The women were curing buffalo hides while the men sat around campfires. Their horses and a small herd of cattle grazed nearby.

"Choctaws?" Willis asked.

"Either Choctaws or Chickasaws," Leroy answered.

"How do you know they aren't Comanche?" Willis lifted his rifle and checked to make sure it was loaded.

"Well," Leroy said with a grin. "For one thing, we ain't crossed the Red River yet. The other thing that leads me to believe they ain't Comanch is that we still have our hair."

Willis groaned. "I hope you're right, cause if you're wrong I don't see us getting out of this."

"We're in their gunsights, that's for sure." Leroy pointed to a cluster of trees. "Let's make camp over there. They'll come to us soon enough."

"We'll take turns sleeping tonight, Leroy. I ain't never comfortable when I'm this close to a bunch of Indians, I don't care what tribe they happen to be."

"Agreed," Leroy nodded his head and grinned. "We'll fix an early supper and see what happens."

"I don't know if I have much of an appetite," Willis muttered. "It's pretty hard to eat while you're waiting for Indians to come calling."

Leroy and Willis lifted the saddles off of the horses, removed the bridles and began gathering what wood they could find for a campfire. Leroy heated some smoked bacon and sliced hard biscuits. "A fine meal we have tonight, Willis."

Willis looked over at Leroy. "I changed my mind. Indians or no Indians, I'm hungry enough to eat a horse. Hell, I'm so hungry I'd even chow down on some more of ol' Cookie's grub. Sure wish we had some coffee."

Leroy kept the first watch, staying out of sight near the horses. He remained motionless, keeping his rifle ready. He changed places with Willis around midnight. By sunrise, Willis joined him for a cold breakfast.

"Watch the horses, Willis," Leroy whispered. "When they start acting up, we'll know the Choctaws are coming to pay a visit."

"I wasn't born yesterday, Leroy," Willis groaned.

Both Leroy and Willis were wrong. The horses hadn't given them any warning when suddenly, four men seem to rise up out of the prairie grass. Cold eyes glared at the two white men. The four Indians had long black hair worn loose over buckskin clothes.

"Lee—roy," Willis whispered as he stared at the Indians. "They don't look too friendly."

"Just stay calm. I'll handle 'em."

Leroy slowly unbuckled his gunbelt and let it slip to the ground while the Indians watched intently. Leroy lifted his hand and raised two fingers, the sign of friendship. When no response came from the Indians, he crossed his arms and pointed his index finger, signaling to the Choctaws that he wanted to trade. Then he rubbed his hands together as a sign of peace. Willis kept his eyes fixed on the Indians.

"They ain't answering you," Willis whispered. "What you plan to do now?"

"Hold my hands up and pray, goddamnit," Leroy hissed. "Got any better ideas?"

For several long minutes, Leroy and Willis sat looking at the stone-faced Indians. They heard riders approaching and were soon surrounded by a dozen or so Choctaw warriors. The leader dismounted and approached the Rangers. Leroy held his hands up to show that he meant no harm.

"I'm one of Corky Kell's cowhands," Leroy began. "He promised to bring you food when he came back to the Red River Station."

He waited for a response. None came so he continued. "I need to speak to your chief about Mr. Kell."

The Indian nodded and motioned for Leroy and Willis to follow him. Several of the Indians crowded around them. He caught a glimpse of their horses being led away by the Choctaws.

Leroy turned to the Indian next to him and asked. "What about our horses?" Leroy asked. He started to ask about his gunbelt but decided it wouldn't do any good. The Indian said nothing, but did give him a shove that caused him to stagger forward. *Not a good sign,* thought Leroy.

A ten minute walk brought them into the village. Women and children gathered around the two Texans, staring silently while Leroy and Willis were led to the long house, as the Indians called the shelter they had constructed of tree limbs, bark and whatever natural material they could find including buffalo hides.

"We are a peaceful people," the tall chief said as he walked up to Leroy and Willis. "We farm and trade to feed our families. But we will fight when we must defend what is ours. Why have you camped so near our village?"

"We're looking for the Choctaw Chief who met with our late trail boss last month. A fellow by the name of Corky Kell," Leroy said. "We come in peace to ask for your help."

The Choctaw frowned and took a moment to gather his thoughts.

"Why do you ask our help and why is Corky Kell late?"

Leroy looked back at Willis who shrugged his shoulders. "By late, I mean he's dead."

The Indian raised his hand and motioned for Leroy to be quiet. Both Leroy and Willis could tell that the man was upset. After taking a deep breath, the Choctaw continued. "Why do you come here? What help can we give you? It is my people who now need help. Corky Kell promised us to bring the food that we need to survive the next cold winter."

Leroy's head dropped for a moment. "Corky Kell was killed and robbed by three men who might have passed this way. One is a big fellow with bushy red hair. The other two are smaller with dark hair. One of the men has a small scar across his cheek."

Several of the Indians looked at each other. Leroy thought he saw a slight expression of recognition cross the Indian's faces. He continued, "Mr. Kell was the most honest man I ever met. He didn't deserve to die this way. The last thing he said was to tell you how sorry he was that he couldn't keep his promise."

Willis frowned and looked over at Leroy who took only a second to return his gaze. His expression warned Willis not to say a word.

Leroy cleared his throat, then went on with his story. "I made a promise to Mr. Kell to hunt these murderers down and I mean to do just that, but I need your help. My friend and I followed these men as far as the Territory before we lost their trail. I figure our only chance of catching and killing them is with your help." He gestured toward Willis, "If you cannot help us, my friend and I plan to ride out of here today and ask at Red River Station if anyone has seen 'em. If the murderers didn't ride through the Station, I don't know where else to look."

The Indians for the most part remained silent. They occasionally exchanged glances with each other and mumbled a few words in Choctaw while they nodded back and forth. Leroy and Willis had no idea what the Indians were saying.

Leroy was about to give up. He decided to make one more plea for help. "Can you help us find the men who murdered Mr. Kell and took his money?"

The Choctaw shook his head. Leroy looked at Willis. Damn these worthless Indians, Leroy thought. They probably wouldn't have been any use anyhow.

Leroy rubbed his hands in a sign of peace and turned to walk away followed closely by Willis. Before they reached the open doorway of the long house, he heard the Indian Chief say, "If you stay here, we will bring them to you."

Leroy and Willis stopped in their tracks. Leroy found himself breathing hard. He slowly turned to face the tall Choctaw Chief. "You know where they are?" Leroy asked.

"Three men passed through here two days ago. One had big shoulders and hair as you say," the Choctaw rubbed his hand around his head in a circular motion. "Big hair. Red hair."

"The others have dark hair?" Leroy asked.

"And one have scar on face." The Choctaw drew an imaginary line down the side of his right cheek.

"That's them," Leroy walked back toward the chief. "Which direction were they headed?"

"South," came the reply.

"Towards Red River Station?" Leroy asked.

The Indian nodded. "One of the men was not well. I think somebody shot him."

"Looks like you did hit one of them," Willis suggested.

Leroy nodded, then turned to the Chief. "Now that we know where they are and when they passed through here, my friend and I can catch them and take them to the nearest Marshall."

"No," replied the Choctaw. "We will bring the white men who shot Corky Kell to you here."

"Better for us and better for the Injuns," Willis whispered. "Those low life bushwhackers will git what they deserve."

Leroy smiled. *These may not be Comanche but they will probably make those killers wish they weren't ever born. Any Indian is damn good at torturing a man, no matter what tribe he belongs to,* Leroy thought. He glanced at Willis who nodded his head in agreement.

"We'll take you up on your offer," Leroy said. "But we'll be glad to help. Remember, your men will be riding into Texas and Willis and I are the law in Texas. We'd like to go with you to bring the men back to the Territory."

The Choctaw spoke to one of the younger braves who motioned to Leroy and Willis that they should leave. The two white men were taken to a blazing campfire in the middle of a cleared area. They were offered berries, nuts, seeds and some wild plants that Leroy had never seen. Then one of the Choctaw squaws brought a large pot containing meat and various kinds of root plants. Although they were hesitant, both Leroy and Willis were hungry and afraid of offending their hostess, who looked as fierce as any woman they had ever seen. Leroy had no doubt that she would have enjoyed putting them into a boiling pot feet first just to listen to them howl. Willis took a big drink from the bowl and declared it much better than anything Cookie had fixed for supper during the cattle drive. Leroy took a small drink and ate a couple pieces of the meat which had a wild taste. He thought it might have been buffalo meat but he wasn't sure. He smiled at the Choctaw squaw. His smile was met with a frown followed by a glare that Leroy thought must have lasted at least five minutes. Now that he had the information he needed regarding the killers, he was anxious to leave the Choctaw camp. He had no reason to hang around a bunch of darn Indians. Just as he was figuring how to get away in one piece, another Indian woman brought cups of tea made from sassafras and as Leroy thought, *God only knows what else.*

While Leroy and Willis were eating, a tribal council discussed their request. The council, made up of the elders of the tribe who were respected for their wisdom, decided to bring the killers to justice.

The Choctaw Chief signaled one of the braves, and a half dozen Indians began to gather up their weapons and prepare for the trip to Texas.

That afternoon Leroy and Willis left the Indian Territory in the company of six Choctaw braves.

The Red River that separates Texas from the Indian Territory was named for the red colored sediment carried along by the rapid current. Willis thought it just looked muddy. Leroy had crossed the river on more than one occasion and seen enough snakes crawling around its banks to make him a bit hesitant to cross it anytime other than during the dead of winter when the darn critters were buried deep in their holes. This time was different. A dozen water moccasins could not have kept Leroy from following the Choctaw braves into the muddy water. He was in a bad mood, and when Leroy Wiley was in a bad mood he was a dangerous man. He had no intention of letting the three men who had murdered Corky and Jimmy get away. *No doubt about it. They deserve killin', and I intend to be the one who sees that they get just what they deserve,* he thought.

The two Texas Rangers followed the Choctaws as they crossed the Red River. Willis turned to Leroy and pointed at the Choctaws.

"Leroy, how are we gonna find out anything at Red River Station riding in with these Injuns?" Willis asked. "We'll be lucky if they don't start shooting the minute they see us."

Leroy laughed, "I'd be disappointed if they didn't take a shot or two at us. But don't worry, Willis. I've just about figured this thing out while we've been riding along with these here talkative fellows."

"Talkative?" Willis snapped. "They ain't said one word since we left their village."

Leroy spurred his horse and caught up with the leader of the Choctaws. "Hey, Chief, you speak any English?" Leroy asked in a friendly tone of voice.

"Hey white man, you speak any Choctaw?" came the reply.

I don't like or trust any Indian as far as I can throw 'em but I'll play along, Leroy thought. "No, can't say that I do. I speak a little Comanche, but not much."

"I not believe Comanche speak with you, maybe they kill you, but they not talk to you. Since you not dead, I not believe you ever speak to Comanche," the Indian snarled.

Well, Leroy thought. *A simple yes or no would have been nice, but I guess that answerers my question. The sonofabitch does speak a little English*

He decided that it would probably not be a good idea to go into detail about his relationship with the Comanche. "I was thinking that me and my friend should ride into Red River Station alone," Leroy glanced back at Willis.

"You leave him with us," the Indian motioned to Willis. "Then you ride into Red River Station. When you come back to us we give him back to you. If you not come back, we kill him."

Leroy glanced again at Willis who was shaking his head and mouthing the word *no.*

"Sounds good to me," Leroy grinned. "I'm sure that my friend, Willis, will be more than happy to keep you boys company while I go on to Red River Station. I'll be back as soon as I hear where them buzzards are headed."

The Choctaw shook his head. "We not here to find birds, we want men who killed Bar S trail boss."

Leroy started to explain what he meant, then thought better of it. "Now, Willis," Leroy said as looked back at his worried looking friend. "You have a nice time with these fine, upstanding Choctaw warriors and don't you worry none, I'll be back real soon."

Leroy gave a huge wave as he galloped away, leaving the Choctaws and Willis camped along the Texas bank of the Red River.

CHAPTER ∞ 26

Yes, sir, I know exactly who you're talking about. They met up with two other men here yesterday," the young stock boy continued, as he poured Leroy a second shot glass of warm whiskey. "One of 'em was hurting real bad. They was headed south to Ft. Worth to find a medical man 'til I told them that ol' Doc Simpson would be able to fix their friend up good as new. Doc's house is just past Clear Creek. After they left, I got to thinking. That's when I remembered that ol' Doc Simpson ain't been right in the head since his wife died. She was part Cherokee, you know."

While Leroy listened patiently, his thoughts turned to Corky Kell and Jimmy Flanagin laying helpless on the dirt floor of the livery stable in Abilene. With one quick motion, he emptied the shot glass, dropped a ten cent piece on the counter and turned on his heels to walk out of the darkened room. *I'll bet you they're at that Indian lovin' Doc's place,* he thought. *We'll go there first.*

When Leroy returned to the campsite, he found Willis sitting alone with his back against an oak tree. The Choctaws were sitting together on the far side of the campsite, cleaning game. Leroy thought by the smell of the dead animal that it must be either a prairie dog or a squirrel. Whatever it was, it didn't exactly excite his appetite.

"Guess who's still alive, no thanks to you," Willis said in a harsh tone of voice between clinched teeth. "Them Choctaws ain't exactly friendly."

"Oh, come on now, Willis," Leroy laughed. "How can you say that? If they weren't friendly, you'd probably be missing some hair."

"You think it's so darn funny, next time, you stay with 'em and I'll go git me a drink at Red River Station."

"Hopefully, there won't be a next time."

"You found the sonsofbitches?" Willis asked.

"Let's just say they don't know it but they're living on borrowed time. Best I can tell they're about fifteen miles south of here," Leroy explained. He didn't worry whether or not the Choctaws heard what he was saying. He knew they would follow him no matter where he went. If they didn't, he figured that he and Willis could take care of the killers by themselves. When Leroy was finished, the Choctaws looked at the white men, nodded, then each one grabbed a fist full of mane and easily swung up onto the backs of their unshod ponies.

It was almost sundown when the two Rangers and their Choctaw companions rode up to the place described by the man at Red River Station. *They were off by a bit,* he thought. *But all in all, pretty darn good directions. We're here and that's all that really matters.*

"Here's the way I see it," Leroy began. He looked around the circle of Choctaws, wondering what they would do in a fight. *Probably shoot my ass off, if they got the chance,* he thought. "Willis, I want you to leave one man down by the creek with the horses."

"You mean one of the Choctaws?" Willis asked.

Leroy took a deep breath and exhaled slowly through his lips. *Damn, Willis,* he thought. "Who do you think I mean? You don't see any dumb Irishmen like Sergeant O'Connor around to leave with the horses do you?"

Willis frowned. The Choctaws looked at each other, but remained silent.

"After it gets dark, we'll sneak up to the house and bust right in the door. Hell, they ain't posted no guards. There's nothing to keep us from ending it fast."

"What makes you so sure there ain't no guards?" Willis asked.

"Cause while you were taking care of the horses I was checking on things," Leroy replied. "Now let's go catch those varmints while they're still at the supper table."

"What about the Doc who lives here? How do we keep from shootin' him by mistake?" Willis asked.

"We ain't got time to be choosy," Leroy said as he reloaded his rifle and checked his pistol. "If you ask me, he's in the wrong place at the wrong time with the wrong company."

One of the Choctaws reached over and touched Leroy's arm. "You stay here. We take care of men who murder our friend."

"Sorry, Chief," Leroy shook his head, "That's not the way it's going to happen. Come on Willis."

The Choctaw shrugged his shoulders and watched Leroy and Willis walk towards the house.

Leroy saw a cluster of trees in the front of the house and whispered to Willis, "You wait there. I'll circle around and go in the back door."

"Shouldn't we wait until it gets darker?"

"Probably, but I think we better take 'em down now. I don't trust these Choctaws. Who knows what they'll do if we try and wait til everybody goes to bed. I'll yell if I need your help. Otherwise, shoot anyone who tries to make a break through the front door."

Willis nodded. "Don't worry, I'll fill 'em full of lead before they can get off the porch."

Leroy disappeared into the brush. *Hell, he's just like one of them Choctaws,* Willis thought. *Them varmints won't hear nothin' until it's too late.*

Leroy circled around the cabin, keeping an eye on the makeshift corral. The last thing he needed was for one of the horses to get spooked and sound an alarm. He rounded the side of the cabin, stepped up on the front porch and motioned to Willis. In the cluster of trees, he saw the tip of a rifle wave back and forth. *Good boy, Willis,* he thought. *Now be sure you hit every damn one of 'em.*

Leroy carefully walked past a darkened window. Just in case someone was in the room, he ducked low and crept across the porch. The next window he came to looked in on a room that was lit by several oil lamps. Inside he saw three men sitting at a table playing poker and the cowboy with bushy red hair named Bright standing over an old man who was tied to a chair. *I bet that's the Doc,* Leroy thought. *He ain't going nowhere, so Willis won't kill him by mistake.* Leroy watched as Bright turned around to the fireplace and picked up a large tin coffee pot. Just as Leroy was getting ready to go around to the back door, two of the Choctaws came out of the bushes on the other side of the cabin and stepped up on the front porch. *Well, so much for my plan,* thought Leroy. *What the hell are they gonna do?*

Leroy didn't wait to find out, he stepped up to the front door and kicked, hard, then fired two shots into Bright as he was leaning over the fire. Bright screamed and fell forward into the fire.

"Who's gonna be next?" Leroy shouted.

The three men at the table looked back at Leroy with terrified expressions on their faces. One dived under the table, the other two jumped to their feet and held up their hands.

"Don't shoot! We ain't armed," yelled one of the men.

By the time Willis reached the porch, the Indians had all three men tied up and stripped of their weapons.

Leroy walked over to the bunks and picked up Kell's saddle bags. Jimmy's saddlebags were laying on the floor beside the doctor. Leroy ignored the struggling doctor and picked up Jimmy's belongings.

"Aren't you going to untie me?" Doc Simpson asked.

"No," Leroy replied. "I don't like the company you keep, so I ain't inclined to help you."

"It's not my fault, you damn fool. I didn't exactly invite them into my house."

"Well, you ought to be more particular about the people you take care of."

"They said somebody from Red River Station sent them, me being a Doctor and all. One of 'em had been shot, but by the time they got here, the wound was so infected there was nothing I could do. Seems like the man was the brother of one of the other men. When he died, they got mad. The red haired one you just killed said he was gonna to leave me here to rot."

"Well," Leroy looked at Willis. "You might be telling the truth, so I'll ask my friend here if he wants to cut your ropes. If he does, fine. If he don't, that's fine too."

Willis laughed. "I'll think about it." He looked around the cabin and asked, "Any biscuits around here?"

"Good God Almighty," one of the outlaws hollered before the Doc could answer. "You riding with Indians?"

"Yep," Leroy laughed. "They're interested in talking to you fellows. You'll be riding with them back to the Indian Territory while my partner and I take this money to the Marshall in Ft. Worth."

"You can't do that, it ain't legal," said one of the outlaws.

Leroy turned and faced the outlaw who had just spoken. It was the cattle rustler that Kell had set free.

"Well, well, who do we have here?" asked Leroy as he walked over to the outlaw. "How did you come to be mixed up with these varmints?"

"Charlie Wilson was my brother," the man answered.

"Ain't that something? You tried to steal a herd of cattle where your brother and his friend are working as drovers. I was told back at the Bar S that the rustlers were getting inside information. I guess that was right."

"Everything would have gone okay and no one would have gotten hurt but you had to go and mess things up," the man snarled.

"I guess I did," Leroy shrugged his shoulders. "I told Kell that he should have hung you, but he wouldn't listen. Now, two of the finest men I've ever known are dead because of you and your worthless friends."

"You ain't taking us to Ft. Worth with ya?" another one of the outlaws asked as two of the Choctaws pulled him to his feet.

Leroy shook his head, "Nope. Like I said, you boys have a date up in the Territory with the Choctaws. You killed a man that was supposed to bring them supplies from Abilene so they could feed their families this winter."

"They can have the damn money," the outlaw cried out. "We can't use it now."

"Oh, I'll give 'em what Kell would have spent on flour and such," Leroy took a few steps toward the outlaws. He leaned over and looked into their terrified eyes. "But, boys, what they really want is you. I figure you'll have more fun with the Choctaws than you would have had dancin' at the end of a rope. Them Indians are plenty mad about you killing a friend of theirs. Somebody they trusted and depended on," Leroy paused and gestured toward the Choctaws. "I don't envy you boys one bit. The only good thing I got to tell you is that you're lucky they ain't Comanch." He turned and walked towards the front door of the cabin.

Doc cried out. "What about me? For God's sake!"

Willis walked over, took out his knife and slipped it through the ropes holding the doctor's arms. He fell to the floor, rubbing his arms to restore the circulation.

Leroy smiled at the Choctaws and tossed a handful of money on the table. "That'll buy your people enough grub to get through the winter," he said. "I'm grateful for your help."

The Indians exchanged glances and nodded, but said nothing. The outlaws, however, were crying out and begging the Rangers for mercy. Leroy and Willis walked out the door into a warm Texas night with heavy saddle bags slung over their shoulders. Both men felt good. Justice would be served, and they were almost finished with their sad mission. After setting up camp by the banks of Clear Creek, they slept until sunrise then headed south to turn in the Bar S money to the United States Marshall in Fort Worth.

CHAPTER ∞ 27

"Leroy, the way you've been pushing me and the horses, you've about wore us out. But we've finally made it home." Willis smiled as he they rode toward the outskirts of Tyler. "Do you think Carter will help me take care of some banking business? I owe the bank some money and I need to clear up my account at the General Store."

"That's about all I can count on that brother of mine to do," Leroy laughed. "Carter's a fancy lawyer now, so you can't get him to do no real work. Let's go see him and make him buy us dinner at the hotel."

"Now you're talking," Willis yelled as he kicked his horse into a full gallop.

The more he thought about home, the more Leroy's thoughts turned to Mindy. He would see her today. *Before the sun sets I'll be able to hold her in my arms.* He smiled as he pictured his wife. He followed close behind Willis until they reached Main Street.

"Willis!" he called out. When Willis didn't slow down, Leroy put two fingers in his mouth and whistled like Jimmy Flanagin used to do on the cattle drive. Willis stopped and turned his horse halfway around so he could see Leroy. "You take the money to Carter," Leroy said, a big grin forming on his face as he handed Willis the saddle bags. "He'll know what to do with my wages. I just want to go on to the farm and see my family."

Willis nodded and smiled. He knew how much Leroy had missed Mindy. The two friends separated at the edge of town. Willis rode on into Tyler, while Leroy rode towards his farm and Mindy.

Carter looked up from his desk when the bell attached to the door of his office rang. The young legal assistant greeted the dirty cowboy then turned to Carter.

"Mr. Wiley," the young man with red hair and a face full of freckles called out. "It's your brother's friend, the Texas Ranger who left with him on the cattle drive."

Where's Leroy? Carter asked himself. *Why is Willis here alone?* He had already lost one brother. For a moment Carter feared the worst but as soon as he saw the smile on Willis' face, he knew that everything was all right.

"Where's my prodigal brother, Willis?" Carter asked. He quickly crossed the open area of his law office and reached for Willis' hand. "You're about as dirty as I've ever seen you. I'll bet that Leroy is twice as dirty and is waiting at the saloon."

"No, he ain't here in town, Carter. He's probably halfway to the farm by now, knowing the way he rides that little Mustang of his."

A frown crossed Carter's face. "I wish he had stopped here first. I needed to speak with him before he talks with Mindy."

Willis laughed. "I'm sure whatever it is, it can wait. Leroy's got Mindy on his mind and little else, I can tell you."

Willis waited for Carter to reply. But Carter appeared lost in thought. Willis decided to get his business tended to so he could go buy some presents for Patsy and his kids. "Carter, can you help me with the money Leroy and I earned on the cattle drive? We had to go to a heap of trouble to earn it, and I want to get my money taken care of so I can stop worrying and go home."

Carter looked at Willis, his face filled with concern. "What kind of trouble?"

"You wouldn't believe it if I told you. I'll let Leroy tell you all about the drive and what all happened to us. The worst part was when our trail boss and the top cowhand were both kilt in Abilene. They was shot dead by some robbers. Leroy and I wound up having to track them sorry buzzards down with the help of some Choctaw Indians."

"Good God!" Carter sighed. "Where's the money?"

"That's what took us so long. Leroy was bound and determined to hand it over to the United States Marshall in Fort Worth. The money should be on its way to the Bar S Ranch, 'cept what was due me and Leroy and what the trail boss paid out in Abilene. He gave each man a little money to tide us over so we could get a bath and a shave. Carter, you wouldn't believe how much it costs to get a shave in Abilene, Kansas."

Carter turned to his young assistant, a man named Terrance Young. "Go with him to the bank." He gestured toward Willis as he walked quickly to the door and pulled his gray Stetson from the hat rack. "I'll be at the farm if you need me." He paused at the doorway and added, "Tell Nancy I'll be late for supper."

"Well gol-lee," Willis exclaimed. "I ain't never seen nothing like it. I come in here to talk to Carter and he runs off before I can tell him what I want. Now, I ask you, what kind of lawyer is that?"

"A worried one," came the reply. "Let's go over to the bank." Terrance said as he hung the sign on the door that indicated that the law office was closed.

Leroy approached the farm slowly, hoping to surprise Mindy. *If that worthless hound doesn't bark, I'll be able to walk right up to the front door,* he thought.

He left the Mustang by the lake and carefully made his way toward the farmhouse. Before he reached it, he spotted Mindy pulling up root vegetables in the garden. *How pretty she looks,* Leroy smiled. He couldn't wait to hold her in his arms. Just as he walked up to the garden fence the hound started barking. *Why don't I just shoot him?* Leroy asked himself. *I'm the only one he ever barks at. Anyone else, he'd lick 'em to death.*

Mindy turned, taking off her wide brimmed straw hat. "Oh," she cried. "I can't believe you're home at last." She reached up to touch her face. "I must look like a mess."

"You look just fine to me," he smiled. "Come here!"

She touched the front of her apron. "I've missed you."

When she didn't come to him, Leroy walked over to her and put his arms around her. "You don't know how much I've missed you."

She looked up at him, remembering how angry she had been for months. "Where have you been? Don't tell me that cattle drive took this long. Didn't you get Carter's letter that he sent to Red River Station?"

Leroy continued to hug her, a look of surprise in his face. "One question at a time, Mindy. First of all, I went all the way from South Texas to Abilene, Kansas and back to Ft. Worth before coming home, and no, the cattle drive didn't take this long, but I had a few other things that I had to tend to. And," he took in a deep breath, "no, I sure didn't get any letter from Carter or anyone else for that matter. That's all the questions for now. Let's go inside and see the folks."

"Wait a minute," Mindy looked up at him and asked, "Did you bring me something nice from Abilene?"

He tried not to smile, but couldn't stop a small grin from turning up the corners of his mouth. "Now, we get down to business. No, but I'll take you shopping for something pretty in Tyler first thing tomorrow."

She stepped back and crossed her arms. She wanted her voice to sound firm but instead her words began to quiver. "All this time away and not one little present? It seems to me that you weren't spending much time thinking of me."

"Mindy," his voice showed a trace of annoyance. "I said I'd take you into town tomorrow and buy you anything you want. That's the best I can do."

"Well the best that you can do isn't good enough," Mindy said, as she turned on her heels and started to walk toward the house.

Leroy realized there was something wrong. *Something's got her upset and it's not me forgetting to bring her a present.* He was about to pull her back to him, but she stepped out of his reach. Before he could catch up with her, he heard his mother shout from the house, "Well, look who's here! Taylor, come quick! Leroy's home."

I'll find out what's going on tonight, he thought. Remembering the wonderful homecomings he had received in the past, he was more than a little annoyed. No matter how mad she was when he left her, she had always welcomed him home with love and tenderness. Now, Leroy felt a chill coming from Mindy that reminded him of a Texas blizzard.

"You missed supper, boy," Taylor laughed. "Never known you to be late for supper."

"I tried to get here as soon as I could, Papa," Leroy glanced over at Mindy who was still pouting. "I wish everybody could understand how long it takes to get here from Kansas by way of Ft. Worth."

"Ft. Worth?" his mother said. "Why in the world did you go over to Ft. Worth? That's out of the way if you ask me."

"Didn't have no choice," Leroy replied as he made his way into the house. "I'll tell you all about it after supper. First, I got to tend to the Mustang."

"I was wondering about him," Taylor walked out to look at the horse. "He looks like some mighty good horseflesh." He turned to Leroy. "You go on into the house, and I'll take him to the barn and rub him down for you."

Leroy looked relieved. "Thanks Papa. I didn't realize how tired I was until I got here."

"Don't you worry 'bout a thing," Verlinda said as she put her arms around her youngest son. "Taylor will take care of the horse and Mindy will warm up some supper."

Mindy frowned as Leroy and his Mother walked by her. Leroy noticed her silence. He also noticed her shiny brown hair and pretty brown eyes. *She's still the prettiest gal I've ever seen. I guess that's worth putting up with her bad temper now and then.* He glanced back at her and grinned. Well, maybe she has some cause to be upset. *I should have brought her a present from Abilene.*

Leroy had just finished putting butter on a couple of biscuits when his father walked through the door wanting to hear all about the cattle drive. Leroy tried his best to put off the story telling, knowing that his parents would keep him up most of the night in order to hear the details of his long trip. "I'll tell you all about it tomorrow. But let me just say that Willis and I got more than we bargained for. We ended up working as both Rangers and cowhands all the way from south Texas to Kansas and back to Texas again. It was a long trip, and I tell you, I sure am worn out."

Mindy poured hot coffee for Leroy and his parents and said good night. Leroy couldn't understand her attitude. *She's never acted this way before,* he thought. *I was gone a lot longer than four months during the war. Sure she got angry every time I left, but she was always happy to have me back home.* He exchanged worried looks with his father.

Verlinda reached over to touch his arm. He looked up and saw his Mother motion that she wanted to talk to him. He nodded and waited for Mindy to go upstairs and close the door to their bedroom.

"When you left, Mindy was with child," his mother whispered. Leroy's face lost all color, his mouth opened slightly, and he took in a deep breath.

His father put his hand on Leroy's shoulder and said in a sad voice, "Carter tried to reach you. He sent a rider to Red River Station with a letter telling you about the baby. Before he got back with any news, Mindy started hurting something awful. Ol' Doc Graham was tending to the Harrison family on the other side of the county. Thank goodness Carter sent for a young doctor from Clarksville. He took care of Mindy. She lost the baby, but he told us that she would be fine. But it seems like Mindy just hasn't been able to get over losing the baby. She stays in her room most of of the time, and at night we can hear her crying. I went into town and asked Carter and Nancy to come out and try to talk to her, but that didn't seem to do no good. Nancy stayed here for almost a month helping us to tend to Mindy. I'm awfully sorry, son. We did the best that we could."

"I know," Leroy said. A wave of sadness swept over him. "I wish I could have been here for her."

His mother reached over and took both his hands in hers. "Go make up with her now. Tell her just how you feel."

He nodded and slowly stood up and walked out of the kitchen.

Standing alone in the darkness of her bedroom, Mindy heard Leroy coming up the stairs and then lifting the latch to open their bedroom door. As he stepped inside, she turned her face to the window and looked out to see the rising moon and a cluster of bright stars in the clear Texas sky.

The room was dark except for the light coming from the full moon but that was all the light he needed to see the slender frame of his wife standing in front of the bedroom window.

"Mindy," Leroy hurried over to put his arms around her. "I'm so sorry about the baby. I didn't know."

Mindy turned to look at him, her dark eyes clearly reflecting the pain in her heart. She lowered her head and asked in a voice so low it was barely a whisper, "Mama Wiley told you?"

"You knew she would," he appeared to be struggling to find the right words. "I can't tell you how sorry I am. I wish I could have been here. I love you so very much."

"Do you honestly love me, Leroy?" Mindy appeared torn apart by emotion. She started shaking and then began to cry.

"You know that I do, sweetheart," he tried to pull her close.

"Then why weren't you here?" Mindy raised her fists and pushed him away.

"I had no way of knowing about the baby. If I'd known, I would have tried my best to get back here in time," he pleaded for understanding.

"I was in pain, Leroy," she shouted. "Never in my life have I felt so alone. Instead of having you here to comfort me, I was left alone with your Mother and Father. Your brother was the one who brought the doctor for me. That should have been you, not Carter."

Leroy had never seen Mindy like this. She looked so sad, obviously shattered by the loss of her child.

"Mindy," he said softly.

"You don't understand. My life will never be the same." Her grief had turned to resentment. "The words you say don't mean a thing to me," she cried and put her hands over her eyes.

Leroy walked over and forced his arms around her. "Come here to me," he said, holding her so close he could feel her heart beating. "We can get through this together. Maybe I wasn't here when I should have been, but I'm here now." He lifted her chin and kissed her cheeks. "I only left you because I had to do what was right for us. I have to take care of my family. That's the only reason I ever leave you."

She leaned against him and said in a quivering voice. "Now you'll be leaving me again."

He frowned and started to ask what she was talking about but decided against saying anything. *Let her do the talking now,* he thought as he gently stroked her hair.

"I heard Carter telling Mama and Papa Wiley all about it. Captain Johnson has been looking for you. The Rangers want you to ride over to West Texas to Comanche country. They're joining up with those awful Yankees to kill off the Comanche and they want you to go with them. I hate the Rangers. After what happened to Clayton, they still expect *you* to go back to fighting Indians."

He looked down at her, searching for the right words. "Mindy, as much as I love you and as much as I hate leaving you, there are gonna be times when I have to go. Being a Ranger is what I do. The Rangers are the only thing that stand between some Texas families and death. What if all the men stayed home and let the Comanche run wild? Texas wouldn't be a fit place for women and children to live. You ain't seen what I have, Mindy, or you'd understand how I feel." He paused, hoping she would respond. He bent down to kiss her, but she turned her head. He felt her body stiffen. "I guess you need some time to think things over," he sighed. "I can tell how much I've hurt you and it breaks my heart. I'd like the chance to make it up to you, if you can ever find it in your heart to forgive and forget."

He gently released his grip on her arms and let her go. As he turned and began to walk away she was sure that she saw tears in his eyes. *He must be suffering too,* she thought. *I've been so wrapped up in my own grief*

I didn't think about how he must feel. She reached out and touched his sleeve. He stopped, turned back, and with her eyes and her tears she told him what she had been unable to say, that she loved him, no matter what. She felt the strength of his body against her, and she raised trembling lips and waited to be kissed.

Early the next morning Leroy saddled the Mustang and rode into town. By the time he reached Carter's home on the outskirts of Tyler, Nancy had already served breakfast and Carter was leaving to go to his law office on Main Street.

"Just in time," Leroy said as he slid off of the Mustang and walked over to meet his brother.

"Willis came by yesterday," Carter reached over and put an arm around Leroy's shoulders. "I started to ride out to see you. I got about halfway to the farm and turned back. I decided that you needed to spend some time alone with Mindy. I didn't want to intrude."

"It might have been better if you had," Leroy shook his head. "It wasn't a very happy homecoming."

"Leroy, I can't tell you how sorry I am about the baby. We did all that we could to take care of Mindy. I think she was distraught over your leaving and then losing the child only made matters worse for her."

Leroy's head dropped so low his chin almost touched his shirt. "God, I feel bad."

Carter said nothing. He opened the door and the two of them moved into the parlor.

"I can ride with the best of 'em. I'll take on most anything that comes my way, Comanche, gunfighters, or hell, even the damn Yanks, but Mindy gets the best of me. Half the time I can't figure her out, and I darn sure can't get it through to her that I have a job to do."

Carter didn't reply.

Leroy shot an angry look at Carter, "I'd be much obliged if you'd say something."

"What do you want me to say?" Carter shrugged his shoulders. "It's your marriage, not mine. You've got to make things right with her. It's as simple as that."

Leroy looked puzzled. Carter face softened. "Take my buggy, fill it with presents and nice things for the house and go home. But that's only a start. Try to become the husband and farmer she wants you to be."

"Carter," Leroy lifted his Stetson up as if to make a point. "I've got the rest of my life to bust sod and milk cows. Mindy knew what she was getting when she married me. As long as Texas needs me and I'm able, I'm going whenever the Rangers call."

"Well said, Leroy," Nancy walked in with a tray of coffee and sweet rolls. "Mind if I add my two cents to the conversation? If that's your attitude, it doesn't really matter at all how Mindy feels, does it?"

Carter frowned at Nancy's interference.

"Morning, Nancy," Leroy waited until Carter took the tray then he reached over to kiss Nancy's cheek. "I can always count on you to sugar coat whatever you have to say."

"I mean it, Leroy," Nancy ignored Carter's disapproving looks and continued explaining Mindy's point of view to her brother-in-law. "You go gallivanting off all over the state of Texas, leaving her here to cope with the farm, your parents and God knows what else. It's time you stayed at home with her. Is that asking too much?"

Carter stepped between Nancy and Leroy. "If it is, it's up to his wife to tell him, not you."

Nancy pointed her finger at Carter's chest. "Maybe the two of you don't want to hear this from a woman, but both you and Leroy know I'm right."

Leroy held his hands up in a sign of surrender. "No argument here, Nancy. I'm going to try to mend my wandering ways."

"Oh, I'm sure that you will," Nancy's words were filled with sarcasm. "I can hardly wait to hear that you've told Captain Johnson that you won't be joining your Ranger Company and leaving for west Texas. What do they call the place?"

"Comancheria," Leroy said. He looked at Carter. "What's she talking about?"

"That's the Leroy I know and love," Nancy said with a smirk on her face.

"Enough," Carter swung around to face his wife. It was clear that he was very angry with Nancy. "If you don't mind, I want to talk with Leroy alone."

"Please call me when I can pour more coffee. That seems to be my important duty today."

Carter pointed toward the door. Before Nancy left the room she smiled sweetly and said, "Goodbye, Leroy. I'll look forward to seeing you when you get back from Comancheria."

Carter pursed his lips and looked down at his boots. Leroy noticed that Carter's face had turned a bright shade of red. "Hell, don't worry about it," Leroy said. "Mindy's just as bad."

"Yeah," Carter gritted his teeth. "But at least she has an excuse. Nancy is just being Nancy."

"Carter," Leroy grinned and leaned back to make sure the door was completely closed, "you knew what a wildcat she was when you met her in Tennessee. Don't tell me you expected her to change?"

Carter started to laugh. "No, I don't guess that I did."

Leroy couldn't resist a jab. "Best I remember, you couldn't wait to go back to Tennessee to marry her after the war."

"If it wasn't so damn early, I'd say let's go over to Suzy's and get drunk."

"Now, Carter," Leroy grinned. "It ain't that early. Besides, I was on the trail for four long months drinking nothing but some brown colored water that the cook called coffee. Most of the time it tasted like mud mixed with cow shit."

"Then you've earned yourself a drink or two." Carter reached for his jacket and hat. "But don't try to tell me a bunch of lies, because Willis has told me the whole story. As a matter of fact, he repeated the story twice ."

Leroy laughed. "That sounds like Willis." Then his voice became serious. "What's this about the Rangers going out to west Texas? Mindy mentioned something about Captain Johnson looking for me, but I didn't think it was a good idea to press her for any details."

"I'll fill you in on the way to Suzy's place, although there isn't much to tell. Your Ranger Company rode out of here two days ago on their way to Fort Belknap to join up with the Federals. I guess the government has finally realized that something has to be done about the Comanche raids. It appears that the fort is undermanned so they asked for help from the state government in Austin. The governor has ordered all the Ranger Companies north of Waco to assist the Federal troops."

"Well," Leroy said as he stepped off of the porch. "That means I've got some hard riding to do if I'm gonna catch up to 'em."

"I've already told Willis, and he was really shaken up about it. He said if you decided to go, he was riding with you."

"You know, Patsy's gonna give me hell over this," Leroy looked away and shook his head as he spoke.

Carter looked up and laughed. "Not as much as Mindy."

"Oh, Christ," Leroy sighed. "For a moment, I'd forgotten about her."

Carter glanced over at his younger brother. *Maybe Nancy's right,* he thought. *Hell, I know she is, but I'll never admit it to her.*

Dawn brought an end to a difficult weekend for both Leroy and Willis. Once again, they said their goodbyes to tearful wives before riding west toward Fort Belknap.

Nancy went to the farm to console Mindy. "The relationship between a husband and wife is supposed to be one of sharing," Nancy said as she and Mindy walked through the vegetable garden. She paused while Mindy reached down to pull up a few sweet potatoes. "Even though we see our husband's faults, if we look deep in their hearts we can also see strengths such as their devotion to family."

Mindy straightened up and lifted her bucket of vegetables. "All I can say is that loving my husband is hard. Mama Wiley told me that to love a rough edged man like Leroy demands patience, and I'm trying my best to be as patient as I can be. What I resent about Leroy is that he seems so restless. He's never happy just staying here with me and JR. He has to be off somewhere doing something dangerous."

"Have you talked to him about how you feel?"

Mindy scowled. "He says that I demand too much of him."

"Oh, let's face it, Mindy. Both Carter and Leroy are selfish." Nancy looked back and Mama Wiley and laughed. "We should have started training them from the beginning, just like Mama did with Papa Taylor."

Mindy watched as Papa Taylor served a glass of lemonade to his wife. "When Leroy gets home, I'll make sure that Mama Wiley gives him a few lessons."

Nancy laughed. "It's too late. I think she spoiled Leroy rotten, him being the youngest and all. But the more I think about it, those lessons might do her oldest son some good too."

The women stood for a moment, looking west. Mindy found her thoughts following the distant hills and meadows that she knew Leroy was crossing on his way to west Texas. She bit her lip and whispered to Nancy. "I'm so worried about him. One of these days he's going to get himself killed. I just know that he will, and I don't think I can bear it."

Nancy took the bucket of sweet potatoes from Mindy's hands. She was reminded of an old saying she had heard while growing up in Tennessee: *Only the good die young.* Nancy thought, *If that's true, you can bet that Leroy Wiley is going to live to a ripe old age.*

CHAPTER ∞ 28

After the Civil War, the Federal government instituted a plan by which the Comanche, along with the Apache and Kiowa tribes, would learn to "walk the white man's road" and become farmers. The selling point of the plan was that a government agency would distribute food and supplies until the Indians were self sufficient. From the start the Comanche didn't like the plan. So rather than accept the plan and see their way of life vanish, the Comanche fought back by launching a series of raids into the settled areas of Texas. During these raids they stole horses and supplies, killed as many settlers as they could, and tried to exact a measure of revenge against the buffalo hunters who were systematically killing off their main source of food.

While Leroy and Willis were working the Bar S cattle drive, the situation had deteriorated to the point where settlement of the western part of Texas had, for all intents and purposes, ground to a halt. Orders came down from Washington to deal with the Comanche problem once and for all. Which in turn led to the Rangers being called up to assist the Federal troops. Leroy and the other Rangers realized from the start that the Comanche were going to put up one hell of a fight.

"Ever hear where the name Comanch comes from?" Leroy asked Willis as they rode toward Fort Belknap in the north central part of Texas.

Willis was dozing in the saddle. "Wake up, Willis. I asked you an important question."

When Willis didn't respond, Leroy reached over with his hat and hit his friends arm. Willis sat high in the saddle, still half asleep. He reached up to remove his hat and mumbled, "I'm wide awake, Leroy," he said, pulling out a large handkerchief and mopping the sweat off of his face and neck.

"I was asking you if you knew where the Comanch got their name?"

"Which Comanche are you talking about?" Leroy knew that Willis was not the least bit interested in the conversation, but he was hot, tired and bored. He watched as Willis put his hat back on and reached for his canteen.

"All of 'em," Leroy said. "I hear tell that to the other tribes, the name Comanche means enemy or somebody who wants to fight all of the time."

"That's good to hear," Willis mumbled. "I could have done without that piece of information, Leroy." He pointed to the trail ahead. "I'll bet you this is some of the best farm land in Texas. This soil would bring in a good crop of most anything you wanted to plant. No wonder the settlers are wanting to move out here."

"Willis," Leroy asked. "Don't you ever think of nothing 'cept farming?"

Willis shook his head and replied, "I'd sure rather think about farming than the Comanch."

"Well, you better enjoy this farming country 'cause pretty soon we'll be in that God forsaken part of Texas where there ain't no rain and there damn sure ain't any trees or shade. Remember the walk back from Glorieta Pass?"

Willis groaned. "I'd just as soon think about the damn Comanch as the walk back from Glorieta Pass. I swear I didn't think we were going to make it through that. Who would have thought that the easy part was going to be the battle?"

Leroy chuckled. "You'll be thinking of nothing else but Comanch when we reach the canyons. Captain Johnson said a whole bunch of 'em are holed up there."

Willis ignored Leroy and continued to stare at the trail ahead of them.

In 1854 the Republic of Texas legislature granted jurisdiction to the United States government over twelve leagues of vacant land that had been set aside for Indians. Fort Belknap had been built in 1851, just north of the Brazos Indian Reservation and forty miles east of the Comanche Indian Reservation. Although the fort served as a trading post and was part of the Butterfield Overland Mail Route before the war, the soldiers garrisoned at Fort Belknap, like all solders stationed on the Texas frontier, endured hardships. They suffered not only from isolation, but also a lack adequate supplies. The fort provided protection against attack from the Comanche, but little else.

As the Regiment stationed at Fort Belknap prepared to ride northwest toward the Tule and Palo Duro Canyons, the soldiers heard rumors that they would be joining up with military units from Fort Sill, located in the Indian Territory and from Fort Union, which was in the New Mexico Territory on the banks of the Canadian River. The soldiers knew that if the rumors were true, they were going to be taking on the Comanche in a fight to the death, something none of them looked forward to.

Only a few Federal troops paid any attention to the arrival of the Rangers when they rode into Fort Belknap. Leroy noticed that several blacksmiths were busy filing hooves and nailing new shoes on horses that carried a U.S. Army brand on their buttocks. *They're getting ready to move out,* Leroy thought.

When Captain Johnson arrived at the fort, he was immediately taken to the office of Fort Belknap's commanding officer, where he interrupted a meeting of the colonel's staff. The officers were going over maps of northwest Texas, paying particular attention to the Tule and Palo Duro Canyon areas.

Johnson reported to the colonel that his Ranger Company was ready for duty before quietly taking a seat in the back of the room and listening to the plans for the upcoming mission. Leroy and Willis stayed outside with the other Rangers. A few troopers milled about, but none approached the Rangers.

"You fellows wait here while Willis and I go over to that store and see if the Yanks have any decent whiskey," Leroy said as he looked around and gave a wide grin. "If the they're in the mood to share, I'll motion from the door. If Willis and I come flying out feet first, you'll know that they ain't feeling hospitable today."

The other Rangers laughed. Derrick and his brother Darryl asked if they could go along. Leroy replied that neither young man was old enough to drink spirits. Derrick started to argue, but quickly realized that it was no use arguing with Leroy once he made up his mind.

Leroy crossed the open area of the fort on his way to a free standing building that served as an off duty gathering place for the enlisted men. He walked into a dark room lit only by the sunlight filtering in through a pair of dirty windows and the wide open door. Leroy and Willis stood there for a moment, allowing their eyes to adjust to the darkness. Leroy could see a few soldiers sitting around barrels playing cards. He rolled a smoke and walked up to a board that was held up by two large supply barrels. Leroy assumed that this was the bar.

"We're dry to the bone," Leroy pointed over his shoulder to Willis, who had taken a position by the door in case of an unfriendly welcome. "You wouldn't happen to have any whiskey?"

"Nope," came the reply. "Got coffee and a few ham biscuits." A Yankee sergeant with a stubby beard leaned over and motioned toward the troops. He reminded Leroy of a mountain man. *Hell,* Leroy thought. *Ain't there no such thing as a skinny Yank sergeant?* "They'll be moving out anytime now. Till then, the colonel says no whiskey for anybody."

"We'd be mighty grateful for whatever we can get," Leroy said. "Got anything to eat in this place? There's twenty Rangers outside just as hungry and thirsty as we are."

"Send 'em in. I'll make some more coffee and see if I can rustle up some more grub," the sergeant said, as his large hands passed Leroy two cups of hot coffee.

Leroy turned to see what was keeping Willis. His eyes met Willis' glare. With a slight nod of his head, Willis pointed out Sergeant Dan O'Connor sitting in the corner of the room. *As sure as hell's on fire, there's O'Connor,* Leroy thought. *I'm gonna have to kill that sonofabitch one of these days, just so I don't have to look at 'em.*

"Coffee, Sergeant?" Leroy asked as O'Connor slowly stood and began walking to him.

The sergeant ignored Leroy's offer of coffee. Out of the corner of his eye, Leroy saw Willis start to move forward.

"This rotten state of Texas ain't big enough for both of us," O'Connor spat at Leroy.

"Oh, I can assure you it is. But you and I just can't seem to stay away from each other," Leroy sat one of the coffee cups down and took a long sip of the hot coffee from the cup held in his left hand. He kept his right hand ready to defend himself in case the sergeant decided to start a fight. *If he gives me an excuse, I'll throw this hot coffee right in his ugly face,* thought Leroy.

"You riding out with us?" O'Connor asked, as he slightly tilted his head.

"Wouldn't miss it for the world," Leroy replied.

O'Connor leaned close to Leroy. His bad breath made Leroy want to step back, but he kept his feet firmly planted on the rough floor. "I'll piss on your grave before this is over."

Leroy hesitated for a moment, then said in a firm voice, "That'll be the day."

"You go to hell," O'Connor snarled as he turned and walked away. O'Connor made a point of bumping into Willis as he walked by him. "And take this stinking Reb with you."

Willis reached out and grabbed O'Connor's arm. He didn't say a word, but his gesture sent a message to the sullen sergeant. He shook free of Willis' grip, then walked out the door.

"I'll take that coffee, now," Willis took a deep breath then blew it out slowly between his lips. "I was counting how many of 'em we'd have to fight in case O'Connor started something."

Leroy leaned over and whispered. "Notice that not one of 'em stood up for O'Connor? I reckon he's as popular with them as he is with us."

"Not so, Texan," the big sergeant standing behind the bar said. He had obviously overheard Leroy's remark to Willis. "They just figured that he could take both of you without too much trouble."

Leroy finished his coffee and grinned. "We'll see about that."

Willis quickly drank his coffee and reached for the ham biscuits before the big Yank could change his mind and take them away.

"The colonel said for us to pick out fresh horses and rest up for the night," Captain Johnson told his men after his meeting with the Federal officers. "We'll billet over there." He pointed to the far side of the Fort. "They're setting up tents for us now."

"When do we leave, Captain?" Derrick asked.

"Not sure," Johnson shook his head and explained. "The colonel said we might leave tomorrow, but probably it's gonna be the day after tomorrow. He's waiting for a rider carrying a dispatch that will tell him where we're linking up with the other troops. In any case, we can all use the rest, and from what I hear the grub ain't bad here at the fort."

Leroy and Willis walked up just in time to hear Captain Johnson's last statement.

"You stay away from O'Connor," Willis said in a low voice.

Leroy nodded. "We better take turns keeping a lookout tonight, just in case that sorry sonofabitch tries to cut my throat."

"Damn good idea," Willis said. "He's up to something that's for sure, but I can't see him trying to bushwhack us while we're here in the fort."

"Probably not, but I'd just as soon not take any chances," Leroy looked around the fort. "Let's go get our pick of the mounts. My Mustang's thrown a shoe."

As soon as Captain Johnson dismissed the Rangers, Leroy and Willis walked towards the corral. Derrick and Darryl followed.

"Don't you boys want to get something to eat?" Leroy asked.

"Sure we do, but first we want to make sure you and Willis don't get all the best horses for yourselves," Derrick laughed.

"Well, come on and show us how good you are at picking out

decent horse flesh," Leroy grinned. "Since we're going up against the Comanch, we might just need some damn fast mounts if we're planning to keep what hair we have." Leroy rubbed Willis' partially bald scalp before adding, "No offense, Willis."

Leroy stopped laughing abruptly and walked directly to a big Appaloosa. Most of horse's body was dark brown, but big black spots on a white background covered his buttocks. Black and white stripes covered all four hoofs, and the horse looked at Leroy through white-rimmed eyes.

"Easy, fellow," Leroy said in a gentle voice. The Appaloosa's coat was as shiny as satin. Leroy rubbed his hands down the horse's strong legs. As he picked up one of the hoofs, he heard the blacksmith call out.

"Hey, what do think you're doing there?" The smithy hurried over to the corral. "That horse is U.S. Government property. He ain't for sale."

Leroy continued looking over the horse. "I'm not buying. Just looking."

"Captain Johnson said that we could pick out some fresh mounts here," Derrick said, hoping to avoid trouble.

"Oh, he did, did he?" the smithy spit tobacco toward Derrick's feet. "Well just who in the hell is Captain Johnson? There ain't no captain by the name of Johnson on this here post that I know of."

"He's a Texas Ranger Captain," Leroy looked the smithy square in the eye. "And he's just following orders given to him by your commanding officer."

The smithy looked toward the headquarters hoping to see the officer on duty. Seeing nothing but enlisted men, he turned back to Leroy and spoke in a harsh voice, "Keep your hands off my horses until I check this out."

"A man's word ought to be worth something," Leroy said. "We're Texas Rangers, not horse thieves, and besides, you just said these horses are the property of the Federal government. That doesn't make 'em your private stock."

The blacksmith frowned. "Word or no word, I intend to check this out just the same. If what you're telling me is the truth, I'll see to your mounts for you until you get back. That is, if you cowboys make it back. From what I hear, it's gonna be rough out there, and if you're lying to me, so help me God," he shook a dirty fist at Leroy. "By the time I finish with you, you won't have to worry about the Comanche."

The Rangers watched the fat blacksmith take huge strides as he stomped across the parade ground.

"Are all Yankees assholes?" Willis asked, as he shook his head.

"I'm beginning to think so," Leroy grinned, then turned his attention back to the horses. "I'm happy with this big fellow right here."

Willis nodded. "I've got my eye on that black and white Pinto. He looks like he could outrun most Comanche ponies."

"Which ones do you think Darryl and I should get?" Derrick asked.

"Take a look at those two over there," Leroy nodded in the direction of a couple of quarter horses standing by the watering trough. Derrick and Darryl stared at the two horses Leroy had pointed out. "The black one with the blaze and that one with the boldface. Their legs are suited for running. See the large muscles in their forearms? They are definitely two fine horses." He turned to Willis and added, "The Yanks know how to take care of horseflesh, I'll give 'em that."

Willis chuckled. "That smithy is going to be mad when he sees you ride off with that Appaloosa. I got a feeling he's partial to that horse."

"Too bad," Leroy laughed. "I'm just following orders. The captain said to get us some fresh mounts, and that's exactly what I intend to do."

They watched the blacksmith arguing with a Yankee Lieutenant, then saw him throw his arms up in the air and storm back to the corral, glaring at the Rangers.

"The way we keep making friends around here, Leroy," Willis said. "We might be better off fighting alongside the damn Comanch."

"Agreed," Leroy said as they walked back to join Captain Johnson and the rest of the Rangers.

Most of the men were so tired after a week of hard riding they ate their super in silence at the mess hall, then rolled smokes while walking to their tents. Inside the newly pitched tents the Rangers found a pair of field cots and a small table waiting for them.

Leroy fell asleep looking at the stars shining through the opening of the tent. He slept so soundly that not even Willis' snoring woke him during the cool summer night and he awoke just before reveille sounded.

The sound of the bugle startled Willis, causing him to jump off of the cot. "Damn Yankee bugle brings back bad memories," Willis snarled. "What an awful way to wake a man up."

Willis was surprised that Leroy hadn't answered with one of his famous wisecracks. It was only then that he spotted his friend standing outside the tent staring at the first glimmers of dawn breaking through the eastern sky. He appeared to be in deep thought. *Worryin' 'bout Mindy,* Willis thought. *No doubt about it.*

The Rangers had scarcely finished breakfast when word came that the dispatch rider had arrived ahead of schedule. Leroy watched two companies of cavalry form up for inspection and receive their orders from Colonel Lewis, the Fort Belknap garrison commander. Leroy nudged Willis and pointed. One of the gates was being opened to allow six Kiowa scouts to gallop out of the fort and into the early morning dawn.

"It ain't gonna be long now," Willis said. "I'm glad I had that second cup of coffee."

Leroy nodded. "Yep, it looks that way to me, too."

After a short meeting with Captain Johnson, the Rangers broke camp and carried their saddles and the rest of their gear to the corral. Leroy climbed the fence, reached back for Willis to hand him a bridle and slowly walked over to the Appaloosa. By the time he and the other Rangers had saddled their new mounts, the two blacksmiths were opening the gate. Their dispositions seemed to match their beards, which were black as a night without stars.

"What's his name?" Leroy asked the smithy he had confronted the day before. The smithy glared, but didn't say a word. Leroy decided to needle the big man. "He's your favorite, ain't he? Well, don't worry, I'll take good care of him." The blacksmith looked away.

"What's his name?" Leroy asked again.

"Comanche," came the surly reply.

Leroy threw back his head and laughed. "I like it. I got a feeling he's gonna bring me good luck."

Leroy grinned as he rode past the blacksmith. The Appaloosa was frisky and ready to run in the cool morning air. Leroy was obviously enjoying himself. Willis watched the blacksmith glare at his friends back before he shouted at him in an angry voice, "Here's hoping he brings you the kind of luck that gets your ass shot off."

Captain Johnson and the Rangers waited for the soldiers to ride through the gates of the fort. The officers of the post were lined up smartly in front of the commanding officer's quarters. A slim young captain mounted his horse and gave a final salute to Colonel Lewis. As soon as it was returned, he wheeled his horse around and faced his men.

"Uncase the colors," the young captain said in his best command voice. When the brightly colored pennant began to wave in the morning breeze, he signaled the top sergeant to move the column forward. Two lieutenants rode to their assigned positions. Dan O'Connor stretched up in his saddle and barked a series of commands. The troopers, in columns of twos, started moving out of the fort.

"They do that right nice," Leroy smirked.

Willis looked at Leroy and frowned, a quizzical expression on his face.

"I mean the Yankees making a fancy ceremony out of going on patrol," Leroy explained.

"I hear tell that Jeb Stuart did the same thing up in Virginia. Charlie Sanders was in the Army of Northern Virginia and he told me they were real fancy up there, what with parades and such," Willis said. "They was all fancy in the Army of Northern Virginia."

Leroy's horse snorted and pawed the ground not wanting to be left behind. "I'm sure all this fancy parading would impress the hell out of the Comanch," Leroy said as he clicked his tongue to tell the Appaloosa it was time to go.

They camped on the banks of the Salt Fork River after the first day's march. The Rangers kept to themselves, watching the Federal troops go about their field chores. Leroy tried his best to convince Charlie Sanders to play *Dixie* on the harmonica.

"Just to let 'em know we're still around," Leroy had explained to Captain Johnson.

Johnson laughed, but told Leroy it wouldn't be a good idea to start trouble. Before going to bed the captain told Leroy the plan that the young Federal colonel had shared with him. "Evidently," Johnson began in a doubtful tone of voice, "they intend to wipe out the Comanche with a surprise attack. Three regiments are supposed to join up at Palo Duro Canyon. Now whether they can coordinate this type of an attack using forces coming in from three different directions remains to be seen."

"How do they know they'll find the Comanch in the canyon?" Leroy asked.

"The Yanks have had Kiowa scouts out hunting them for weeks," Johnson replied. "The scouts reported that the Comanche are camped near the center of the canyon."

"How old is this report?" Leroy raised his eyebrows. He had questions about the reliability of the Kiowa scouts that he had seen at Fort Belknap.

Johnson shook his head. "Colonel Lewis didn't say. He just said that his orders were to proceed to the southeast side of the canyon and be ready to attack on the 12th. That gives us plenty of time to reach the canyon. Another regiment from Fort Sill in the Indian Territory will attack the village from the northeast rim of the canyon. The third regiment is coming in from Ft. Union in the New Mexico Territory. I assume that bunch will attack from the west."

Leroy sighed. "Sounds a bit too complicated for my liking."

Johnson nodded in agreement. "You're right, Leroy. The plan is too damn complicated. It depends on three different forces arriving at the right place and at the right time. I ask you, back during the war, how many times did that ever happen?"

Leroy laughed out loud. "You just answered any doubts that I may have had, Captain. We better hang back and take care of ourselves in this fight."

"We'll do our job, Leroy," Johnson said. "But I am going to make sure that I know what we're getting into before we ride into Palo Duro Canyon."

The morning dawned bright and warm with only a few clouds dotting the sky. Willis swallowed a last gulp of hot coffee. Leroy had already finished his breakfast. Neither Ranger was confident about the upcoming battle. *Guess it's time,* he thought as he watched the Yanks pack up the campsite. He closed his eyes, leaned against a sturdy tree trunk and let his mind drift back to his east Texas farm and Mindy. His thoughts whirled as he felt a slight breeze ruffling his hair.

"You all right, Leroy?" Willis asked. His eyes narrowed as he looked closely at his friend of many years. "You've been standing there for at least ten minutes."

Leroy forced his mind back to the present. "Yeah," he answered. "A little confused, that's all."

Willis stepped forward and handed him a freshly filled canteen. "Confused about what?"

Leroy shook his head and took the canteen. "Just leave it," he said. "Nothing worth talkin' about."

At daybreak, the men mounted their horses and started the day's march. Leroy couldn't help but chuckle when Willis described a typical day's riding alongside the Federal cavalry as "starting, then stopping, then walking the horses and stopping again." The long blue line stretched across prairies and sandy plains. After several days of this, most of the troopers appeared to be completely worn out but the column pushed on. The Rangers were chafing under the restraints the Federal commanders had placed upon them. *We would have already gotten there, whipped the darn Comanch and been on our way home if we were in charge,* Leroy thought as they passed mile after mile of piney woods. *Yankee cavalry ain't no match for the Texas Rangers. When we set our mind to do something, we get it done. Still, who knows, what with all the confusion going on around here, I might just get the opportunity to settle an old score with O'Connor.*

Leroy passed the time thinking of Mindy, planning Sunday picnics and trips into town to make her happy. He also took time to plan a few practical jokes to liven up life on the trail just a little bit. Each night when the campfire was blazing bright, the coffee steaming hot and the Yankee cooks dishing up whatever rations they had time to prepare, Leroy found ways to needle the Yankee cavalrymen.

"All in good fun," he would explain to Captain Johnson. But as the days dragged on, most of the men, including Leroy, were too tired to do much more than swallow their rations before going to sleep.

When the column arrived at the Prairie Dog Town Fork of the Red River, the commanding officer, Lt. Colonel Lewis, ordered the horses turned loose to graze on the abundant soft grass and sweet clover. The campsite was situated at the edge of a narrow valley thickly studded with cottonwood, willow, mesquite and salt cedar trees. In spite of his homesickness for Mindy, Leroy took a few moments to enjoy the natural beauty and to collect his thoughts. *The Yankee officers have their plans, and I'm gonna have mine in case things don't go right,* he thought. *Any time you're dealing with the Comanch, fancy plans have a habit of going by the wayside mighty fast. Whatever else happens, Willis and I are gonna make it out of this and go home to Patsy and Mindy.*

The next day the Kiowa scouts rode into camp. They reported that the column from Ft. Sill had camped just north of Palo Duro Canyon and was making preparations for the upcoming attack. The scouts also confirmed that the Comanche were still in the canyon and apparently unaware of the approaching Federal troops. Lt. Colonel Lewis sent a dispatch rider to the commander of the column from Ft. Sill, Lt. Colonel Matthew Hathaway. Hathaway was the senior officer of the expedition, due to his date of rank, and would assume command once the coordinated attack began.

Captain Johnson relayed the information to his men and told them to use this time to rest up. "When the Yanks say go, we'll go," Captain Johnson said.

More wasted time, thought Leroy. *The damn Comanch just might find us before we find them. Then who's gonna be surprised?*

Lt. Colonel Hathaway was a tall, slim, immaculately clean man who looked every inch the military officer. He had been given command of the troops at Fort Sill only two months before the start of this campaign. Never having served on the frontier prior to his current assignment, he had no appreciation of the fighting spirit of the Comanche warrior.

Hathaway had served under General Philip Sheridan and idolized the general. Under the general's leadership and influence, Hathaway had advanced in rank quickly during the War Between The States. Lt. Colonel Hathaway now thirsted for the general's stars he had lost during the post-war reduction in force. When Sheridan was sent west, Hathaway had pulled every string he could to be able to follow him.

General Sheridan's plan to solve the current "Indian problem" was to converge upon the Indians and destroy their camps, lodges, horses, and food supplies and then to pursue them until they surrendered. At which point, those that hadn't been killed or starved to death would be moved to reservations.

When Colonel Hathaway received his orders to march to Palo Duro Canyon, the plan was in it's initial stage.

General Sheridan had given him the mission to find and eliminate several bands of Comanche thought to be camped in the Palo Duro Canyon. He had emphasized that the Comanche must be taught the lesson that "war is hell" and that no quarter was to be shown. By the end of the meeting it was clear to everyone present that the general believed that the only good Indian was a dead Indian.

The three companies of Federal troops from Fort Sill, about three hundred men in all, rode in a column of twos across the dry, sun-seared prairie. Despite the grass covered soil, the horses kicked up a cloud of dust, heavy enough that men riding near the rear of the column had to wet their kerchiefs and cover their noses for protection.

Stopping just at sunset, the men prepared their evening meal. Because of the recent drought there was the ever present danger that the prairie grass might erupt into a prairie fire that could consume the whole Texas Panhandle. Consequently, no campfires were allowed.

Colonel Hathaway lay silent in his bed roll and tried to ignore the sounds outside his tent that continued throughout the night. His mind began to go over his plan for the upcoming battle. He felt no dread. In fact, if the battle went as he planned, there wouldn't be much of a fight. He hated Indians, especially the Comanche. *They are savages,* he thought, *of less value than a dog.* He had followed in their wake where they had raided settlers and wrecked havoc upon the families. He had seen the remains of such terrible acts as ruthlessly murdering helpless women and children. The more he thought about the upcoming battle, the more excited he got. Eventually, he fell asleep.

Sometime during the night, clouds covered the sky and rain began to fall, at first lightly, then in a heavy downpour. Men got up to see to their horses and gear. September was a month when fall rains began in the Panhandle.

Good, thought Hathaway. *Now the men can have their coffee.*

The rain continued to fall gently as the men readied for the day's ride. By noon the sky was again full of dark threatening clouds.

The rain soaked grassland made traveling a little more difficult for the horses, but much easier for the men. The horses' hooves no longer kicked up the choking dust.

By nightfall they were within a few hour's ride of the canyon's rim. Hathaway decided to bivouac where he was and attack just before dawn.

"Scouts report Lt. Colonel Lewis is just south of us, sir," a young lieutenant said after having his salute returned by his commanding officer.

Lt. Colonel Hathaway nodded and smiled. "Get one of the troopers to carry orders to Colonel Lewis."

CHAPTER ∞ 29

The Texas Rangers watched from the south end of the canyon.

"Look at all them soldiers, Leroy," Willis said. "This ain't gonna be much of a fight."

"Nope," Leroy sighed. "But still I'll be darn glad when it's over."

Captain Johnson gathered his men together and gave them their orders.

"Lt. Colonel Lewis sent me a message that he's made contact with the other Yanks. He says they'll attack once the other forces begin firing from the east side of the canyon. When the Yanks move forward, we'll be the only ones left to hold this end of the canyon. Our job is to keep any escaping Comanche from getting past us. But," he removed his hat and wiped sweat from his brow, "from what he says, he doesn't expect any Comanche to escape from the village."

"What about the squaws and kids?" Willis asked.

Captain Johnson shook his head. "From what I understand, the Yanks intend to finish 'em off—all of 'em."

"Well," Leroy said emphatically, "I got no love for the Comanch, everybody here knows that, but I ain't gonna take no part in shooting women and kids. I don't care what the Yanks say, I ain't gonna follow no orders that tells me to shoot women."

Willis and most of the other Rangers said nothing, but nodded in agreement.

"I don't think I could," Derrick shook his head. "Me and Darryl weren't brought up to do something like that."

He looked over toward Darryl. Darryl lowered his head.

"I'm not giving any orders that tell you men to do that," Johnson said. He looked around the area and added, "Let's spread out and find some cover. I have a feeling if any Comanch makes it this far, it won't be squaws or kids."

The Rangers took their positions and checked their weapons. "Goddamn Yanks," Leroy said as he knelt down beside Willis. "They're just as bad as the Indians. I wish they'd both just kill each other off and leave Texas to us."

The sky had begun to lighten in the east when the first shots were fired. Moving quickly with little opposition, the troops soon had the Indian camp surrounded.

Leroy and Willis could see the Federal troops move into the village. They were obviously not taking any prisoners, as they killed every man, woman and child they came in contact with. After while, Willis got sick and turned away. Leroy watched intently, reminding himself of the massacre of his brother, Clayton, and the other Texas Rangers who were with him that day that seemed so long ago. Suddenly, a group of twenty Comanche warriors broke through the Federal troops and make their way on horseback toward the south end of the canyon. The Rangers were right in their path.

"Here they come!" Captain Johnson shouted. "They're gonna be desperate to get past us so make sure both your rifles and pistols are loaded."

Just out of range, the Comanche dismounted and headed for the cover of rocks and brush. "Damn Comanch," Leroy muttered. "You never can count on 'em to do what you expect." He turned to Willis and said, "Keep an eye out and pass the word from now on, no talking, no matter what."

Leroy's attention was drawn back to the area around him. Several Rangers shouted as the Comanche found their mark with arrows and tomahawks. Near the canyon floor, a wounded Ranger cried out for help but Leroy knew that there was no way to reach him. He momentarily rested his head on his arm. The man's cries for help were almost more than he could take. Willis suddenly pointed to their left where Captain Johnson was engaged in hand to hand combat with a Comanche warrior. Leroy quickly aimed his rifle and fired. The Comanche arched his back and dropped his weapon as he fell to the ground. Captain Johnson looked up to see what direction the shot had come from. Just as Leroy motioned with his rifle, he saw another Comanche coming up fast behind the Captain.

"There's another one!" Willis cried out.

Leroy tried to aim his rifle at the Indian but Captain Johnson was between him and the charging Comanche. At the last minute, Johnson must have heard the Indian because he turned around, but before he could react, the Comanche used one powerful blow to split his head open with an already bloody tomahawk.

"Damn," Leroy said. "I couldn't get a clear shot."

"It don't matter now," Willis shook his head.

"That's enough for me, Willis. I'm going home," Leroy spat out the words and started working his way out the canyon. "I'll kill any fightin' Comanche that crosses my path, but I ain't got the stomach to shoot squaws and kids and I don't wanna watch it happening either. I'm sick of Yanks, Indians and Longhorn cattle that trample a man to death."

Willis said in a low, tired voice. "I guess you're right. It's time to go home."

Leroy drew Willis' attention to the cluster of rocks and trees that seemed to be hanging on the wall of the canyon. "Derrick and Darryl are over there hiding behind them rocks. I ain't sure where anybody else is now."

"How do you know Derrick and Darryl are there. I ain't seen nothing move?" Willis asked as he leaned over to look in the direction of the rock formation.

"Cause that's where I told them to stay put, that's why. They're both scared to death and probably sick of all this killing by now, just like we are."

"What about Charlie Sanders?"

"What about him?" Leroy replied in a hostile voice. "To hell with Charlie. I can't save everyone on this battlefield. The last time I saw him, he was over there where we heard them fellows cry out. I figure the Rangers over by that bluff are all dead by now."

"You mean we're gonna leave Charlie?"

"Willis, I ain't gonna stick around here long enough to find him or anyone else for that matter."

"Leroy, I swear that Yankee Colonel is a worse commander than Whiskey Keg Sibley," Willis sighed. "Did you see O'Connor during the battle?"

"I had the sonofabitch in my sights awhile back," Leroy thought about the missed opportunity and grinned. "I'll probably wind up having nightmares about not pulling that trigger and blowing his damn head off."

Willis laughed. "Maybe there will be a next time."

"Oh, I'm sure of that, Willis. But for now, let's hightail it on out of here."

Willis went to get the horses while Leroy crept down the side of the canyon towards Derrick and Darryl.

"We're out of cartridges!" Derrick shouted. "There's nothing we can do 'cept throw rocks at 'em."

"Can you go get us some?" Darryl called out.

"No time for that now," Leroy's hands tightened around the rifle. Two Comanche were running towards Derrick and Darryl. He carefully aimed the rifle at one of the Indians and squeezed the trigger. The man's arms flew out to his sides and and his knees buckled. The second Comanche warrior kept coming. Leroy swung the rifle slightly to the left, aimed and fired again.

Derrick and Darryl watched Leroy's movements. "Heck, you'd think he was shootin' rabbits," Darryl said in awe. "He's so smooth, he ain't gonna miss even with the Comanche comin' right at 'em." Just as Derrick started to reply, an arrow whizzed by his head, then a second.

"Jesus," Darryl yelled.

"Come on!" Leroy called out. "There's probably more of 'em coming up that ravine behind you."

Without hesitation, Derrick and Darryl kept low while moving as fast as they could toward Leroy. Leroy kept firing, if only to slow the charging Comanche down. After he emptied the rifle, he drew the Colt and waited. As soon as the first Indian cleared the brush, Leroy cocked the hammer and fired. "I'm running out of time and bullets, boys," Leroy called out. "Keep going until you get past the ravine. Willis should be right above the rim. He'll have the horses with him."

"Yes, sir," Derrick hollered. "We'll be waiting for you."

"Fine," Leroy muttered as he fired again. "You do that." He turned and started making his way up the craggy red rock canyon wall. He kept low, crouching behind sagebrush and rocks, not wanting to give the Comanche a target. The steepness of the path forced him to traverse back and forth, making for slow progress up the canyon wall. He paused now and then to look over his shoulder to see if he was being followed by Comanche.

Willis waited, hidden at the top of the mesa. "They ain't following you, Leroy," he called out as soon as Leroy had pulled himself up over the rocks just beneath the rim of the canyon.

Leroy stopped in his tracks. He looked up toward the sound of Willis' calm voice and squinted into the sunlight. "Damnit Willis, tell me who ain't following me."

"The Comanch, that's who," Willis replied. "There's ain't nothing coming up the canyon 'cept Derrick and Darryl. Those fools are climbing up the canyon wall in plain sight. If the Comanch were anywhere around here, there'd be enough holes in them boys to pour a horse trough full of water through 'em."

Leroy turned to see Derrick and Darryl scrambling up a particularly steep part of the canyon. "See anyone else?"

"Nope," Willis said. "Ain't seen nothing since you took care of those three Comanch that was after you. Notice we ain't hearing no gunshots. I figure the Yanks have finished off the rest of the Comanche down in the Canyon."

Leroy sat down and unfastened his canteen. After taking a long drink, he wiped his mouth and looked around the rim of the canyon. He had skinned his wrist raw climbing up the rock ledge. He poured a few drops of water to clear the dirt from his burning wound.

Vultures were circling. Their wings made a loud thud with every flap. He closed his eyes tight. *They'll be busy today,* he thought.

As soon as Derrick and Darryl had climbed over the ledge, Willis ran over to untie the horses. Leroy handed the young Rangers his canteen. From the ridge he could see smoke coming from the site of the battle. He didn't care anymore. *It's time to leave all this behind and go home to Mindy.* he thought.

"We're ready to go, Leroy," Willis said as he led the saddled horses up to the edge of the canyon.

Derrick and Darryl eagerly grabbed their horse's reins. "We ain't never leavin' home again," Darryl said.

"I wish we could keep riding and not have to stop 'till we get there," Derrick whispered, still out of breath from the climb up the canyon wall.

Sunlight poured through the clouds, almost pointing the way home. Leroy closed his mind to everything except the words that seemed to come from far away, in another voice. A pretty woman with shiny brown hair tied back with a blue ribbon was calling to him in a soft voice that only he could hear.

Leroy took the reins from Willis' outstretched hand, climbed up on the Appaloosa and turned the horse east toward home and Mindy.

Thick black smoke clung to the hillside but Sergeant Dan O'Connor managed to make his way up the ridge line. Moments before he had seen Leroy and several other Rangers climbing over the ledge of the canyon. Moving as quickly as he could and determined to overtake the Rangers, O'Connor put all thoughts of the Comanche out of his mind. The battle had been confused and ugly. Not a single prisoner had been taken. Smoke had been so dense that no one knew where the firing was coming from but O'Connor was sure that the Rangers had shot at some of his men.

O'Connor passed two wounded soldiers still alive but weak from loss of blood. One reached out and asked for water. The sergeant threw down his canteen but keep going.

"I'll be back," O'Connor promised, as he passed more men asking for help. "First I got a job to do." He turned his attention back to the Rangers. "Damn 'em to hell," O'Connor struggled through the brush. "Cutting out on us."

Finally O'Connor pulled himself over the top of the canyon wall only to see Leroy and the other Rangers riding away. He raised his rifle. The open, flat terrain gave the sergeant a clear shot, but Leroy and the others were out of range. O'Connor looked in vain for a horse but the Rangers had taken the mounts.

"I'll find you and I'll put a bullet right between your eyes," O'Connor shook his fist at the cloud of dust stirred up by the galloping horses. "I've said it before and I'll say it again. If it's the last thing I do, I'll piss on your grave, Leroy Wiley. It ain't over between us."

Leroy tried to turn his mind away from the battle and think of home and his waiting family. But the expression on his face was hard as rode past the desolate landscape. In his mind's eye he saw a shadowy figure with a gun in his hand. *O'Connor,* he thought to himself. *You and me are gonna meet up again, just you wait and see.*

CHAPTER ∞ 30

The hot and thirsty Rangers rode toward Fort Richardson, which was located in the north central portion of the Texas frontier. As the gates to the fort swung open, Leroy paused for a moment. *Something ain't right,* he thought. He fought an overwhelming urge to turn around and go back to the scene of battle. But he knew his horse was as tired as he was. He also knew he needed a night's rest in order to clear his head and take stock of things.

Fort Richardson was built after the Civil War and named for General Israel B. Richardson, who died in the Battle of Sharpsburg. The fort was the northernmost line of Federal forts established after the war and consisted of a small hospital, officers' quarters, barracks housing the garrison of enlisted men, a guard house and a bakery. The small outpost provided defense for the nearby farmers and their families against attacks by hostile Indians, mostly Comanche.

The four weary Rangers tied their mounts to hitching posts outside the building that housed the headquarters and supply rooms for the fort. The rectangular stone and wood faced building had a wide portico supported by white washed columns. The center section consisted of a two storied stone structure that served as the command center of the fort.

"Boys, let's go inside and partake of Yankee hospitality," Leroy said as he nodded to several soldiers resting along the portico.

"I ain't never liked Yankee anything, but right now I'd sure like some biscuits and gravy, and I can smell biscuits cookin'," Willis said as he stretched his back and shoulders. "Think they'd let us rest up a spell before we ride on to Smith County?"

"Yeah," Derrick added. "I'd sure like that. Me and Darryl are hungry and tired to the bone."

"Yeah," Darryl echoed his brother's request.

"Well, it never hurts to ask," Leroy laughed. "After all, the Yanks are here reconstructin' Texas. Let 'em start with constructin' some biscuits and gravy."

"How far is Jacksboro?" Willis asked. "In case the Yanks don't have no room for us."

"Too far," Leroy said. "I ain't leaving."

Leroy stepped up onto the stone walkway and opened one of the double doors leading to the fort commander's office. Inside he found a large room with rough beams covering a high ceiling that topped walls made of pine logs. A pot bellied stove stood in the middle of the room. It was surrounded by square shaped tables and ladder backed chairs.

"Howdy, fellows," Leroy said as he took off his hat and tapped it against his knee to remove some of the trail dust.

A slim, clean-shaven lieutenant in his mid-twenties, walked toward the Rangers. He was dressed in a dark blue officer's uniform trimmed in cavalry gold. He mirrored all the other Yankee officers Leroy had seen since the end of the war. The lieutenant, right out of the military academy at West Point, gave the appearance of a man in a hurry to command troops in the field of battle.

"You Rangers headed west?" the lieutenant asked, taking in the silver badges worn on each Ranger's vest.

Leroy looked around the room at the tough looking men gathered in small groups of four to six. They stared at him, he stared back, then turned his attention back to the young lieutenant.

"Just come from Palo Duro Canyon," Leroy said. "We were fighting

Comanche alongside troops from Fort Belknap and Fort Sill."

The lieutenant frowned. Every soldier in the room stopped what he was doing and listened intently.

"I haven't received word of the outcome of the battle. I'd appreciate it if you'd fill me in on the details." The lieutenant motioned to a desk at the far side of the room. "I'm Lieutenant Benson. Captain Weeks is in charge of the fort right now. Major Smith died three months ago."

"My name's Leroy Wiley," Leroy turned and gestured toward the other Rangers. "This here is Willis, and them two younguns' is Derrick and Darryl. We're with a Ranger company from east Texas. Sorry to hear about the major. Where's Captain Weeks?"

"Out on patrol," the lieutenant answered. "I'm in charge right now, and I'd appreciate a report of the action at Palo Duro Canyon."

"Not much to tell," Leroy shook his head. "All the Comanch were pretty much wiped out. That included men, squaws and babies." Leroy paused before adding, "Not a pretty sight, I can tell you. But it's over now, and the troops are probably headed back to Fort Belknap and to Fort Sill, up in the Indian Territory."

"Well, it's all for the best," Lieutenant Benson sighed. "Their way of life is over now. It's time to settle the frontier."

Willis muttered, "If them Injuns had any doubts, they don't anymore."

"What did you say?" Benson leaned over to look past Leroy at Willis.

"Oh, never mind him," Leroy grinned. "He's just tired and hungry like the rest of us."

"Well, you're welcome to rest up here. There'll be plenty to eat in the mess by now. We have our own bakery here at the fort, and our cook makes the best biscuits in Texas. I'll send someone to show you where you can bunk and where the mess hall is located." Benson turned and motioned for one of the sergeants to step forward.

The man silently nodded toward Leroy and the Rangers, then walked toward the door.

"I'll join you directly," Lieutenant Benson called after them. "I'm eager to hear about the battle."

Well you can damn sure hear about it from somebody besides me, Leroy thought. *I ain't in the mood to talk about it.*

"My name's Billy," the sergeant said as they stepped out into the fading Texas sunshine. "After you see to your horses, I'll take you over to the mess hall."

"The horses can wait a spell," Willis said. "I'm hungry."

The sergeant stopped in his tracks and turned to face Willis. "Them horses are in need of grain. In the army, they come first."

"Same in the Rangers," Leroy said. "Willis, you come with me. Derrick, you and Darryl take the horses over to the livery stable. I want you to feed, water 'em and brush 'em down real good."

Derrick's eyes grew wide. He looked at Darryl, then back to Leroy. "Hey, Leroy, we're hungry too. That's gonna take a long time and there might not be nothing left."

"Yep, that might be the case but after you feed the horses, you can eat everything the Yanks and Willis leave on the table." Leroy gave the boys a hard look before adding, "Remember boys, them horses do all the work. You just sit on 'em."

"Darnit," Darryl whispered.

The sergeant laughed. "Same thing goes on in the army, son. It appears this fellow out ranks the two of you."

"Darnit," Derrick said, resigned to eating what was left over.

Leroy and Willis followed the sergeant called Billy. As the bugler summoned the soldiers to the mess hall for their evening meal, Derrick and Darryl, both miserable, turned around and headed toward the hitching posts.

"There probably won't be much left," Darryl sighed.

"Not after Willis gets his fill," Derrick answered in a sad tone of voice.

As a young bugler filled the evening sky with sound reverberating from the bell of a treble wind instrument made of copper, Leroy and Willis joined the soldiers in a hearty supper of boiled beef, potatoes and beans. Hearing the call of the fort's bugler, Derrick and Darryl hurried toward the livery stable to unsaddle and feed the mounts.

"There ain't gonna be nothin' left unless we hurry," Derrick said.

"You start unsaddlin' 'em and I'll get the feed bags ready."

Darryl nodded as he pulled his horse along with Leroy's toward the open stable doors.

Following the trail of the four Texas Rangers as it wound through creeks and shaded areas, Sergeant Dan O'Connor laid whip to his tired horse and rode like the devil himself was behind him.

They gotta be headed to Fort Richardson, O'Connor thought. *It's right on the way to east Texas. That's where I'll find them stinkin' Rebs and Leroy Wiley is gonna be with 'em. I'd bet my last dollar on that.*

The sergeant paused just long enough to insure that his horse would make it all the way to the fort. He finished the last water in his canteen, wiped his mouth with his rolled up sleeve, and stored the empty canteen. Out of the corner of his eye, he saw movement in a nearby cluster of bushes. He lifted his rifle up to fire, then heard the deep growl of a dog. "Well, come on out, you son of a bitch," O'Connor roared. "You being here means I ain't too far away from people."

The big brown and black dog slowly moved out from the brush, shying away from the intruder.

"Come on, dog," O'Connor called out as he motioned to the animal. The dog kept his distance and watched the sergeant with wary eyes. "Come on out. Hey, I think I'll call you Buddy."

The dog snarled and flashed fierce teeth.

"Oh, what the hell," O'Connor said as he aimed the rifle. The dog turned, but the bullet caught him right in the ribs. The dog fell on his side and began to whimper, O'Connor mounted his horse and rode with his back to the setting sun. *He might howl awhile,* the sergeant thought. *But it ain't worth wastin' another bullet to put 'em out of his misery.*

The bunkhouse walls were lined with rows of army issued cots. Between each cot was a metal trunk where each trooper stored his belongings. Leroy picked a cot from the pile of extras stacked near the door. The last words Leroy heard before falling asleep was Derrick complaining to Darryl about his supper of potatoes and beans. The beef had long since disappeared by the time before the young Rangers arrived at the mess hall.

The bugler assigned to Fort Richardson was fortunate that Willis was unarmed when he sounded reveille at 5:00 a.m. Willis, clad in his wornout red drawers, sat up so fast that he hit his head against a shelf that hung above his cot.

"Good God Almighty!" Willis said. "I swear the Yanks have the loudest bugles in the world."

Leroy pulled the blanket over his face and muttered, "If I could get my hands on that sonofabitch, I'd kill him and put him out of his misery."

"How long does it go on?" Derrick asked. "Seems to me, he's starting his tune all over again."

"Breakfast, Rebs!" shouted one of the sergeants, then he corrected himself by adding, "I mean, you Rangers better get up and eat breakfast while there's still something left to eat."

Leroy yawned, wiped the sleep out of his eyes and looked around. The soldiers were already up and getting dressed.

"I'd rather get up than listen to any more Yankee buglin'," Willis sighed. He reached over and gave Darryl a slap on his back. "Git up, boy. Let's go git some grub."

Willis led the party of Rangers out into the predawn. When they arrived at the mess hall, most of the soldiers had filled their plates with generous helpings of biscuits, ham, eggs and red eye gravy.

Willis gave Leroy a poke in the ribs to get his attention before asking, "Ever see this much grub in your life? At home, Patsy has to slice a piece of beef so thin you can see through it, and still everybody ends up leaving the table hungry. And that's on a good day. 'Round here, there's enough food to feed this army and two more besides."

It was too early in the morning to get Willis started, so Leroy nodded in agreement, then got in line behind Derrick and Darryl. After enjoying a full frontier breakfast, the Rangers headed to the stable to retrieve their rested mounts. Leroy stopped by headquarters and thanked Lieutenant Benson for the use of the bunks and meals. The lieutenant glanced up from his paperwork and told Leroy to feel free to fill up with supplies before leaving the post.

Maybe I can get used to Yanks being in Texas after all, Leroy thought. *Especially if they feed Willis and me like they have here at Fort Richardson.*

By the time Leroy had filled two sacks with supplies from the mess hall and crossed the parade ground, he met Willis and Derrick leading the horses out of the stable.

"Where's Darryl?" Leroy asked.

"Gone back to the mess hall for more ham and biscuits," Willis answered. "I figured we could use extra grub for the trail."

Leroy smiled, showed Willis the contents of the two sacks, then climbed on his horse and rode out. Derrick waited for his brother, but Willis followed Leroy. While they waited under a large, spreading elm tree for the two young Rangers to catch up, Leroy shared his thoughts with Willis.

"We got to find away to spend more time at home with the womenfolk," Leroy said. "The way I see it, we're missing out on too much."

Willis took a deep breath and leaned on the saddle horn. "I don't wanna have to go on no more cattle drives. If I can't make it on the farm, I'll take Patsy and the kids and go west. I hear there's land for the taking in the New Mexico Territory."

"Oh, Willis," Leroy sighed, sounding tired and worn out. "Out in New Mexico there's just more Indians to fight, and I'm talking about Apaches. If there's anything worse than a Comanch, it's an Apache. No matter what I have to do, I ain't leaving east Texas. I want grass and trees and water, and that don't sound like New Mexico to me. Hell, Willis, don't you remember the walk back home after the battles of Valverde and Glorieta Pass?"

"What about up in the Indian Territory? I hear there's lumber work up there," Willis asked, trying not to remember the hard times they endured during the war.

"More damn Indians. And up in the Territory, they run things. Hell, no," Leroy said. "That's the real badlands. There ain't no real law there in the Territory. The outlaws we can't catch in Texas go up into the Territory and hide out. It ain't a fit place for women and kids, that's for sure."

"Then what are we gonna do?" Willis looked Leroy right in the eye. "We can't carry guns and do Ranger work forever. 'Sides, it don't pay enough to make it."

A very slight smile creased Leroy's lips as he reached over to give Willis a playful shove. "We'll just have to become damn good sod busters, Willis. Just think how happy that'll make Patsy." He paused for effect before adding, "Or Paulette, whichever one you end up with."

Willis sat straight in the saddle and snarled at Leroy. "That ain't funny. You hear me, Leroy Wiley? Don't you go mentioning that fancy gal's name again or we'll both be in a kettle of hot water. Mindy's gonna ask how you know so much about Paulette and that'll bring up the Lady In Lace Saloon where you spent a lot of your time while in the fine city of Abilene." He pointed toward the gate of Fort Richardson. "There comes Derrick and Darryl so consider the subject of Paulette closed forever. That's final, Leroy. You hear me?"

Willis continued to ramble on while Leroy pulled his hat low over his brow and rode east toward home and Mindy.

"Hey, Leroy," Derrick called out. "Some Yank rode past us in a mighty big hurry, almost ran into Darryl."

Leroy abruptly stopped his horse and turned back to face Derrick. "What did he look like?"

"Big ugly guy with a salt and pepper beard. He was covered in dirt. His horse was about dead, but he kept on whippin' it until they rode through the gate."

Willis looked at Leroy. Leroy's eyes met his. "Did you see what regiment that Yank was assigned to?"

"Nope," Derrick replied. "Not that I would have known any of 'em. Only thing I noticed was the salt and pepper beard and one of them flat hats the Yank sergeants like to wear."

"Infantry or cavalry?" Leroy asked.

"Cavalry," Darryl replied. "I seen the yellow trim on his Yankee shirt."

"Let's get the hell out of here," Willis said. "It don't sound good to me. Whatever's happened, we don't wanna be part of it."

Leroy thought for a moment, then nodded his head in agreement and tapped the ribs of his horse with his spurs. Rays of sunlight were only now filtering through the eastern sky.

Most Texas Rangers believed that a camp should be located near water. But Leroy disliked low, damp ground, that attracted crawling critters like snakes and flying ones such as mosquitoes. Even before joining the Rangers, Leroy had decided that the best place for a camp was on ground, not too far from a source of water. He knew that on the high ground, the currents of air are often strong enough to keep the insects away and at the same time allow him to observe anyone or anything attracted to the water.

What Derrick and Darryl had reported as they left Fort Richardson worried him. He had that nagging feeling of doubt that always plagued him before something bad happened. With this in mind, he chose their campsite that night with particular care.

"Why are we making camp here, Leroy?" Derrick asked. "Seems to me we're a long way from the water and from firewood too. I know you and Willis ain't gonna be carrying it, that's gonna be left up to me and Darryl. I think we ought to have a say where we're settin' up camp."

"I'm trying to avoid the dead wood and heavy underbrush, Derrick," Leroy explained. "The ground has an easy slope and that's just the way I like it."

"Build us a crisscross fire, Derrick," Willis said as he spread his horse blanket on the ground covered with pine straw. "That way it'll last overnight. Them star-shaped Indian fires will be out by midnight."

Why me? thought Derrick. *How long before Darryl and I are senior enough in the Rangers that somebody else has to do all the work?*

"It ain't cold, Willis," Derrick argued. "It don't matter if the fire goes out. Fixing a darn crisscross fire means finding and picking up a lot of wood. You gotta lay a row of sticks, then a second row on top of that. That's a lot of work, and we ain't cooking, so we don't need a bed of coals."

"Do what he says, Derrick," Leroy said. "And get birch bark. I saw plenty of birch bark just over that rise and it looked tender. It'll burn even if it's wet." Leroy always liked to start the fire as soon as the campsite was located, and he wanted to make sure this fire burned through the night.

Removing his spurs and boots, Leroy pulled on a pair of Indian moccasins he kept in his saddle bags. He turned to Willis. "I keep thinking about being ambushed. I don't know why, but I can't shake a bad feeling I got hanging over me."

Willis nodded. "Your instincts have been pretty good in the past, so I'll weigh in on the side of caution."

Leroy laughed. "Since when did you pick up fancy words like that?"

"Oh, I remember things Mr. Kell said back during the cattle drive. He sure was a smart man and a good one to boot." Willis sighed. "Seems like the good ones all meet the same end."

"So do the bad ones," Leroy grinned. "I just ain't got around to all of 'em yet." Then his tone turned deadly serious. "You take the first watch up on that ridge. I'll relieve you. Let's leave Derrick and Darryl by the campfire."

Willis laughed. "You ain't using the boys as bait are you?"

"Maybe," Leroy replied in a low voice. "But I ain't seen nobody that could sneak up on either you or me yet. Not even a damn Comanch. If either one of us is set up in good cover on that ridge, Derrick and Darryl are as safe as if they were in their mama's arms, or Paulette's, for that matter."

"Leroy!" Willis yelled as he stood up, rifle in hand. "Cut it out. I don't wanna hear her name again. She cost me five dollars."

"Keep your eyes peeled in the direction of the fort," Leroy said, ignoring Willis' complaints about Paulette. "If there's trouble, it's gonna come from there."

Willis raised his hand and waved Leroy off as he walked into the trees. "I'll find some good cover like you did at Shiloh, remember?"

"Was it poison ivy or poison oak?" Leroy laughed. "I was so busy trying to find cover from the Yanks, I didn't take time to see what I was covered up in, but I found out by nightfall, didn't I?"

"You were broken out all over," Willis laughed as he remembered.

"I still remember you scratching your butt for two or three days."

"More like a week," Leroy said. "I've kept an eye out for leaves of three ever since." He continued watching until Willis was completely out of sight, then turned his attention to Derrick and Darryl as they cleared an area to build the crisscross campfire. *It's gonna be a long night,* he thought. *And I've got a feeling it ain't gonna be a peaceful one.*

Sergeant Dan O'Connor knelt down and closely examined the hoof print of one of the shod horses that had recently traveled over the hard packed trail.

"It's them all right," he said to himself. "I'd bet a month's pay on it."

Looking up, his eyes followed the trail into a range of gentle sloping hills. "It won't be long until I have that sorry Reb in my gunsights."

At Fort Richardson, O'Connor had talked the blacksmith into giving him the strongest and best mount at the post. He had slipped the smithy a twenty dollar gold piece and the quarter horse was well worth the money. Now, he felt sure that he would overtake the Rangers before dawn. He climbed back onto the fast quarter horse, "Let's go git 'em boy."

Two hours later, he begin to smell smoking wood burning on a campfire. He swung down from the saddle, slipped out his rifle, and tied the horse to a low hanging tree branch, but forgot to remove the spurs from his cavalry boots, a mistake he would later regret.

Ambushing men is dangerous business, and O'Connor sweated through his uniform blouse as he made his way toward the smell of the smoking wood. His eyes took in the rocky terrain leading to the campsite, as well as the cover of trees, and he paused and listened after each step.

O'Connor knew that this would probably be his best chance to end the blood feud between him and that smart assed Reb named Leroy Wiley. He was determined to surprise the campers thus giving him three, maybe four shots to kill as many sleeping Rangers as possible. The more Rangers he could kill, the better the chance would be that one of them would be Leroy. When he saw the clearing, he gripped his gun and slowly raised his head, searching for a clear line of fire. He didn't hear Leroy, clad in moccasins, moving slowly in position behind him.

O'Connor smiled. The Rangers were fairly close together, increasing his chances of killing them all before they could scatter. He aimed and took a deep breath, preparing to squeeze off one shot after another.

"Drop it, you bushwhackin' son-of-a-bitch," Leroy said.

The sergeant whirled around, clutching the rifle, ready to fire. At the same time he tried to dodge what he figured would be a shot aimed at the center of his back. For a split second, he thought he had succeeded in dodging the expected bullet, but then he felt a stinging sensation in his arm. He grunted as the bullet entered, shattering the bone in his upper arm and finally coming to rest in his shoulder. His left arm became heavy and useless. Still holding his rifle in his good hand, he tried to aim at Leroy. The shot went wide, splintering a nearby pine tree.

For Leroy, time seemed to pass slowly as if in a dream. He lunged forward and reached for the rifle. O'Connor struggled, cussing Leroy even while realizing his strength was fading fast.

"God help me, I'll kill you somehow," O'Connor spat at Leroy.

Leroy kept silent as he fought to free the rifle from O'Connor's hand. With all the strength he could muster, O'Connor was able to roll Leroy off him into the thick pine straw. Leroy's pistol was knocked from his hand. O'Connor lifted the rifle butt and tried to slam it into Leroy's head. Leroy rolled to his side, just in time to see the rifle butt jam into the ground, then stretched his fingers out trying to find his Colt pistol. By this time Dan O'Connor's body was shaking so hard he could barely focus on Leroy, but all the hate carried since the battle at Palmito Ranch kept him fighting. He didn't have much time; he knew he was probably a dead man. Now his only wish was to take Leroy Wiley to hell with him.

Willis raced down the hill followed closely by Derrick and Darryl. Just as they reached the two men, they saw a muzzle flash. It was Leroy's Colt. He had found the weapon and fired into O'Connor's broad body.

The sergeant's eyelids fluttered, he fell to his knees, then reached across his belly and felt warm, sticky blood. "I'm gut shot." He tried to raise his head, but searing pain enveloped his insides. "Finish me off, goddamn you."

Leroy looked up at Willis who stood stone faced, silently watching, his rifle ready to fire if needed. Derrick and Darryl looked stunned.

"Who is he, and why did he try to bushwhack us?" Derrick asked.

Willis shook his head. "Go on back to the campsite, boys. Ain't nothing you can do here."

"Finish me off, Reb," O'Connor moaned.

Leroy rolled his eyes and looked up at the heavens. The stars dotted the clear Texas sky like lanterns. He thought of all the men he had seen die. Those were not memories that he wanted to keep. O'Connor's moaning brought him back to the present. He looked down. The big man appeared smaller now, all curled up holding his insides and bleeding like a hog during slaughter. He hated Dan O'Connor and everything he stood for. Leroy wasn't about to do him any favors.

"Sorry, Sergeant," Leroy said, his voice husky, but the tone was clear and cold. "You just ain't worth the trouble. I'd rather put a dog out of his misery than waste a bullet on you."

He stepped back as O'Connor grabbed for his leg. "Please," he cried. "Don't leave me like this, finish me off or give me a gun and let me do it."

"Give you a gun?" Leroy said. "And let you bushwhack me again? I don't think so." Leroy walked past O'Connor toward the trees where Willis stood, still holding the rifle aimed at O'Connor.

As he passed by Willis, Leroy heard the rifle explode. He didn't turn around, just reached out and put a hand on Willis' shoulder.

"It was the right thing to do," Willis said, his voice void of emotion.

"I know," Leroy sighed. He heard Willis breathing hard.

"It's damn hard to kill a man, even if he's asking you to do it," Willis turned his head and looked at Leroy.

Leroy saw that Willis was in pain. He decided that the best thing he could do for his friend was to get him home to Smith County as soon possible. "Come on, Willis," he said as he draped an arm over Willis' shoulder. "Let's go home."

As they walked away, Willis asked, "I did the right thing, didn't I, Leroy? I mean, he was helpless and he wanted to die. I don't want to face the Almighty or Patsy with any killing on my conscience that wasn't necessary."

"You did the right thing, Willis," Leroy said, then in an effort to make Willis feel better, he added, "Just think, if you hadn't killed him, we'd have to listen to him howl all night. The Almighty would understand that, but Patsy wouldn't understand about Paulette. Paulette is an entirely different matter."

Willis pulled away from him and said in disgust, "I swear, Leroy. You sure do try my patience. You ain't supposed to joke about important things like that."

"What important things? You talking 'bout Patsy or killin' O'Connor?" Leroy asked, showing Willis a wide grin.

"Both of 'em," Willis said angrily.

"It's not my patience you have to worry about, Willis. I'd be thinkin' 'bout Patsy's patience if I were you." He turned a deaf ear to Willis' complaining and looked again up into the big, clear Texas sky. He felt a sense of relief he hadn't felt since the war ended.

Yep, he thought. *Time to go home and bust some sod.*